DISNEY

MULAN

BEFORE THE SWORD

❋

GRACE LIN

DISNEY PRESS

LOS ANGELES • NEW YORK

Printed in the United States of America
First Hardcover Edition, February 2020
1 3 5 7 9 10 8 6 4 2
FAC-020093-19361

Library of Congress Control Number: 2019943876
ISBN 978-1-368-02033-6

Designed by Soyoung Kim

Visit disneybooks.com

SUSTAINABLE FORESTRY INITIATIVE Certified Sourcing
www.sfiprogram.org
SFI-00993
Logo Applies to Text Stock Only

FOR MY PARTNER, ALEX, WHO KEEPS
OUR REAL LIVES WORKING WHILE I WRITE
ABOUT IMAGINARY ONES
–G.L.

PROLOGUE

SHE DISLIKED when they transformed into spiders. When she was a spider, her sight dimmed and everything became shapes of smoke. But she saw well enough to follow Daji. Even in the shadows, the white spider seemed to glow. One of Daji's nine translucent legs brushed against her, and she felt the pain of a slapped face. Daji was irritated they had failed so many times. How many times had they done this? How many years, only to be thwarted?

The white spider tapped a leg on the floor impatiently, and she knew the message behind the flashing eyes. *Get the right girl,* the eyes said. Daji found the other girl an infuriating nuisance, always in the way and always somehow stopping them with her clomping feet or sudden movements. "Obviously," Daji had said, "she is not the one we want. That clumsy calf could never save the Emperor. We want the other one."

So it was the other one they crept toward. The girl that smelled of embroidery threads and woven cloth. The one with clean, half-moon fingernails and smooth hair that glistened almost as much as the poison dripping from their spider fangs. They pushed against the floor and moved out of the shadows. Crawling. Watching. Crawling. Unnoticed, they stole across the floor and up the leg of the table. Then, Daji's spider legs, like the craggy petals of a white chrysanthemum, disappeared into the folds of the girl's dress. They were closer than they had ever gotten before. And getting closer.

Then, the white spider leapt from the sleeve onto the girl's hand — the skin as soft and delicate as a freshly steamed dumpling. The girl gasped, but it was too late. Daji had already stabbed her needle fangs deep into flesh. *At last,* said the glint in the beady eyes. The girl screamed.

The door flew open. The other girl, the one that smelled

of horse and chicken feathers, rushed in. "What happened?" she called out. "Xiu! What's wrong?"

"The nine-legged spider!" the stricken girl said, grasping her sister's strong arms. "The spider! It bit me! Oh, Mulan!"

CHAPTER 1

Hua Mulan

HUA MULAN felt Black Wind's mane whip her face as she pressed the horse to run faster. The man who sat behind her was tall but did not seem heavy, for Black Wind quickened his stride with ease. Still, Mulan worried. *Faster,* she thought. *We need to go faster.*

She urged the horse through a field, a shortcut that only she knew, while the dust Black Wind's hooves kicked up behind them rose like smoke. They galloped up the slope, the sun-tipped stalks stretching on either side of her as terraced rice paddies and farmlands below came into view.

This would be faster than following the road, she knew. But she also knew that if Ma or any of the villagers saw her, they would shake their heads with annoyance. Mulan always seemed to veer off the road.

But Mulan could not forget the look on Old Auntie Ho's face. When Auntie Ho had seen Mulan's sister, her wrinkles had frozen as if carved of wood, and Mulan felt a dread come upon her. Xiu was as pale as the moon and as hot as fire, and she lay motionless with eyes that could no longer open.

"Mulan," Auntie Ho had said, the worry clear in her voice, "your sister needs more help than I can give. In the Lu Family Village, there is a visiting healer. Take your horse and get him. If you go now, you will be back before dark. Go now. Quickly!"

Her parents had sensed the urgency, quickly waving Mulan off. Her mother had not even frowned at the reference to Mulan's skill at riding. Just before, Ma had been chiding her for riding Black Wind so often. "You try the patience of an Immortal! What girl rides a horse all the time?" Ma had scolded, as Mulan flushed with shame. "And it's given you wind-cold sickness. You can't even breathe out of your nose anymore."

Maybe this healer will be able to clear my nose, too, Mulan thought. But she knew she was only trying to distract herself from thinking about Xiu. How Xiu's eyes, so full of panic and fear, had dulled to be as unseeing as stones and how her hands had fluttered and fallen to stillness, like the petals of a dying magnolia flower. *It was only a spider bite,* Mulan thought. She had teased Xiu hundreds of times about spiders. She had joked about spiders in her hair, spiders in her teacup — with Xiu screaming as if the mere thought of a spider would kill her. *But a spider bite couldn't . . . Xiu couldn't . . .*

Mulan leaned forward. "Faster, Black Wind," she murmured into the horse's ear. They finally clambered onto the road, thundering past the layers of rice paddies. The plants swayed in their wake, waving thin leaves in greeting as if compensating for the farmers who had already left for their dinners. Mulan squinted in the early evening light, hoping to see her home in the distance.

At least the healer had been easy to find. The Lu villagers had immediately pointed her to the right home, and when she had burst in, she had gasped in surprise as well as exertion. Mulan was used to Auntie Ho with her bent back and dappled skin; she had been expecting another wizened, plain-clothed healer. But while this healer had a silver beard, he wore a lord's robe of brilliant red trimmed with blue. His eyes were strange, unusually light-colored. They were amber with pupils that burned like two black coals, which Mulan found disconcerting yet also oddly familiar. He had stood as if expecting her, his yellow bag already looped across his chest.

"My . . . my . . . sister . . ." Mulan had stuttered, "bitten by a spider . . ."

In return, he had given her a long, hard stare before simply nodding. "Let's go," he said.

And, finally, they were almost there. Now, she could see her village tulou, the large, round community building, bathed in the golden glow of the dipping sun. The villagers must have been watching for her, for the doors of the tulou were already opening. She was home. Mulan felt a surge of gratitude and warmth as they raced through.

Neighbors stared out from their windows and stood at their doors, and she could see the worry etched on all their faces even as they held up their hands in greeting. Big Wan, the village blacksmith, met Mulan at her door.

"I'll take Black Wind out for you," he said. Big Wan was so large that Mulan could meet his gaze even while sitting on the horse. So when she saw that his face held not only concern but sadness, Mulan felt herself turn cold.

The healer slid down from the horse behind her and his

feet hit the earth like a heavy weight. "Is Xiu . . ." Mulan choked on her words. "Is she . . . is she worse?"

Instead of answering, Big Wan gently took Black Wind's reins out of Mulan's trembling hands and helped her off the horse. "Better go in," he said. "They're waiting."

Mulan looked at the door and windows, closed and shuttered as if the house had been forsaken. Mulan gulped. She was home.

CHAPTER 2

The Healer

"WE'RE HERE!" Mulan cried out as she pushed open the door and stepped over the entryway. Her congested nose muffled her voice, but it sounded loud in the still house. She blinked to adjust to the darkness, holding the door open so that the light from the sinking sun cascaded over the floor like a translucent banner. "Here's . . . um" — Mulan realized that she did not even know her companion's name — "the Healer!"

He entered and scowled at the scene that greeted him, but

somehow Mulan knew his anger was not for them. They had created a makeshift bed for Xiu and she lay as still upon it as if she were a clay figurine. Mulan's eyes burned with tears when she saw that an embroidered cloth rabbit hung from a pole leaning on a nearby wall. In desperation, Old Auntie Ho must have fallen to old superstitions and dangled Xiu's favorite baby toy over her in hopes of luring her wandering spirit.

Mulan's parents had risen at the Healer's entrance, their eyes full of hope and gratitude, but the Healer waved them back down again. He walked to Xiu's bed and Auntie Ho lifted Xiu's limp hand to him, showing him the wound. His glare darkened. The two small pinpricks would have been impossible to see, except that a viscous, honey-colored liquid slowly oozed from them.

"Do you have many spiders here?" the Healer asked, checking the pulse of Xiu's left wrist and then her right.

"A few," Auntie Ho said. "But just the usual."

"Maybe not," Mulan's mother broke in. "Maybe there were more, or maybe something is strange about our spiders, after all. It would explain why Xiu has always been so afraid of them."

"She's been scared of spiders her whole life," Mulan said when she saw the Healer's eyebrows rise. Her mother's eyebrows rose as well, and Mulan knew it was because she was speaking out of turn again — not what a young girl, quiet and obedient, should do. But this seemed important to the Healer, so Mulan pressed on. "Xiu always acted as if spiders were chasing or hunting her." Then Mulan's voice faltered. "I teased her about it."

"Hunting her?" The Healer's voice held only the faintest question. "Do you know for certain that it was a spider that bit her?"

"Well, she said so," Mulan said, hesitating. "But maybe she just thought that because she's so scared of them? She said it had nine legs, and I don't think any spider — "

"Nine legs?" the Healer interrupted, dropping Xiu's arm and standing. He towered over them, the glint reflecting from his eyes like lightning. "The spider had nine legs?"

Mulan stared up at him and nodded. "That's what she said."

The mournful howl of a restrained dog somewhere in the village drifted into the room. As her father limped unevenly over to the Healer, Mulan realized how upset he was. He usually hid the pains of his old war injuries. She remembered seeing him limp like that only once before, when she was a child and had accidentally chased a chicken onto the roof. She remembered his faltering, unsteady steps as he ran toward her, so afraid she would fall to her death.

"Tell me," her father said. "This is not an ordinary spider bite, is it?"

The Healer hesitated. "No," he said, finally. He reached into his bag and turned to Mulan. "Put these in hot water," he said, handing her a small packet.

She took it to the kitchen and, as she suspected the Healer had given her this job so that he could talk to her parents and Auntie Ho in private, left the door open. When she opened the packet, she found a small bundle of dried, greyish-green herbs. They were so delicate, Mulan feared they would crumble before she could get the water heated.

She tended to the kettle, but could not help continuing to steal glances over her shoulder. She heard her parents recount Xiu's scream, how she had clutched at them and cried about the spider, and then how she had suddenly wilted in Mulan's arms. The Healer replied in low murmurs, and as Mulan gently placed the fragile plants in a bowl, she strained for the words. *Poison . . . reaching vitals . . . destroying her chi . . . death.*

Mulan felt an icy wind fly down her throat as the boiling kettle softly hissed, a thin snake of steam coiling from the spout. Slowly, she poured the water into the bowl.

The herbs seemed to dissolve into smoke, for as soon as the water touched them, Mulan saw a cloud billow up like the dust of swept ashes. She grabbed the bowl with both hands, hoping she had not accidentally done something wrong. The mist thickened, curving into her face and enveloping her. It grew into a heavy veil of fog that hid everything from view and dampened all sound. Suddenly, all was silent, and Mulan could only see whiteness. Her world had disappeared.

Chapter 3

The Frozen Village

MULAN SHOOK her head wildly, her hair whipping at the mist. She blindly set down the bowl, hoping the table had remained in front of her. As she released it, the fog began to thin. She rubbed her eyes and slowly began to see the familiar kettle and stove.

But when she turned, she had to rub her eyes again. It was as if her world had become a still painting. Through the open door, she saw the Healer's back and her parents' faces looking up at him. But their mouths were open as if struck silent midsentence and their outstretched, pleading arms were frozen in the air. Auntie Ho stood static next to the bed, her hands still clutching a red cord as she waited with the hope of tying Xiu's spirit back to her body. Everything seemed swathed with a soft silver light; even the scarlet robe of the Healer, which had been so brilliant before, was now the more muted color of a frosted hawthorn berry.

What had happened? Why was everything frozen? Mulan crept forward soundlessly, unwilling to disturb the suddenly hushed world. She was beginning to feel as if she had somehow slipped into a moonlit dream, where all — except her — slept.

But then, without warning, the Healer stirred. His arms dropped from his conversational gesture and, in a swift motion, he turned from Mulan and her parents, his robe swirling behind him. The sound of his boots echoed in the silence as he stalked out the door.

Mulan stared, openmouthed, and then stole out after him. Yet, the instant she stepped over the entryway, she stopped. Her mouth fell open even wider than before as she gazed, dumbfounded. Her parents were not the only ones suddenly still. All the villagers looked as if they had turned into statues. Big Wan held a dog by the scruff of its neck, the dog's wide-open mouth revealing he had been silenced while detecting a foreign animal outside. Boys, frozen in play, stood on one leg — a ball impossibly balancing on one child's toe. Above, a woman leaned over the balcony and a falling piece of her newly clean laundry floated just out of reach of her outstretched hand. Even the chickens stood tilted in their half-waddled steps.

The silver mist veiled everything, as if it were a sugared coating holding the world motionless. Mulan's head slowly spun as she continued to gape. It was everyone and everything she knew, yet it was not. For they all seemed fixed in a real place and time, while she was wandering alone in this dream. And here, there was no sound, no movement . . . except for the flapping red robe of the Healer as he wove his way around the stationary villagers and out the door of Mulan's village tulou.

CHAPTER 4

The Rabbit

MULAN DARTED around the frozen villagers, chasing the Healer's fluttering red robe as if she were trying to catch a butterfly. The crimson silk flapped out of view through the tulou's open entry and Mulan rushed forward, tripping over the doorway. Her arms splayed wildly and she fell, face-first, onto the ground.

As Mulan gasped into the dirt, she realized that outside her village, the sounds of the world were unchanged. Even as her feet had pounded on the floor of the tulou, the thuds had been muffled. Here, the wind's gentle roar and the warbles of the dusk-singing birds filled her ears. As she raised her head, Mulan saw that all was still tinged with a muted light, but unlike inside her village, everything was moving and alive. The grass and trees swayed, and black silhouettes of birds flew against the amber-colored clouds.

She could still see the Healer. He was far ahead of her — he had crossed the village's well-worn path and walked in the light-frosted grass toward the forest. His crimson cloak was streaming behind him like spilled wine, and with every step he took away from her, he seemed to grow smaller. Mulan squinted. No, the Healer did not *seem* to be growing smaller — he *was* growing smaller.

The Healer had been tall and lean, but now it was as if the sky pressed an invisible weight upon him to make him shorter and stockier. His silver hair was shortening, too. It spread over the skin of his neck like fur. His clothes adapted to his size, and when he appeared almost egg-shaped, two pointed forms sprouted out from his head. They were long and white, like two crane feathers. Were they ears? Yes, they were! *This is impossible,* Mulan thought. *I must be imagining this.*

But her eyes continued to show her senselessness. Because the Healer was shrinking even further! He was now the size of a dog. Mulan stared, her mouth gaping and her hands still pushed into the ground. The sky filled with the yellow light of the sun casting its colors behind the distant forested mountains as it fought its fade to darkness. The Healer's new pointed ears were tipped in this last golden light, but the grass mostly obscured his diminishing, round figure. The Healer stopped suddenly and shuddered. His clothes fell from him like the petals of an opening peony flower, and for a moment he seemed a soft mound of silver fur, brushed with the colors of the sunset. But then, in a sudden motion, he straightened, his long ears pointing upward, and Mulan's eyes widened to echo her perpetually open mouth. For against the orange-and-pink-streaked sky, the Healer's figure made an unmistakable silhouette. He had turned into a rabbit.

CHAPTER 5

The Foxes

THE RABBIT bounded forward in a smooth, fluid motion, and Mulan saw that the Healer's robes had also somehow transformed, becoming a bag that was slung across the rabbit's back like a thin crescent moon. The sky was now tinged purple, the night finally winning its struggle with the sun. The rabbit leapt again, a silver, sinuous curve soaring above the grass.

But then, as if made from the shadows of dusk, two canine

creatures burst forth and surged toward the rabbit like shooting arrows. Foxes!

One was small and dark. The other was larger and gleaming white, even in the dimming light. It was the larger one that shrieked so viciously that Mulan flinched. It attacked first, its sharp claws glinting as it pounced upon the fleeing rabbit. Mulan watched in horror as the rabbit collapsed, crumpling to the ground like an autumn leaf.

"No!" Mulan heard herself shout. She momentarily forgot about the Healer's strange transformation, the sleeping village, and her sister and parents, and saw only the pouncing foxes — savage beasts about to kill a helpless animal. She bolted up from the earth and rushed toward them.

Oddly, however, instead of devouring the fallen rabbit, the foxes were circling it as if watching for a return attack. Their snarls became a combined growl that seemed to grow larger and larger in the wind, filling Mulan's ears with a menacing melody punctuated by the drumming of her heart and feet.

She squinted. Perhaps it was the dimness of the night or the quickness of the foxes, but did the white fox have more than one tail? Mulan couldn't count them all and did not even try, for the white fox had pulled itself upward. She could see it preparing to strike again; its bared teeth and extended claws glittered against the now-black sky.

"No! Stop!" Mulan shouted again. Without thinking, she reached to the ground, grabbed a stone, and threw it at the white fox — just as she had thrown at thieving crows hundreds of times before. Even in the dark, she was a good shot, and the white fox yelped in anger and surprise. Mulan scooped up another handful of stones and wound her arm, ready to continue, when both foxes turned to her.

Their eyes met and Mulan froze. The moon broke through the night gloom, casting a soft light onto the quivering shape of the helpless rabbit. Now she could see that the smaller fox was red, the color of cinnabar. But it was the other fox, the white fox with many tails, that had startled her to stillness. The white fox's eyes glinted like black diamonds, cold and hard, and Mulan felt them bear into hers with the sharpness of a knife. A chill of terror crawled up her neck, but Mulan clenched her teeth and forced herself to raise her chin.

The white fox's piercing eyes narrowed, glaring with such fury that Mulan tightened her grip on the stone, tensing all her muscles. Then, with a toss of its head, the white fox dismissed her, spat in the direction of the rabbit, and shot away into the night.

When Mulan turned back, she saw that the red fox and the rabbit were locked in an unreadable gaze. Mulan glanced back and forth between the two animals, the red fox's eyes flickering like a wavering flame, while the rabbit's were as steady as moonlight. Finally, the rabbit shook its head sadly.

"Will you ever find your place?" the rabbit said, still looking directly at the fox.

Mulan's eyes bulged. *The rabbit talks?* she thought. She suddenly remembered all the oddities she had just seen and began to feel almost dizzy with shock. The stones dropped from her hand, thumping onto the ground like a dull rain.

The red fox swiveled its head toward the sound and hissed at her with spite. Then it turned and ran away, disappearing into the darkness just as the white fox had.

CHAPTER 6

The Rabbit Heals

MULAN STOOD in a daze. What was happening to her? Was she still Mulan, the older, untalented daughter of the Hua family? Once, when she was younger, her father had told her the story of the Jade Rabbit on the moon who used a mortar and pestle to make medicine. She had been so enthralled by the story that she had wheedled the job of pounding the rice into flour just so she could pretend to be the great Jade Rabbit. Mulan tried to do her job dutifully, but there had been one grain that repeatedly escaped her.

Determined to do well, she had struck at the grain with all her might. And then, *crack!* From the force of her blow, the mortar split in two and the rice flour flew up into the air, covering her in white dust. Ma had run out, crying, "Mulan! What are you doing? Control yourself!"

Maybe I have lost control of my mind, Mulan thought. *Or maybe it's not that everyone else is asleep; maybe I'm the one who's sleeping, and all this is a dream.*

"Could you help me?" a voice called politely. It was the rabbit. "Please?"

Mulan hesitantly walked over to the fallen rabbit. But as she came closer, she tried not to gasp. What she had thought were spots on the rabbit were really blotches of blood. Four black gashes on the rabbit's hind leg were seeping, staining the fur like spilled crimson ink. The rabbit looked up at her with serene eyes even while his body trembled with pain and weakness.

"You?" the rabbit said, sounding more amused than annoyed. His voice was still the Healer's voice, but somehow smoother and more flutelike. "You should be asleep with the rest of the village. But I am glad for your help. Could you get my bag, please?"

Mulan shook away all the confusion and reached for the rabbit's bag. It had fallen off during the foxes' attack and lay unharmed in the grass, gleaming pale and silvery in the twilight. As she grasped it, the rich silk felt as smooth as water in her rough fingers.

"Take out the blue bandage," the rabbit said, and stretched out his wounded leg, "and tie it here."

Mulan reached into the bag and found a blue cloth in her hand. It was light and soft as goose down, and when she held it up, it was like holding a piece of the sky. She knelt next to the rabbit and, as gently as she could, lifted his leg. Dark liquid continued to drip from the evil-looking slashes, so she quickly wrapped the cloth around the leg, making sure she covered the entire wound. As she tied the cloth securely, she saw a strange look in the rabbit's eyes — a mixture of admiration and respect. Mulan smiled to herself. Somehow, she had impressed this extraordinary talking-rabbit-healer being.

"Well done," he said, nodding.

Mulan stood up, but then began to gawk. For the cloth she had just tied was now melting into the rabbit's leg. As it disappeared into the fur, the ugly marks of blood also disappeared. In the space of a breath, the rabbit's hair returned to silver, shimmering in the light of the moon. The only remains of the violent attack were four long dark marks on his leg that looked as if someone had drawn them with a burned branch.

Mulan continued to stare, her eyes as round as rice bowls.

Just when she had begun to think that she couldn't be more surprised. . . . "Who . . ." she choked, "who are you?"

The rabbit gave a wry smile, and Mulan found herself even more bewildered to see such a human expression on an animal's face.

"Who do you think I am?" the rabbit said, gazing up at her with the same tranquility as before. *His eyes are like a cat's,* Mulan thought, *or maybe more like a tiger's?* They were round and amber with pupils as black as a starless night, leaf-shaped eyebrows jutting above. *They seem familiar somehow.* But she couldn't remember how. Her thoughts felt as stuffed as her nose. Perhaps she just needed to clear her head? Mulan sniffed and began to hunt among her clothes for a handkerchief.

"Ah, that's it," the rabbit said, in the tone of a mystery solved. Mulan gave up her search, for, as usual, she had no handkerchief. She looked at the rabbit quizzically.

"You didn't breathe in the herbs," the rabbit said, answering her look. "That's why you didn't fall asleep."

The rabbit stood, and Mulan saw that he was larger than she had thought, his ears reaching the height of her knees. She watched as the rabbit hopped slowly to the bag, favoring his injured leg. Then he pulled out a small embroidered pouch, the color and shape of a persimmon. The rabbit handed it to Mulan. "Smell this."

Mulan hesitated, looking at the pouch. A purple flower surrounded by the five poisons — viper, spider, toad, centipede, and scorpion — had been stitched into it with silk threads. That, too, seemed slightly familiar.

"It's not going to put you to sleep," the rabbit said, the amusement returning to his voice. "It'll clear your nose."

Mulan grimaced and then took a deep sniff. To her wonder, her nose did clear. She breathed the cool wind into her chest and marveled as air rushed out of her nose. She smiled. "So," she said hopefully, "you really are a healer, then?"

"Yes," the rabbit replied, taking back the pouch and returning it to the bag, "among other things."

"And those foxes weren't normal foxes, were they?" Mulan said. "I mean, they didn't even try to eat you!"

"No," the rabbit said with a laugh. "She wouldn't eat me now. That would be much too barbaric for one as cultured as her."

"As her?" Mulan said. "You know one of the foxes?"

"I know them both," the rabbit said, and a shadow passed over his face. "But it was the white one I was referring to."

"How do you know her?" Mulan said. She couldn't help asking, even though she knew it might be rude. She could hear Ba's quiet but firm voice reproving her. *A young girl like you should not be asking questions like that. Try to remember your place.*

But the rabbit did not seem offended. Instead, he was looking at Mulan thoughtfully, as if unsure where to begin. "I have known her for a long time," the rabbit said, finally. "But I only truly knew who she was when I died."

CHAPTER 7

The Rabbit's Story

"YOU . . . YOU died?" Mulan stammered. Everything from the silver light to the talking rabbit was giving her a dizzy, dazzled feeling, as if she had suddenly stepped into an imaginary land. She sat down on the ground, glad to feel the solid earth beneath her, and shook her head in wonder. Then she looked again at the rabbit standing before her.

He had been gazing off into the distance, lost in a dream.

But at Mulan's words, his head turned and his eyes refocused upon her.

"Yes," the rabbit said, "I died. It was a long time ago. It was like this. . . ."

The Rabbit's Story

When the land was young, the Supreme August Jade Emperor, the Ruler of the Heavens, decreed that the night of the full moon of the seventh month was to be sacred. On that night, those of the spirit world and of the Heavens could roam freely on Earth, and all mortal creatures were to prepare generous feasts in their honor. No person or animal, no spirit or Immortal was to feel hunger that night; anyone in need was to be given food if they asked. To refuse would not only be shameful, but bring dishonor to one's family and ancestors.

The beasts, too, were given this decree, and all planned accordingly. The monkey gathered chestnuts from the trees. The otter caught a supply of fish. The dog dug up a pile of taro roots and radishes.

But the rabbit worried about his feast. The rabbit ate only grass and realized that would be a poor offering to the hungry. So the rabbit decided to prepare differently. He went from animal to person and, with much bartering and wheedling, collected a grand assortment of food—from the monkey's chestnuts to a pot of milk from the cow.

But no matter what the rabbit promised or said, there was one being who refused to contribute to his feast. It was the white fox.

"Look at you," the fox mocked, "scurrying around like a peasant slave! Some dirty beggar is just going to gorge himself with your hard work, you know."

"I would rather work hard than risk the shame of dishonor," the rabbit said, stiffly and with a bit of haughtiness. "What about your own feast? Or does disgrace mean nothing to you?"

"Oh, I'll provide a feast," the fox said, in her sly way, "and mine will be the best of the lot. I'm not going to have to work like some poor drudge, either. Don't you worry about me."

The rabbit shook his head in disdain, his low opinion of the fox not improved by this interaction. The rabbit and the fox had never been friends—the fox often mocked the rabbit for being so serious and fastidious, and the rabbit found the fox shallow and unscrupulous. But the rabbit had never realized just how unscrupulous the fox was until the night of the full moon.

While it was still light, all the people and beasts arranged their displays of food. And what displays they were! Such an abundance had rarely been seen before. Tables seem to sag from the weight of the plates of noodles and dumplings and steamed buns. Heaps of lotus seeds and golden longan fruits sat next to bowls of wrinkled red dates. But the most lavish, the most bountiful—the jewel of all the displays—was the one the rabbit had prepared. His feast was an overflowing banquet. Mountains of blushing wax apples, pale round pears, and vibrant oranges rose over a landscape of soups and steamed rice.

Many mouths watered, and all wandered from neighbor to neighbor to take note of what would be on the night's menu.

One animal seemed especially curious about everyone's feasts. That animal was the fox. She went to each array of food and stared at it as if trying to balance each load with her mind. When she reached the rabbit's display, she stared so intently that the rabbit began to feel irritated.

"Why are you looking at my feast that way?" the rabbit demanded.

"Oh," the white fox said, that familiar, scheming smile beginning to curve on her face, "I'm just admiring it. I think yours is the best, actually."

The rabbit distrusted the fox's compliment, but could only nod in thanks. "And where is your feast?" the rabbit asked.

"Over there," the fox said, nodding her head at a covered mound. She saw the rabbit frown at the drapery. "It's still a long way until night, you know. I don't want all my food getting dried up and flyspecked. I'm surprised you're leaving yours all out in the open like this."

As she left, the rabbit's nose twitched and he looked up at the sky. The fox was right; there was still a while until nightfall. The rabbit hopped away and returned with a cloth of his own. Quickly and carefully, he covered his food as well.

So when night finally fell, the rabbit felt quite confident about his food offerings. And with this assurance, he was almost eager when the first beggar arrived in the animals' area. The beggar was obviously a pauper—an old bent man, with unattractive boils on his face and a long dirty beard. His clothes reeked so much of dung and dirt that the dog, sitting a *li* away, perked up his nose in interest.

"Supposed to be food for me tonight," the pauper cackled, his voice like a crow's. "What do you animals have for me?"

The monkey presented her chestnuts while the old man inspected the otter's fish.

"Can't eat those," the beggar yawped. "Raw nuts? Raw fish? How am I gonna eat that? I should've stuck to the people's area. Stupid of me to come here. You animals don't know how to be hospitable."

The animals looked at each other anxiously. Would they all face dishonor this evening?

"If you only give us a moment," the monkey chattered nervously while giving the otter a panicked look, "we'll get your meal cooked right away."

The man grunted as the monkey and otter rushed to set up a fire. He investigated the dog's radishes and the pig's turnips. "RAW!" the beggar bawled again, which caused those animals to join the monkey and otter in building an even larger fire.

"If you please," the rabbit said, speaking over the man's various noises of disgust, "I have food that you might enjoy."

The rabbit led the beggar to his covered feast. With a flourish, the rabbit removed the sheltering cloth, only to hear all the watching animals gasp in unison. Alarmed, the rabbit moved to take a quick look at his feast, then stared in horror.

All his food was gone!

Instead of mounds of rice and fruit, there were only bundles of grass. They were strewn across the ground cloth like fallen leaves, and the aghast rabbit felt as if he had turned to stone.

"GRASS?" the beggar howled. "YOU EXPECT ME TO EAT GRASS?! YOU ANIMALS ARE—"

"Come with me." The fox's coaxing voice broke the beggar's rant, and he turned to look at her. Giving him a beguiling look, she led him over to her covered display. Then, with a wink in the rabbit's direction, she plucked off the cloth.

It was the rabbit's feast!

There was no mistaking it. The pink apples, the white rice, the pot of milk . . . it was the rabbit's hard-won collection of food. The fox had somehow stolen the rabbit's offering. The beggar fell upon the feast with ravenous voracity, bits of rice and juice falling as he chewed openmouthed. The rabbit could only gape, struck dumb by shock.

"Don't know what that rabbit was trying do," the beggar grunted between bites. "It's insulting! Giving a man grass to eat!"

"Well, the rabbit does have a poor sense of propriety," the fox said, her voice dripping with condescension, "but we must pity his worthlessness. He has nothing he could feed you."

At that, the rabbit stirred. The grey rocks, the beggar's bellow, the blazing fire—everything seemed to be swimming around him faster and faster, a rope suffocating him with shame and humiliation. *He has nothing he could feed you.* The fox's words drummed in his ears. *He has nothing he could feed you.*

"Sir!" the rabbit spoke. He did not speak loudly, but the intensity in his voice cut through the crackling of the fire, and all, including the beggar, turned to him.

"I apologize for having nothing to feed you," the

rabbit said, looking directly at the beggar. "But, perhaps, you could eat ME!"

And with those words, the rabbit leapt into the fire.

For the rabbit, there was pain and blackness and then death. Which should have been the end. But it was not.

Because as the rabbit perished, the beggar stood in alarm. His matted beard suddenly began to smooth and darken; the blemishes on his face disappeared. The beggar raised himself to his full height and his filthy robes fell from him, revealing sky-colored, dragon-embroidered clothes. Imperial robes! He lifted his head, pearl tassels swinging from his hat, and began to shine with a radiance stronger than the fire. All could see that he was no beggar. This was the Jade Emperor. The Ruler of the Heavens himself.

As everyone fell to the ground in humble kowtows, the Jade Emperor approached the fire. With a wave of his hand, the fire extinguished with the charred form of the rabbit lying among the vestiges. The Jade Emperor looked down at the sea of bowed heads and spoke.

"Yes, it is I," the Jade Emperor said. "I disguised myself to test you, to see if you would follow the decree and how generous you would be. I see I have discovered the most unselfish of you, as well."

He bent down and plucked the blackened remains of the rabbit from the ground with a grotesque tearing sound. Ashes and coals fell from the wretched mass, but the Jade Emperor looked at it with tenderness. He pressed his hands around the sooty, misshapen form, and the burned body of the rabbit began to change. The scorched, brittle limbs softened and plumped. The covering soot turned to fur that lightened to silver and grew fine and lush. The rabbit's chest began to rise and fall gently, like the tender rocking of a sleeping baby, as breath returned to his body. Then the rabbit's nose twitched and his eyes opened, wide and wondering. In the time it would take for an incense stick to burn, the rabbit had returned to life.

"Rabbit," the Jade Emperor said, shaking his head at the newly woken animal in his arms, "you should not have harmed yourself. But I am truly touched by your generosity."

The rabbit's head rose. The full moon had scaled the sky and its soft light embraced him, basking the rabbit in a gentle glow.

"Ah, yes," the Jade Emperor said, looking up at the moon, "that would be a good place for you, now that

I've made you immortal. She's been lonely up there, and you'd be the perfect friend. I will take you to her."

Five-colored clouds suddenly appeared, and the Jade Emperor stepped upon them as if entering a sedan chair. Then, illuminated by the splendor of the Heavens, they began to float upward into the night. As the Rabbit crossed the sky, all the animals watched in awe and wonder—except for the white fox.

Instead, she burned with jealousy and fury and vowed to become as powerful as the newly immortal Rabbit. Her eyes glittered with a cold light that gleamed as brightly as the Rabbit's new home, the moon.

"You're the Rabbit on the Moon? The Moon Lady's companion?" gasped Mulan. "My father told me stories about you! You're . . . you're the Jade Rabbit!"

"That's what some call me," the Rabbit replied, the amusement returning to his eyes.

"Why are you here?" Mulan asked. She felt like a pot of water put to boil, her words and ideas bubbling over. "Why were you pretending to be a healer?"

"I am a healer," the Rabbit said. "You see me working with

a mortar and pestle when you look up at the moon, right? I've been mixing medicines for centuries. The Moon Lady often sends me to Earth to cure the sick and dying."

"So, you come to Earth," Mulan said, her thoughts connecting like stars in a constellation, "and transform into the Healer — "

"Not just the Healer," the Rabbit interrupted. "I take other forms as well."

"And you cure people!" said Mulan, too excited to acknowledge the Rabbit's words. "Like Xiu! You're here to save her."

The Rabbit did not answer. When Mulan looked at him, she saw that he was looking intently away, and a cold dread began to creep into her.

"You . . . you are going to save her, right?" Mulan said, her voice squeaking in the night air.

The Rabbit finally met Mulan's eyes. "No," he said, shaking his head. "I don't think I can."

CHAPTER 8

The Essence of Heavenly Majesty

"WHAT?" MULAN said, her voice rising. She pushed herself forward, her hands pressing into the ground. "What do you mean you can't save her?"

"Your sister was bitten by the nine-legged spider," the Rabbit said, meeting Mulan's eyes directly. "That means she is dying of *hupo* poison. To cure *hupo* poison, she needs to drink a decoction of Dragon Beard Grass and a freshly picked blossom of the Essence of Heavenly Majesty before the poison reaches her vitals."

"Well, can't you make it?" Mulan asked. "You're a healer."

"Of course I can make it, if I have the ingredients," the Rabbit replied, a bit snappishly. "But I do not. While I have the Dragon Beard Grass, I do not have the Essence of Heavenly Majesty."

"Where can you find it?" Mulan asked, jumping to her feet. She was ready to search under every rock and tree in the forest if it would save Xiu. This was her little sister! Xiu, gentle, shy Xiu, who had always looked to Mulan whenever she was scared. Mulan cringed inwardly when she thought about how she had teased her about the spiders. Xiu would forgive her, Mulan knew. That was the way Xiu was, always kindhearted and understanding. Mulan could not let anything happen to her.

"You can only find it," he replied, and then met her eyes with a pointed gaze, "in the garden of the Queen Mother of the West."

"Queen Mother of the West . . ." Mulan choked. "The Queen of the Immortals?"

The Rabbit nodded. Mulan sat back down.

"Well, you're an Immortal," Mulan said hopefully. "You must know how to get there. Can't you go?"

"I was going," the Rabbit said. "That's why I put your village to sleep. I was just about to start when those foxes attacked."

"But you can still go," Mulan said. "You're fine, now, right?"

"Unfortunately," the Rabbit said, looking down at the four dark marks on his leg, "I am not. The wounds the fox inflicted upon me are much deeper than you see."

"What do you mean?" Mulan said. A cloud drifted over the moon, dimming the light.

"I had planned to summon a cloud to fly to Kunlun Mountain, to the Queen Mother's palace," the Rabbit said. "And even then, getting the Essence of Heavenly Majesty would not have been easy. The Queen Mother tends to be protective about what is picked in her garden."

"You can't fly to the mountain now?" Mulan asked. More clouds gathered in front of the moon, making the Rabbit into a small, silver-lined silhouette.

"No," the Rabbit said. "As I told you, that was no ordinary fox. Her attack has all but destroyed my powers. I cannot even change forms now, and I cannot reach Kunlun Mountain as a rabbit."

"Yes, you can!" Mulan said, sitting up straight. "I can take you! We can ride on Black Wind."

Mulan stuck up her chin, bracing herself for another amused look from the Rabbit. But instead, the Rabbit was frowning.

"No," he said, shaking his head. "No."

"Why not?" Mulan asked stubbornly. "Black Wind is the fastest and strongest horse of all the villages here. We could get you to Kunlun Mountain almost as fast as your cloud!"

"It's not just the distance," the Rabbit said. "The White Fox . . . It's not a good idea."

"What other ideas are there?" Mulan said, feeling desperate. She remembered how Xiu had clung to her before she'd fallen unconscious. *Oh, Mulan!* Xiu had cried out, a beseeching plea for help. And now the Rabbit said there was poison eating away at her. Mulan knew they had to do this. There was no time to waste. "How else can we save Xiu?"

The clouds in front of the moon thinned. Mulan could see the Rabbit staring past her, up at the moon, his face troubled and slightly confused. He shook his head again.

"It would be a mistake to bring a mortal again," he said, mostly to himself. "Last time . . ."

"You can!" Mulan said. She knew her insistence was too brazen for a young girl and she could almost hear both Ma and Ba admonishing her, but she couldn't stop. This was too important. "If you don't let me take you," Mulan said, her words cracking, "what will happen to Xiu?"

The Rabbit met Mulan's eyes again. The moon finally pushed through the clouds, and its light swept down upon them both.

"Very well," he said. "It seems I have no other choice. The only way to save your sister is to have you come with me. You'd best go gather your things for the journey, for we should leave as soon as possible."

Mulan nodded, feeling as if she were full of chicken blood—a mixture of relief, excitement, and fear simmering inside her.

"When will the poison reach Xiu's vitals?" Mulan asked, standing up. "When do we have to have the plant by before it's too late . . . ?" Her voice trailed off and Mulan swallowed.

The Rabbit looked upward. The moon was in her full glory, a luminous pearl on black silk. "We must have the Essence of Heavenly Majesty in our hands before the night of the new moon," he said. "We have until then."

CHAPTER 9

The Red Fox

I T WAS not easy for her to attack the Rabbit. Of course she remembered him. How long ago was it? The sea had turned to mulberry fields, but she had not forgotten. She had been such a child then. So naive, so foolish. She had still believed that there was a place for her somewhere, a place where people would not look at her with narrowed eyes as if disgusted to live under the same sky. Or worse, cringe away as if expecting her to swallow them whole.

The Rabbit had done neither of those things, she recalled.

"Let me come!" she had said to him. "I can help!"

He had looked at her with those amber eyes that seemed to pierce into her. His expression was one that she had never seen before, at least not directed toward her. She had not quite understood it. But when he had nodded his head in agreement, she had pushed away all discomfort and questions.

She had been so eager to leave, to leave the place where she was unwanted. She had filled her head with dreams of returning as a hero, of her mother embracing her with gratitude, of her family and villagers clamoring around her with joy. She had thought going with the Rabbit would bring her that.

But he seemed to have known that it would not. He was kind to her. That in itself had been enough to disquiet her, but whenever he looked at her, there had been a trace of . . . something. Something sad and slightly rueful. Through all the land they had traveled, all the meals they had shared, all the conversations — she had felt it, a scalding needle constantly jabbing into her heart until it finally burned black.

"Will you ever find your place?" he had said to her, his eyes boring into her and uncovering a hundred years of memories. It was only then, seeing him again after so long, seeing him bleeding on the ground, that she realized what it was he had felt that made her turn from him.

Pity.

He had pitied her and she, unknowingly, had hated it. She had hated it so much that when Daji . . .

The White Fox hissed at her impatiently, her tails swaying as she stalked away.

She shook her head, trying to force aside her thoughts. Then, quickly, she ran after the White Fox. She knew better than to keep Daji waiting.

CHAPTER 10

Xiu's Toy

MULAN CREPT into her house, even though the Rabbit had told her the villagers would not waken even with the loudest of noises. The moonlight trailed into the house, the delicate light shielding the sleepers from the darkest part of the night.

Quickly, she gathered supplies — food, clothes, blankets — and shoved them into her pack in a disordered manner that would have horrified Ma. But Ma didn't see her now. As Mulan quietly passed her parents, they both stood silently with their eyes closed, wheezing peaceful sounds of slumber. Ba was leaning over awkwardly and Mulan could see the bindings that held his bad leg. "After we defeated the evil Emperor Zhou, the new emperor needed warriors to fight the invading Rouran, and my leg was badly damaged," he had once said to Mulan, recounting his mighty warrior days as she listened with starry eyes. "But I would do it again, and more. Nothing is too much to sacrifice to bring honor to our ancestors."

Would traveling with the Rabbit be honorable? Mulan wondered. She knew Ma would not approve of her going on a journey. "You must learn to diligently care for your family, Mulan," Ma had said to her. "A girl brings honor by care. Not by boldness." Mulan looked at Xiu and the cold, clammy whiteness of her sister's cheeks. Whether this was care or boldness, she knew she must go.

"I'm going to help get something that's going to save Xiu," Mulan said to her parents. She gulped uneasily and then said, with more hope than force, "I will not dishonor our family."

Her last words seemed to hang in the air as they all remained still. Mulan felt as if her chest was cracking — it was so full of love and worry and fear. She looked at the cloth rabbit dangling from the pole behind her motionless sister. Mulan reached out to touch the toy's soft, worn silk, the shabby threads as delicate as a newborn's hair.

Mulan slipped the cloth rabbit out of the loop of string and pressed it to her chest. She would take it with her. It would remind her of home while she was away. Mulan swallowed, wondering how far away she would go.

She turned back toward the static figures of her family. She bowed a farewell to each of them, feeling slightly as if she were honoring shrine statues. Then, grabbing Black Wind's riding gear, Mulan left her home to find the Rabbit.

The Rabbit was waiting for her just outside the tulou's doors. It was strange how ordinary he looked, just a rabbit sitting in wait by a silk bag. Though, Mulan realized, if you looked carefully, you could see the difference. There was an unusual luster to his fur, a silvery iridescence. But it was more than that. It was the way he sat so calmly and proudly, his head arched upward with a kind of regal majesty. *Not much like a common rabbit, after all,* Mulan thought.

"You can call Black Wind," the Rabbit said, in way of greeting. "He's awake."

Mulan nodded without question as she realized that rousing a horse was probably well within the powers of an immortal rabbit. She whistled and heard the sound of a faraway whinny. She knelt down and began to rummage in her bag, various items falling out as she finally pulled out the blanket.

"What's that?" the Rabbit asked, pointing at the cloth toy.

"It's Xiu's," Mulan said hurriedly as she shoved it back into the bag, embarrassed to be caught with a toddler's plaything. "Just to remind me of her."

"Oh," the Rabbit said, giving Mulan a strange and pointed look. Mulan felt her cheeks burning. Did the Rabbit think she was a child who needed a stuffed doll? She was surprised when he asked, "How did she get it?"

"Actually, it was given to me," Mulan said, "but I gave it to Xiu."

"How did that happen?" the Rabbit asked. "Tell me."

The Story of Xiu's Toy

When Xiu and I were children, my father and I were herding the chickens into the coop. I was very excited because my father told me that it could be my new job. I wanted to show him and everyone else that I could do it well.

However, as we were rounding up the chickens, one ran away. I rushed after it, determined to get it. But I was so busy chasing the bird, I didn't pay attention to anything else. I dashed through the courtyard, through the crowd of villagers, causing many to fall over. Soon, behind me, there was a trail of sprawled people, upset bins, and tangled laundry, with everyone shouting and yelling. But I didn't notice any of it. All I could see was that runaway bird. Even when the hen ran into the village shrine, I kept after it. And, to my great shame now, I accidentally broke the shrine statue.

Yet that still did not stop me. The hen jumped onto the balcony of the tulou and onto the roof. I climbed up as well, as fast as I could. I charged after the chicken, running along the slanted roof. But just as I was about to grab it, the bird flapped off the roof down into the courtyard, and waddled toward the coop. Xiu closed it in.

I was stuck on the roof. I saw my father below, hurrying toward me, worried. He called to me, telling me to climb down slowly. I tried to do what he said, but with my very first step, I slipped! Luckily, I was able to wedge a stick I was holding into the balcony and use that to break my fall. Somehow, I was able to twist in the air and land on my feet safely.

No one was pleased with me. All around me, people were shocked, shaking their heads and grumbling. When

I looked at my father, I knew I had disappointed him. I had, again, acted improperly and forgotten my place as a young girl.

The crowd slowly broke up, and, shamefaced, I began to scuffle to my father. But before I reached him, a peasant woman swept in and came up to me.

She was not from our village—she was someone I had never seen before. She was old, hundreds of wrinkles lining her face, and so sun-darkened that her eyes seemed light amber in her face. "Mulan," she said, "for you."

And she handed me this cloth rabbit. It's all old and worn now. But back then it was bright reddish orange with all the regular poison-fighting animals—the viper, spider, toad, centipede, and scorpion—embroidered in bright colors on it around some flowers. I remember thinking it looked so brilliant and new in her old, dappled hand.

I took it, and before I could even say thank you, she turned and left. She hadn't yelled at me or shaken her head or looked at me with disapproval like everyone else. Instead, she had given me a gift. I was confused.

My father was waiting for me, so I quickly put the stuffed toy in my sleeve and continued to him to begin my apologies. Later, I showed it to Xiu. She loved it right away. She hugged it and played with it, so I let her take it to bed. After that, I just let her keep it.

And it was for the best, too. That rabbit was Xiu's favorite toy, so much so that even now, years later when she's outgrown and almost forgotten about it, Auntie Ho still hoped it would lure her spirit back.

As Mulan said those last words, a wave of sadness and fear came over her, like an icy wind. The memory of her past disgrace stung, as did the thought of her sister, rosy and happy, when now she lay in the darkness, as white and as still as death. Tears burned in Mulan's eyes, and she was glad when the sounds of Black Wind galloping grew louder and he came to her, his black form outlined by moonlight. Hiding her tears, she avoided looking at the Rabbit and, instead, outfitted the horse with his saddle, tying her bag with the toy in it securely. Then she began to twist and knot the blanket around her waist and shoulders.

"What are you doing?" the Rabbit asked. "What's that for?"

"It's for you," Mulan said, scooping up the Rabbit and placing him in the folds of her blanket. As she adjusted the sling so she could carry him on her back, she heard him make noises of disgust.

"Like a baby," he said grumpily. "A baby!"

Mulan grinned to herself as she climbed up on Black Wind. The moon's splendor overflowed onto Earth, brightening it almost to daylight.

"Which way?" Mulan asked the Rabbit.

"Since I am stuck in this shape," the Rabbit said, still grumbling, "we'll need help. We can find an old friend of mine in the City of Rushing Water."

"The City of Rushing Water?" Mulan faltered.

"You've heard of it?" the Rabbit said. He pushed his paw free of the sling and waved. "That way."

"Ah, yes," Mulan said, not willing to admit that she had heard of it only as a place so far away that it was rumored to have a different sky. She clicked at Black Wind to start him moving. "It's quite a distance."

"Yes," the Rabbit said as Black Wind galloped. The land was soaked with moonlight and their figures swooped across it like shadow puppets pulled by an unseen master. "That is why we are leaving now."

CHAPTER 11

Daji

THE NIGHTS and days melted into each other. Black Wind seemed to fly, galloping so quickly and effortlessly across the earth that Mulan suspected that it was the Rabbit's manipulations. Rice terraces, the stacked layers of land jutting out like a dragon's backbone, made way to jagged mountains softened by greenery. They passed small villages and the huts of friendly farmers, all left curious by the vague answers given by the girl traveling with her pet (which further irritated the Rabbit and amused Mulan). Then, to Mulan's awe, the landscape brightened as trees turned coral and amber. Fan-shaped leaves fluttered around her like golden butterflies and the pounding of Black Wind's hooves was quieted by the tree-created carpets.

They rode deep into the night and then rose at sunrise to ride again. As Mulan traveled through lands she had never seen before, she began to think about Ba's old stories of when he was a warrior, traveling through the empire to help defeat the evil Emperor Zhou and fight the Rouran invaders. He would have raced through these same fields and passed these same trees. How magnificent Ba must have been! A great warrior who had brought such honor to their ancestors. Mulan felt a wistful guilt. If only she could do the same.

The air chilled, and one evening, as the sky was beginning to bid a somber goodbye to the sun, Mulan found herself shivering.

"You're cold," the Rabbit said in Mulan's ear. "We should stop."

They were traveling on a little-used forest path, and Mulan slowed Black Wind in a small clearing. She got off the horse and helped the Rabbit wiggle out of the pouch.

"It's colder in this area," the Rabbit said. "We should make a fire. It's not good for a mortal like you to get chilled."

Mulan nodded, her teeth beginning to chatter slightly.

"Go get some wood," the Rabbit said, reaching for his bag. "I'll make you something that will help."

Mulan nodded again, wrapped the blanket around her shoulders, and left the Rabbit rummaging in his bag with Black Wind supervising. She wandered into the light-dappled forest, searching for fallen branches among the fallen leaves. The leaves crunched under her feet, making a crisp, welcoming sound, but dry sticks were surprisingly rare, and Mulan meandered from tree to tree like a hungry sparrow looking for seeds.

She was getting colder and colder and beginning to despair of ever finding enough wood for a fire when a sunbeam temporarily blinded her. Mulan shaded her eyes and then saw that a stream of light, a glistening radiance slipping through the rampart of trees, was creating a path. On the ground in front of her, a stretch of leaves was lit by the sun like unrolled yellow silk. The air shimmered, the curtain created by the dying sun glittering and beckoning. Mulan could not help following.

It led her to an enclosure of trees. Bending tree trunks and gnarled branches had grown and twisted together, making an arched, glowing doorway. Mulan peeked in and then gasped.

There, in the center of the glade of trees, stood the most beautiful woman Mulan had ever seen. She was as exquisite as if she had been carved of jade, her face as delicate and as fine as a flower petal, and her black hair floating gently like a cloud. Her white robes flowed around her, waves of silk billowing. The brilliance of the sun cascaded down upon her, and her eyes sparkled as she saw Mulan.

"Hello," the fairylike creature said as if expecting her, her cherry lips curving into a smile.

Mulan stood silent for a moment, dumbfounded. She herself had given up on trying to be pretty long ago. "You always look like a wild crow, Mulan!" Ma would say when Mulan rushed into the house, her hair flying. She was so different from Xiu, whose hair was always smooth silk neatly framing her gentle face. Everyone in the village, including Mulan, admired Xiu, but even Xiu was a common blade of grass next to the lotus-flower face of this woman. Truly, no mortal, no *normal* person could be so incredibly lovely. Mulan threw herself onto the ground in a humble kowtow. This must be some sort of Immortal or goddess! What else could she be? As Mulan prostrated herself, she heard the woman laugh, a tinkly sound like the ringing of tiny bells.

"Stand up, child," the lady said. Mulan pushed herself up, feeling like a scrubby chicken as she tried to brush away the leaves clinging to her clothes and hair. "But you're not a child, are you?" the woman continued. "You're almost a young woman. Now, who do you think I am?"

Mulan gawked, her mind racing through names of fairies and goddesses. Who could she be? Who would be this beautiful and smile at her with such delight, as if actually pleased to see someone so graceless and gawky? Mulan realized she had never seen anyone look at her with such delight and approval. Even Ba, with his loving smiles, always looked at her with a shadow of worry.

The graceful being laughed again. "Well, you may not know who I am," the woman said. Her voice was like the strumming of a zither, lulling and smooth. "But I know who you are."

Mulan stared as if her tongue had been broken. Her eyes could only widen in wonder as a response.

"Yes, Mulan." The woman smiled, revealing her small teeth, like pearly pomegranate seeds. "And I know you are traveling with the Rabbit to save your sister."

Mulan nodded, but her mouth felt clumsy and numb. Why was she as mute as a gaping fish? Words had always come easily before — too easily, as they usually burst out of her mouth before she could stop them. Ma often despaired of her, and Mulan had tried many times to be as quiet as Xiu. But she had never been able to, until now.

"I'm here to help you," the woman said. "That rabbit has his points, but he's quite limited. He doesn't know mortals the way I do. Why, look at you, half-frozen! He doesn't care about you!"

"No," Mulan protested, the thought of the Rabbit loosening her words. "He sent me for wood so we could make a fire."

"He sent you, shivering and cold," the woman said, "into the forest — not worried if you got lost or if wild animals attacked. You poor thing! Don't worry, I'll take care of you."

The woman waved her hand in an elegant gesture. Mulan followed her motion and saw a heap of wood on the ground. Mulan jerked in surprise, unsure if the magical woman in white had made the wood appear or if it had been there the whole time.

"Yes, it's for you," the woman said to Mulan's astounded eyes. "Take it."

Mulan quickly began to gather the wood into her arms. It made an awkward collection as the knobby sticks refused to pile evenly, jutting and shifting. When she finished, she saw the woman was still smiling at her as if highly entertained.

"I have another gift for you as well," the beautiful woman said. From her sleeve, she took out a small glossy flask of creamy ivory. With a willowy movement, as if she were dancing in water, the woman stepped to Mulan. Her white hands whisked off the top and she brought the flask to Mulan's face, a sweet aroma wafting.

"Honey," the woman said. She dipped a long, slender finger into the flask. "Your rabbit might use it for medicine, but I think you should savor its sweetness."

She brought her finger toward Mulan's mouth, the honey clinging like golden dew. The fragrance seemed to encircle them, and Mulan was swathed by perfume and light. She suddenly felt lost in its splendor, as if floating on rushing water. Spellbound, Mulan raised her face, awaiting the anointment of the honey on her lips.

But before the white finger could reach her, a stick dropped from the clumsy bundle in her arms. Its bulbous knot struck her foot sharply, and Mulan yelped, jerking back. More sticks escaped, clattering to the ground with the clumping sound of an ox.

Mulan hurried to gather the fallen wood, catching a flash of annoyance on the woman's face. The enchanted moment was broken, and Mulan found herself clutching the wood tightly. But when Mulan looked up, the woman was smiling at her again. She laughed another tinkling bell laugh.

"Here," the woman said, slipping the flask into Mulan's sleeve. "You can enjoy it later."

Mulan nodded, the strange muteness coming over her again.

"You'd best go now," the woman said, "or the Rabbit might actually worry about you. But I will see you again."

Mulan, arms full, bobbed a farewell like a humble peasant to his lord. *What is wrong with me?* she thought, mystified by her own behavior. She was filled with uncomfortable feelings of shyness and timidity — feelings she had never quite felt before.

"If you need me," the woman said, "just call for me and I will come."

Mulan stopped and turned. "What should I call you?" she asked, forcing the words from her lips.

The woman smiled again, so radiant that it dazzled Mulan even from this distance. "You may call me Daji."

CHAPTER 12

The Red Fox

HIDDEN IN the shadows, underneath the falling leaves and crooked trees, she could feel herself trembling. She told herself it was fatigue — scuttling about and gathering all the fallen branches in the forest for Daji had been exhausting. But deep down, she knew it was not the labor of collecting wood that made her shudder. It was the honey.

She remembered that honey. The golden drop like a pendant of amber hanging from Daji's finger, glistening and glowing. The soft brush against her lips, the overwhelming sweetness, the sticky syrup clinging to her lips — she remembered all of it.

And just like this girl — this girl who was now disappearing into the falling darkness, stumbling with all the wood — she, too, had seen Daji as a goddess. So beautiful, so graceful and kind. *I'll take care of you,* Daji had said to that girl. Daji had said those same words to her, as well, long ago. How long ago had it been? All she could remember was the intoxicating feeling that had overwhelmed her. To be taken care of meant to be wanted. And how she had yearned for that! She hated when they called her the Unwanted Girl. But that was before she found out what they would call her as Daji's servant.

"The girl's gone!" Daji snapped. "Come here!"

She crept from the cover of the trees, keeping her copper-colored fox head bowed.

"I want to talk to you!" Daji said impatiently.

She willed the sickening feeling in her stomach to burst through her blood as she transformed, her black hair streaming from her head as her pointed fox nose melted into a human face. In a moment, she was kneeling before Daji, just as she had when she'd been as young as the girl who left a moment ago.

"Yes, Mistress," she said.

"The girl didn't eat the honey," Daji said in annoyance. "She's such a clumsy ox, I couldn't place it on her lips."

"Yes, Mistress," she repeated. She knew Daji didn't really want to talk to her. Daji just wanted someone to unleash her temper on.

"But the bottle will keep her quiet enough," Daji said grudgingly. "Yes, the girl will taste it soon. I will simply have to bide my time."

She nodded, unwilling to repeat herself a third time.

"Though it is time that I must not let them have," Daji said thoughtfully. "I will have to slow them down." Then Daji looked sharply at the woman before her.

"Yes, Mistress," she said, swallowing her sigh. She had learned long ago not to offer suggestions or voice any opinions. They were never wanted or needed and usually resulted in a scathing insult or a box of the ears.

"Come!" Daji ordered, clapping her hands. "You have things to prepare for me."

Daji waved her sleeve, and as it swirled in the air, she changed into the White Fox, her tails swaying.

She had no choice but to follow, returning to her own red fox form. But for the first time in a long time, she felt a resentful wave rush inside her. *I am not just your servant. I have a name,* she thought. *I am Xianniang.*

CHAPTER 13

Dragon Beard Grass

WITH THE wood she'd been given, Mulan was soon able to sit at a crackling fire, sipping a concoction brewed by the Rabbit. Whatever it was, the drink warmed her from her toes to her vitals. She watched the sparks fly from the fire in what should have been reasonable comfort, but her buzzing thoughts made her uneasy. The strange encounter with the beautiful Daji had left Mulan puzzled and unsettled, as if she were being woken from an enchantment.

She kept looking at the Rabbit, willing herself to tell him, but her lips stayed closed.

Her sleep that night was also uneasy, the small bottle of honey in her sleeve resting heavily in her head. Visions of a giant, attacking spider filled her dreams, and she found herself running through a river of honey in an attempt to get away. Just as the terrifying creature was about to catch her, Mulan woke up, gasping. She could still see the spider's evil black eyes, the giant sharp teeth, the nine pointed white legs . . . Mulan straightened, a cold breeze brushing her face. This was Xiu's spider! Mulan remembered Xiu's lifelong fear of spiders — had Xiu been plagued by these same dreams? Her heart twisted as she thought of her sister, tormented. Poor Xiu! She was always so awestruck by Mulan's daring. *Not that it's ever been something to be proud of,* Mulan thought ruefully.

The fire still crackled, casting a dim light on the Rabbit, who was in the deep sleep of the guiltless. Black Wind nickered as if feeling her unease, and she patted his nose. Then, careful not to disturb the sleeper, she crept to their bags and untied the red string the Rabbit had used to fasten their belongings together. She groped through their things, finally pulling out Xiu's stuffed toy. Her fingers stroked the silk embroidery threads, smooth and fine like the hair of her gentle sister.

Mulan hugged the toy to her, wrapped herself with a blanket, and lay back down. This time, when Mulan closed her eyes, sleep fell upon her heavily, swaddling her so tightly that she did not even stir when Black Wind's squeal filled the air.

❀

Morning came abruptly. The sun glared into Mulan's face, but it was the Rabbit's sound of dismay that forced her up.

"It's gone," the Rabbit groaned.

"What's gone?" Mulan said, alarmed.

"Everything!" the Rabbit said.

And everything *was* gone. The Rabbit stood forlornly next to the burned-out fire, ashes blowing in the wind like snowflakes. Mulan's plain cloth bag with the food and clothes and supplies was nowhere to be seen, as was the Rabbit's rich silk bundle.

"Where's Black Wind?" Mulan asked, panicked. She whistled and was relieved to hear a whinny and approaching hooves in the distance.

"Smart horse," the Rabbit said approvingly. Black Wind nuzzled at Mulan, who gratefully wrapped her arms around him. "He ran away before they could get him, too."

"Before who could get him?" Mulan asked, clutching the

horse close. "Did someone steal our things? Who would do that?"

"The foxes, of course," the Rabbit said. "They've been following the whole time, you know."

"They have?" Mulan said. She released Black Wind and fixed her gaze on the Rabbit.

"Yes," the Rabbit said, "just waiting for the right time to cause mischief. I wonder how she was able to finally undo the red thread?"

"Red thread?" Mulan said, a stone in her throat. "I . . . I untied the red thread. . . ."

"You?" the Rabbit said with surprise.

"I — I wanted to get something . . ." Mulan stammered, "in the middle of the night . . . so . . ."

The Rabbit sighed. "She seems to always know how to do the most damage with the least effort," he said, shaking his head.

"What do you mean?" Mulan asked. The Rabbit had made no admonishments, but Mulan felt the way she had when, as a child, she had once again accidentally broken the village's guardian statue — this time playing ball with the boys. "Why can you not play dolls with the girls?" Ma had asked impatiently. "Why can you not be like Xiu?"

"They took everything," the Rabbit said. "But she knew my bag was the most valuable thing. All my medicines and herbs were in it."

"Was there a medicine you needed?" Mulan asked, concerned.

"Yes," the Rabbit said, "the one that I needed for your sister. Remember, to cure *hupo* poison, I need both Dragon Beard Grass and the Essence of Heavenly Majesty. I had the Dragon Beard Grass. Now, I have neither."

Mulan's heart suddenly had the weight of a mountain in her chest. "Is the grass hard to find?"

"It only grows on Green Island," the Rabbit said, "but it is abundant everywhere there."

"Can we go there?" Mulan asked, trying to swallow.

"We will have to," the Rabbit said, sighing again. "She's trying to slow us down. She knows we only have until the new moon."

"Who?" Mulan asked. "The White Fox? Why is she still after you, after all this time?"

"She's not after me," the Rabbit said. "She is after you."

CHAPTER 14

Prophecy of the Hua Sisters

"ME?" MULAN gasped. Another gust of wind blew over them and the chilly breeze swirled the ashes over Mulan like a grey cloud. "Why?"

The Rabbit hesitated. "I am not sure I should tell you."

The ash that had settled on her began to itch. As she brushed it away, her hands were dusted a dull white, the same color as a funeral robe. "I need to know," Mulan insisted. "Tell me."

The Rabbit sighed. "It is another long story," he said.

The Story of the Prophecy

Through trickery or cleverness, the White Fox was able to gain many favors, and with her various guises, she lived often among mortals, enticing one to become her attendant: the Red Fox. She created havoc and drama wherever she went, and almost all the incidents ended with her fleeing while the Red Fox was left behind to safeguard her escape. After one such affair, the White Fox found herself alone at the site of the ancient bonfire.

Centuries had passed and the trees and moss had long claimed ownership of the place. But the White Fox, her keen nose heightened by magic arts, knew where she was. She could still smell the acrid odor of the Rabbit's burning flesh and the tiny particles of ash in the air. And something else . . . Her nose wrinkled and she began to sniff furiously, smelling the earth. *Yes,* she thought, *it is here.*

And then, she began to dig. It was difficult digging—roots and tubers clung to her claws and fought to keep what she was searching for in the earth. But the White

Fox was persistent, and finally she had pulled out what she wanted—a bone.

It was an ancient bone, cracked and crumbling, yet the White Fox treated it as if it were a phoenix feather. By then the Red Fox had rejoined her, and she could not help shivering when she saw the glint in her mistress's eyes. The Red Fox knew how the White Fox resented her latest forced departure, and this was the start of a vendetta.

And soon enough, the Red Fox found herself on the docks of a verdant island, again in the form of an attendant to the White Fox's noblewoman. The White Fox had adorned herself in opulent splendor; embroidered peonies gleamed on her silk sleeves and elaborate gold ornaments dangled from her hair.

"Him!" the White Fox hissed to the Red Fox, nodding toward a young man disembarking a ship. He was obviously a scholar, and a poor one, judging from the plainness of his robes.

The noblewoman glided toward him with her maid dutifully following, carrying her mistress's trailing finery above the many bird droppings decorating the ground, as well as ensuring that her fox tails were hidden. The noblewoman's willowy body swayed as she moved, and the faint scent of sweet honey rose around her; all eyes, from fishermen to fish, turned in admiration. The Scholar bowed as they approached him, the surprise evident in his face.

"May I help you?" the man asked.

"Yes," the noblewoman said, her rank and refinement displayed with every enunciation. "I have heard that you are a great scholar, the only one with the talent to do the job I need done."

"I will help you if I can," the Scholar said. "What is it that you require?"

"I need you to transcribe and translate this," the noblewoman said, waving her hand.

The maid stepped forward and presented a small gold casket, elaborately wrought and encrusted with jewels. With a nod from the noblewoman, the maid opened it, revealing an ancient, blackened bone.

"An oracle bone!" the Scholar said in disbelief. He stepped closer and peered at it keenly. "Very old . . . extremely old . . ."

"You will do it?" the noblewoman said. She framed it as a question, but spoke it as an order.

The Scholar stepped back.

"I'm sorry," he said, shaking his head. "A bone like

that . . . it isn't a small job. To transcribe, translate . . . it would take years. . . ."

"I can pay you well," the noblewoman said. "I will make you a rich man."

"I'm sorry," the Scholar said again. "I have to return home. I'm only here because my ship went astray. We are docking now to get supplies. I was not supposed to be gone for so long. My wife must be worried; I must return to her as soon as possible. I promised her."

He backed away, and the maid studied him. Did he suspect that they were not what they seemed? Was he distrustful? But his eyes, though regretful, were sincere to the point of naivete.

The Scholar bowed, and the women watched him as he walked away. "Very well," the noblewoman said. "This way will be more fun, anyway."

The Scholar went to a teahouse to wait for his ship to resupply. It was a lovely place with a view of the island's lush green hills and the azure sea. *Yes, a lovely place,* the Scholar thought, *but not as lovely as my wife's face.* He had no qualms in refusing the rich noblewoman's offer.

He was thinking so deeply about his wife that he

almost did not recognize the woman refilling his teapot. And when he did see her, he almost dropped his cup.

"Suhling?" he gasped. It was his wife! She smiled at him as she turned to go. He stood, upsetting the tea tray, the porcelain shattering into hundreds of pieces. But he did not even notice. She was leaving the room. In the doorway, she glanced over her shoulder at him and smiled again. "Suhling!" he yelled, and ran after her, his feet crushing the broken china.

He followed her out of the teahouse and down the path, past the green grasses to the rocky bluffs. Her slim figure was in the distance, but always in view—her white robes fluttering as if beckoning him. Then, as she walked the uneven coastline, she disappeared behind a craggy rock. He ran after her, but she was gone.

All he saw was the steep, rough rock face . . . wait, there was an opening in the jagged stone. Was there a cave? Had she gone inside? He stepped closer, peering into the darkness. Then he felt a sharp pain, and all was black.

When he woke, he saw his wife looking down at him, smiling, holding a tray with tea and delicacies. "Suhling?" he said in wonder.

"Ah, awake," she said. "Sleepyhead! You know you have work to do!"

She set down the tray and helped him up. It was then he saw he was in his own house.

"I'm home," he said, surprised.

"Of course," Suhling replied, and then a shadow passed over her face. "Oh, no, you haven't forgotten again, have you? Ever since you returned from your trip, your memory keeps disappearing."

"It does?" the Scholar said, shaking his head in confusion.

"Oh, dear," she said, handing him a cup of tea. "You still don't remember coming home, do you?"

He shook his head. She clucked worriedly. "Here, eat something," she said. "Maybe that will help."

She brought the Scholar a plate of honeyed plums. As he bit into one, he could not help a small groan of delight—its rich sweetness was a delicacy they rarely enjoyed.

"How are we able to have this?" he half mumbled, his tongue savoring the luxurious flavor.

She smiled at his pleasure and shook her head. "Don't you remember how that noblewoman gave you that job?"

"The noblewoman?" he said, swallowing. "She wanted me to transcribe an oracle bone."

"Yes," his wife said, relieved. She urged him to take another treat. "At least you remember that."

"But I refused," the Scholar said, bewildered, waving the sticky plum. "I needed to come home to you."

"Yes." She smiled lovingly at him. "But remember? She gave the bone to you to translate here at home."

And Suhling motioned to his desk, where a golden casket sat. The opulent jeweled box was out of place in the humble room, and he felt himself being drawn to it like a bee to a flower. He opened it. Yes, there was that ancient oracle bone.

"You said it would take a long time," his wife said, pushing him into the chair. "You had best start right away."

And so it began. The Scholar worked at his desk, hour after hour, day after day. As soon as he woke in the morning, his wife pushed him to his desk. Whenever he stopped to rest, his wife was there urging him to continue. She made sure he never had any need to leave, bringing him his meals and endless cups of tea and sweets. He ate mindlessly and noticed nothing else, for the work was all-absorbing. The bone was older than he could imagine, and he was fascinated by it. What secrets did it hold?

But one day, when he had to brush aside his beard from his papers to continue writing, he stopped. He touched his chin, curiously, feeling the long, coarse strands. He'd had no beard when he began this work. He looked up, and there was his wife, as she always was when he stopped working.

"Have you finished?" she asked him eagerly.

He shook his head, and her face fell in disappointment. "How much more is there?" She pouted.

"Not much more," he promised. "I have been able to translate most of the part that tells the prophecy."

"Prophecy?" the wife said, her eyes lighting. "What does it say?"

"It is incomplete," the Scholar said, "But so far it says:

"In the Family of Flower,
A bud.
In the Tenth Moon
Of the Rabbit

Begins to bloom.
A flower
Which will shield
The Son of Heaven."

"Son of Heaven!" the wife said. "That means the Emperor!"

"Yes," the Scholar said. He was looking at his fingers, wrinkled and frail. *They are the hands of an old man*, he thought. He stroked his beard again, this time looking at the white strands streaking the dark hair. He could not remember the season or year. He could not remember anything outside his desk and this room. He looked again at his wife, who for once was not smiling or looking at him.

"A bud . . ." she was saying to herself. "Someone who is a child now . . . but in the Year of the Rabbit, in the tenth month . . . starts to no longer be a child . . . will save the Emperor . . ."

The Scholar looked at his wife. A crafty, cunning look had come over her face, and he suddenly felt a chill of suspicion. He looked at her unlined, jade-like face and black hair, her smooth, soft hands. He picked up the oracle bone and stood.

"What is it?" Suhling looked at him, startled. Her face returned to its loving expression. "Darling, is something wrong?"

"Yes," he said, pushing away from his desk. "This bone must be cursed. It has brought evil spirits here."

"What do you mean?" Suhling cried. "Be careful! You'll damage the bone."

"The bone is evil," the Scholar said as he marched toward the door. "I must destroy it."

"NO!" the woman shrieked, throwing herself at the Scholar to stop him. She clutched at him, clawing at him like a wild beast to retrieve the bone. He grabbed her shoulders with a force that surprised them both.

"If the bone is not evil," he said, his jaw squaring and a fire flaring from his eyes, "then it must be you. Tell me, why is it you care so much for this bone? Why is it that the only words I have heard from you are to tell me to keep working? Why is it that I have a silver beard and you are still young and unchanged?"

He pushed her away from him, and as she fell, a white fox tail poked out from underneath her robe.

"A fox spirit!" the Scholar exclaimed. "You are not my wife! I want nothing to do with you or this bone!"

And in his outrage, he crushed the crumbling bone

in his hand and threw the dust at the woman on the ground. She snarled, all her loveliness replaced with a malevolent look of fury. He strode to the doorway and threw open the door. But as he stepped out, his feet took on a sudden heaviness.

He glanced down and, in shock, saw they had turned to stone! He felt the cold pressure grow up his legs and realized all of him was turning to numb, hard rock. He opened his mouth to call out, but no sound came from his lips, which had already turned hard and cold. All he could do before losing himself as an unfeeling statue was stare out into the green-blue sea around the island he had never left and yearn for the sight of his real wife.

❁

"The White Fox turned the Scholar into stone!" Mulan gasped. "That's cruel!"

"She is not one who cares for more than herself," the Rabbit said. "To be discovered and thwarted by the Scholar must have enraged her past the point of reason. And since he had eaten a great deal of her poison over the years, she was able to punish him with her most malicious of powers. Luckily, she has been too busy chasing your sister all these years to do that again."

"All these years . . ." Mulan trailed off. "The White Fox has been after Xiu for years?"

"The White Fox can change not only into a woman. She can change into any beast or bird or insect," the Rabbit said. He looked at Mulan pointedly. "Even a spider."

"The spider!" Mulan said. She felt as if a firecracker had burst inside of her. "With nine legs! The White Fox was the spider that bit Xiu!"

"Yes." The Rabbit nodded. "No doubt, she has been trying for quite a while to get your sister."

"Years . . ." Mulan said again. Xiu, and her fear of spiders! Mulan felt a flash of guilt. How she had teased Xiu about it! She had laughed and joked, while Xiu had truly been tormented by them.

"You couldn't have known," the Rabbit said, reading Mulan's anguished face. "No one would have guessed how the White Fox was trying to thwart the prophecy."

The prophecy. Mulan's mind spun like a yo-yo.

"Are we the prophecy?" Mulan asked. "Our family name is Hua — so are we the Family of Flower? Are Xiu and I buds?"

"So it would seem," the Rabbit said.

"And then . . . the tenth moon of the Rabbit," Mulan continued, slowly, frowning with concentration. "That must mean the tenth moon of the Year of the Rabbit. It's the ninth moon of the Year of the Rabbit now. That means by the next moon, a bud will . . . Does the prophecy mean one of us will grow up to save the Emperor?"

"That is a logical conclusion," the Rabbit said, "and the White Fox knows better than to add legs to a snake."

"Xiu!" Mulan cried out. "That's why we need the medicine by the new moon, right? Xiu needs to live past the new moon so she can grow up and save the Emperor!"

"That seems to be how the White Fox has interpreted it," the Rabbit said, his face expressionless. Then he looked directly at Mulan. "The White Fox probably also knows that if we have the Essence of Heavenly Majesty in our hands by the night of the new moon, the prophecy will be set."

Xiu's prophecy, Mulan thought. For, of course, it was about Xiu. She was the perfect daughter—conscientious, attentive, and obedient. Not like herself, so careless and headstrong. Mulan felt a rueful pang as she thought about the numerous scoldings and sighs she received, how worried Ba's eyes were when he looked at her. Mulan again felt that wistful shame, the air around her suddenly as heavy as rocks.

But as she thought of Xiu's ready, gentle smile and kind heart, the weight lightened. A pride began to fill her. Her little sister would save the Emperor! What honor she would bring!

What service to their country! Mulan knew Xiu must fulfill her destiny.

"We can't let the White Fox get her way," Mulan said, raising her chin. She jumped up and began twisting her blanket into the Rabbit's carrier. "We need to get both those plants and save Xiu."

"I agree," the Rabbit said, and as she placed him in the pouch, he looked at her with an odd expression.

"What is it?" Mulan asked, even though she knew the more proper response would be to say nothing.

"Nothing important," the Rabbit said. "I was just thinking how you do not give up easily."

Mulan flushed. "You can never give up, can you?" Ma had said to her so long ago, right after the chicken-chasing mishap. "Must you be as stubborn as a stone?"

"That will work well for us," the Rabbit continued.

"It will?" Mulan said, surprised. For once, could something about her be helpful? She pushed herself up onto Black Wind, now unhampered by any bags or supplies.

"Yes," the Rabbit replied. She could no longer see his face, but she could hear the amusement return to his voice. But the levity disappeared with his next words. "Let's go."

CHAPTER 15

The Red Fox

XIANNIANG HELD a robe — that girl's robe — and rubbed her fingers against the rough texture of the cloth. She used to wear clothes like this. Plain, homemade, humble. These days, with her magic, she could wear rich silk and jewels just by willing it. Strange how little that seemed to matter to her now. In fact, right now, her soft, delicate robe felt as heavy as iron armor.

"Destroy it," Daji ordered. Daji herself was crushing the

Rabbit's dried herbs to a powder, scattering it like the ashes of the dead.

So Xianniang grasped the robe in her fists and — *RII-IIIP!* — tore it in two. The hundreds of broken threads trembled from the force of the split, and she found herself thinking of the hands that had woven it. Most likely it was the girl herself who had made it. Hours and hours of sitting in front of a loom. She remembered doing that, making cloth not only for herself but her sisters and brothers, resenting each of them as they wore their robes.

Well, maybe not Bouyue. Her youngest brother was the only one of her siblings that did not look at her with disdain. Perhaps because he was so young and had not yet learned how to scorn her. But it was also his nature. With child-like generosity, he would drop his bamboo shoots into her bowl with his grubby hand. And once, when she was being yelled at, he placed one hand over his own ear and the other over hers.

This girl reminded her of Bouyue, she realized. They were different ages, of course, but when the girl looked back at Daji with that clear, earnest gaze of sincerity — those had been Bouyue's eyes. Xianniang felt an odd twinge inside her, something she had not felt in a long time.

"The honey wasn't in the bags," Daji said. "That means the girl has it."

"Perhaps the girl has tasted it already," Xianniang said, in mild reply as she realized that the strange ache in her chest was sadness.

"Yes," Daji said slowly. She was holding the flask that Mulan and the Rabbit had used for water. "But in case she hasn't," Daji continued, "I will give her another reason to."

And with that, Daji transformed back into her fox shape — her white neck arching against the blue sky — and began to growl. But it was not the rasping growl of an ordinary fox. No, this was a low, echoing roar that made the heavens moan. The growl grew louder and louder, and then the White Fox opened her mouth, her sharp teeth glistening in the bright light, and screamed — a scream of rageful command that seemed to split the sky. The sun itself dimmed as if in fear.

The White Fox brought the flask of water to her mouth, the liquid dripping down her peaked face and drenching her fur. When the flask was empty, she let it fall to the ground and raised her pointed nose up toward the darkening sky.

Then, like a cannon, the White Fox spat the water into the air. The water burst upward, and where the droplets touched, the sky filled with gloom.

The White Fox shrieked again, the violence of the sound

thrusting forward that murky black piece of sky. Swiftly, it flew to find its victims as her fury echoed against the land.

As the screeching, thundering cloud sped away, the White Fox changed back to Daji—her head held high with satisfaction.

"That will slow them down," Daji said, her mouth curving with malice.

"Yes, Mistress," Xianniang replied dutifully, but she was thinking of her long-dead youngest brother, Bouyue.

CHAPTER 16

The Storm

T HEY HAD been riding half a day when they saw the storm. Though, truthfully, Mulan heard the storm before she saw it. The trees had thinned and the earth now rolled out before them in waves of muted green and gold. She had been fighting pangs of hunger (and wondering what their next meal would be) but was determined to be stoic. *Ba never complained when he went to battle against the evil Emperor Zhou,* Mulan told herself, remembering the stories Ba had told her about his time as a warrior, and how she had secretly longed for those same adventures. *He had to ride for days without food and only a little water. I can do the same.* But her stomach refused to cooperate and whined continually. So when the thunder first rumbled, Mulan thought her stomach was making its loudest protest yet. The Rabbit, however, suspected otherwise.

"Behind us!" he said into Mulan's ear.

When Mulan looked, she immediately urged the horse to a fast gallop. For behind them, all had turned dark. An evil, thick cloud had risen over the land, blotting out the sun. Black Wind dashed across the vast expanse, but he was like a child's toy against the massive, relentless shadow. It seemed to be racing toward them, a beast charging across the sky for its prey.

"We can't outrun it!" Mulan said. Already the rain was pelting them — sharp, cruel rain, like thrown stones. The wind was filled with shrieks and roars, as if the sky were battling itself, and the Rabbit, though close to Mulan, had to shout to be heard.

"Over there!" he said, pointing. "That house! Go there."

The ceaseless rain was blinding, and Mulan could only barely make out what the Rabbit was indicating. It was more of a hut than a house and had obviously been abandoned. The earth had half swallowed it, and many seasons' worth of vines were entwined over the rough wooden walls and thatched roof. But it was shelter, so Mulan steered Black Wind to it.

Mulan left Black Wind under an overhang and entered the house with difficulty, the door crumbling and falling to the earth as she pushed. Mulan grimaced, remembering how she had often broken the door at home like that by accident. It would crash against the wall like thunder from a clear sky, with the sound echoing as the door clattered to the ground. "Not again, Mulan!" Ma would wail. "You are too strong for your own good." Xiu would try to keep her mouth from curving in amusement, and even Ba, in his patient way, would say, "Perhaps a bit gentler next time, Mulan."

However, now, as the door hit the ground with a dull thud, there was only silence inside the house. Silence and darkness.

Outside, the wind continued to howl and the storm beat against the house as if frustrated by their escape. But the house was strangely still, as if hushed by years of slumber. When her eyes finally adjusted to the dim light, Mulan could see the outlines of a stove, chairs, and containers; the house was so small that the main room shared the kitchen.

"Light the lantern," the Rabbit said. He was still bound to her, the carrier clinging with uncomfortable wetness. "There are probably fire-making tools by the stove."

Mulan lit the stove and the lantern, then released the Rabbit from her back. The light showed her the entry to the bedroom, where she found a wooden bed and cabinet blanketed in dust. She went to the cabinet and was grateful to see some clothes. They were all moth-eaten, with many missing pieces that were likely now part of mouse nests, but she found a tunic and dress that were mostly whole. Mulan stripped off her dripping garments and changed, slightly amused by the old-fashioned style of the dry clothing. As she gathered her sodden robes from the floor, the small flask of honey fell from the sleeve. Mulan picked it up. Her stomach groaned and she thought of how luxuriant it would be to let the sweetness coat her mouth, to let golden syrup slowly seep down her throat. But as she went to unclasp the flask, she stopped. *I should share it with the Rabbit,* Mulan thought. Yet, somehow, she could not bring herself to show it to him. She found herself frozen in the room, clutching the flask in puzzlement. Finally, she placed it on the ground next to the bed, like a shrine figurine.

She brought her wet clothes to the main room, leaving the honey behind. The Rabbit was already in front of the stove, enjoying its warmth.

"Good thing I made you the Nuanhuo medicine before my bag was stolen," the Rabbit remarked as Mulan draped her wet clothes near the fire. "You shouldn't be cold."

And she wasn't, though Mulan realized that she probably wouldn't have noticed if he hadn't mentioned it. She wondered what other things the Rabbit had managed without her knowledge. Had he made this house magically appear? Though, as she glanced at the thick-dust-covered room and the climbing weeds growing out of the broken windows, she imagined that he probably would've created a place a bit less shabby.

"Whose house was this?" Mulan asked. She felt sudden misgivings, helping herself to someone's house and clothes even though it all seemed from a time past. It didn't seem like the owners had meant to abandon their home — there were still clothes in the cabinet and a blanket on the bed. What had happened to them?

But the Rabbit didn't answer her. He was busy hopping away from the stove and springing on top of a covered vat to inspect the storage containers. "Vinegar," he said, nosing some small jugs. "Salt." He tapped the large bin he was sitting on. "This is probably rice," he said. "It's closed pretty tightly, so we might be lucky."

Mulan pried open the lid and was delighted that it did hold rice, just as the Rabbit had guessed. With her grumbling stomach, those white grains were more glorious than an ascending Immortal. She quickly pushed some large empty bowls out the door to collect the beating rain, her guilt of pilfering from lost owners forgotten with the needs of her belly. The Rabbit continued to snuffle around all the jars. "Tea!" he called out.

"But I smell . . . They're here somewhere. . . . Ah! Here!" He patted a deep pot, this one covered with a tied cloth. Mulan left the filling bowls and went to remove the top, only to see it was filled with what looked like dried mud. She grinned, grabbed a spoon hanging from the wall, and began to gingerly poke through it. She was soon rewarded with an egg, grey and speckled like a stone.

"Ha ha!" the Rabbit laughed triumphantly as Mulan peeled off the drab eggshell, revealing a glossy black preserved egg. "That is a hundred-year-old egg that probably *is* a hundred years old!"

However many years old they were, the eggs in the pot were perfectly preserved. And in the time it would take an incense stick to burn, Mulan had prepared a delicious meal of rice porridge — the steaming bowls making an aromatic cloud as the floating pieces of egg shone like lustrous black pearls. The storm shrieked the primal screeches of an attacking cat, with angry wind gusting through the cracks in the walls, but both Mulan and the Rabbit felt as if they were awaiting an emperor's banquet.

As Mulan placed the food on the table, she noticed a scrap of paper.

"What's this?" Mulan said, gently blowing off the dust. The sheet was brittle and old, with parts already destroyed by age or invading rodents. Faded words, like shadows of the past, lined the page, and Mulan squinted to read:

> . . . I fear he has met with some calamity. I will return with him or not at all. If I do not return, I leave this house as shelter for all travelers, man or beast, in hopes that the comfort it gives those in need will avail me mercy on my own journey. . . .

Outside, the wind wailed and the wooden slats of the closed windows rattled together like clattering bones. Mulan looked up blankly, confused, as the rest of the paper had long crumbled away. But the Rabbit was nodding knowingly, as if he had read the entire message.

"Ah, it's her house," he said. "Odd."

"The White Fox's?" Mulan exclaimed. "Was this her house?"

"No, not her," the Rabbit laughed. "This place wouldn't be fine enough for one of her whiskers."

"Then whose?" Mulan said, relieved. "Why is it odd?"

"Well, it's odd considering I just told you that story this morning," the Rabbit said, cocking his head thoughtfully. "It makes me think a highly eminent Immortal is influencing part of our journey."

"Wouldn't they tell you?" Mulan asked.

"One should not be told their fate," the Rabbit said, giving her another peculiar look. "Destiny works best when unforeseen."

"Well, what does this house have to do with this morning's story?" Mulan asked, shrugging off the Rabbit's stare. "Whose house is this?"

"I suppose she deserves to have her own story told," the Rabbit said. "After all, she, too, was an Immortal."

CHAPTER 17

The Waiting Wife

"THE OWNER of this house was an Immortal?"
Mulan asked. She glanced again at the home. Even
imagining it without the years of dust and grime, it was a humble place with plain, modest furnishing. It was not a place she
envisioned an Immortal living.

"Do you think we all live in jade palaces?" The Rabbit
laughed, and then added, "Though I suppose she did live in
one for a while."

"She did?" Mulan said. "Who was she?"

The Story of the Waiting Wife

In the Jade Palace of the Queen Mother of the West, there are many Immortals—all there for the glory of serving the queen. Those with the highest honor are the Immortals who are chosen to be her attendants.

At one time, a butterfly fairy was bestowed with such favor. She soon became a great favorite, accompanying the Queen Mother almost everywhere, usually holding the feathery fan over the queen's head.

But even in this exalted position the Butterfly Fairy felt strangely discontent, and she found herself often visiting the mountains underneath the Heavens. One day, during one of her wandering flights, she was amused to see a young man sitting against a tree, engrossed in a book. He was obviously there to cut wood; his ax and binding rope lay on the ground next to him. But this labor had clearly been long forgotten. She fluttered around him in her butterfly guise.

"Get to work, lazy egg!" she giggled. "Or you'll be cold tonight."

The man continued to read, the butterfly unnoticed.

"You'll be hungry," she teased, "if you have nothing to cook with!"

The man turned the page in his book.

"You are such a silly melon!" She burst out with exasperated laughter and landed herself right on the page he was reading.

"Butterfly!" the man said, finally seeing her. He waved his hand. "Please move. You're blocking my reading."

When she refused to budge, he shook his head and gently pushed the butterfly onto his fingers, bringing her to the ground. There, he saw his ignored ax and grimaced. He looked at the butterfly and smiled. "Were you trying to remind me to cut wood?" he said. His stomach growled, and he gave the butterfly a gentlemanly bow. "Thank you. If it were not for you, I'd be forced to go without dinner again."

The Butterfly Fairy was touched by his courtesy. When he knelt to pick up his ax, she transformed into her human form, a basket of food on her arm.

"How many days have you been without dinner?" she asked.

The man gasped and dropped his ax, very narrowly missing cutting his own foot.

"Wh-who . . . where . . ." he stuttered. "You must be a fairy!"

"Why?" she asked with a playful smile.

"You put the flowers to shame," he said, his face flushing.

She found herself touched again, and a softness began to bloom inside her. She looked again at the man. He was handsome enough for a mortal, but it was the kindness and sincerity that shone on his face that charmed her.

She sat down against the tree and patted the ground next to her. "Tell me about yourself," she said, offering him a warm steamed bun.

They both soon learned about the other—his lack of family and his lifelong ambition to take the Emperor's examinations, and her restlessness despite all the honors and wonders of the queen's palace. They discovered they shared a fondness for poetry and began quoting lines to one another. And, in the time it took to eat a meal, they were deeply in love.

Speedily, they prepared to marry. However, when the Butterfly Fairy asked the Queen Mother if she could relinquish her position in the palace, all the Immortals were aghast.

"How dare you! You would rebuke Heaven and your Immortal powers for a mortal man?" they gasped. "You insult our queen!"

But the Butterfly Fairy was steadfast, and even the disgust of the queen could not move her.

"Go then," the queen said, waving away her favored attendant with a flick of her sleeve. "Be a clay ox entering the sea, if you insist."

Yet even with such an inauspicious start, the marriage of the fairy and mortal man was happy. They were undeniably poor, wearing robes of rough cloth and surviving on plain rice. But the two were deeply devoted to each other, and if the Butterfly Fairy ever missed the delicacies of fruit and flowers served on golden platters or the silken luxuries of the jade palace, not a hint of regret ever passed her lips or showed upon her face. Instead, she dedicated herself to helping her husband prepare for the Emperor's examinations—studying with him and, she laughed, making sure he ate dinner.

But one night, the Butterfly Fairy was disturbed by an unexpected dream. As she slept, one of the queen's other attendants, an Immortal who had been her dear friend, visited her.

"Sister!" the Butterfly Fairy said in surprise.

"I fear I am not here for joyful greetings," her friend said soberly. "The Queen Mother bade me give you a warning. She says there is a shadow on your mortal husband."

"A shadow?" The Butterfly Fairy gasped. "What is it? What will happen?"

"You know I cannot answer your questions," she said, shaking her head sadly. "The Queen Mother says his spirit will depart unless you are by his side before the magnolia blooms."

"Does that mean he will die?" the Butterfly Fairy demanded. "What does the Queen Mother mean?"

"You must be by his side before the magnolia blooms," her friend repeated, embracing the Butterfly Fairy lovingly. "The Queen Mother still carries a heart for you and fears the upcoming winds and waves will drown you, too."

The Butterfly Fairy woke greatly troubled. The Emperor's exams were at the Imperial City, a great distance from where they lived. The most practical way to get there was to travel to the port village and take a boat. But they had only enough money for one fare. He would have to travel without her. She spoke with great concern to her husband, who did his best to allay her worries.

"The Emperor's exams are in the autumn. I will leave directly after," he promised. "I will be home before midwinter, with plenty of time to spare before the flowers bloom."

She reluctantly agreed, and when he departed in the summer, he repeated his promise to her.

"Even if the Emperor himself asks me to stay, I will decline," he vowed to her. "I will let nothing delay me. As soon as the examinations are done, I will return."

She smiled at him, but was unable to hide her fear.

"Don't worry," he said, catching her hands in his. "My spirit will never depart this earth unless you are with me."

Yet as she watched him leave in the summer sunset, she could not stop a sense of foreboding. The misgivings only grew as the days turned into months and the bitter winds of winter arrived. She kept vigil during the long dark nights of the season, but he did not return. And as the days began to grow longer and her husband still did not arrive, a chilling terror began to overtake

her. Then one morning as she heard the icicles melting—
their droplets falling to the ground like beads from a
broken necklace—she knew she could wait no longer. She
packed traveling supplies, closed the house, and left for
the port village where her husband had caught his boat.

And when she got there, she stood where the boats
docked, day after day. In the wind, in the rain, in the
sun and sleet, she waited—not caring or noticing that
her clothes had become torn and ragged. The villagers
whispered about the woman who remained at the river's
edge like a statue and watched for her husband. They
called her the Waiting Wife, and the few that dared to
meet her eyes were forever haunted. "It was like watching all the hope of the world die," one old woman said,
her own eyes misting.

Few plants grew by the river's edge, but the Waiting
Wife saw the mountains in the distance grow green, the
emerald color spreading like slowly poured honey from
the sky. The air grew warmer, and more and more boats
arrived at the village, but none carried her husband. One
day, a family ran to greet an approaching boat, carrying
an armful of flowers to welcome their visitor. As they
dashed by, a branch from their bouquet fell at her feet.
She reached for it as if in a dream, but when she saw

the delicate pink flower blossoming from it, she dropped it as if it were a poisonous viper. For it was, of course, a magnolia in full bloom.

No one saw her blanch or grab her chest; none saw her turn ashen or crumble to her knees in a despair too sorrowful for tears; but all noticed when she was no longer there. The Waiting Wife, the constant, solitary woman by the river, had been replaced. Instead, there was large rock—as white as bone and strangely shaped with twisted layers, hollow eyes, and ragged holes like those in the tattered clothing of the Waiting Wife.

"She turned into a rock?" Mulan exclaimed. "She couldn't have! She was a butterfly fairy! Immortals can't die!"

"Well, Immortals can't die," the Rabbit said, shifting slightly. While he had been speaking, the rain had misted onto him through the open window slats, and now a single droplet of water fell from one of his whiskers like a tear. "But they can be killed."

"What do you mean?" Mulan asked.

"Being an Immortal only means you are immune to sickness and aging," the Rabbit said, another peculiar look appearing on his face. "Just like mortals, we can be killed by blade or poison."

"You can?" Mulan said. "But the Butterfly Fairy didn't poison herself."

"Not exactly," the Rabbit said. "She turned herself to stone rather than exist with a broken heart. And while it is not exactly death, it is close enough."

"So she's not dead?" Mulan pushed. The wind, in between shrieks, was hushed as if holding its breath.

"No," the Rabbit said slowly, "but she's not alive in any way we would call living. That could only happen if she reunited with her husband. . . ."

"Her husband," Mulan said as the low hiss of the wind began to strengthen to a shriek. "He's the scholar you told me about this morning, isn't he? That's why you thought it was odd we're here."

The Rabbit nodded. "It cannot be coincidence that we just happened on her house," he said.

"You think another Immortal is doing something?" Mulan asked. "Who? And why?"

"I don't know." The Rabbit shrugged. "But to maneuver this — it must be someone quite powerful." He hopped over to the window and pulled aside the mostly whole curtain, a thick coating of dust flying into the air as he did so. "But it's nothing to be troubled by," he continued. The storm outside had returned to its enraged, fevered rush of screams and rain, but it was now muffled by the house's ancient stillness. "So far, whoever it is has helped us."

I'm here to help you, Daji had said. Mulan thought about the beautiful creature and the magic that seemed to sparkle in the air around her. Was Daji the powerful Immortal influencing their journey?

CHAPTER 18

The Date Tree

THE STORM raged until nightfall, giving one last shriek — an angry farewell full of bitterness — as the moon entered her dominion. The storm had seemed determined to destroy the house, so the hush of night was a relief. However, sleep still did not come easily. Mulan had dusted and cleaned the bed and had even found a blanket that was mostly intact. Compared to the cold ground she had been lying upon during the journey, it should have been a luxurious chamber. But being in someone's home reminded Mulan of her own; and when she closed her eyes, she saw Ma's and Ba's faces. What would they think if they knew she was here? Ma would be aghast. Mulan could easily imagine her eyebrows raised to the sky, her face incredulous with shock and displeasure. "Mulan!" Ma would say, just as she had when she'd seen Mulan try to shoot an arrow from one of her father's old bows, pretending to be a warrior. "What kind of girl are you? If you continue like this, you will never bring honor to our ancestors!"

But Xiu would. Mulan could never be the kind of girl Xiu was — so quiet, attentive, neat, and graceful. She was glad that her kind, soft-spoken sister would bring such honor, but alone in the darkness of this ancient room, she felt the twinges of shame and longing. How she wished she were good enough to be a pride to their family, too.

It was not to be, Mulan told herself. She hugged Xiu's stuffed toy. She, with her clumsiness and impulsiveness, would never amount to much, but she could at least make sure Xiu fulfilled her destiny. Yet it was poor consolation, and as she twisted and turned through the night, she found herself thinking about the Waiting Wife, who must have had her own sleepless nights upon that same bed.

So Mulan was awake when dawn arrived, the pink and gold light fringing the curtain of darkness. As the sky thinned to silver and then blue, Mulan rose. Quietly, she crept out of the house, careful to step over the sleeping rabbit — though, given the way he was snoring, she suspected that even a treading foot would not wake him.

Black Wind's whinny welcomed her as the damp wind chilled her face. Mulan patted his head and led him out from the sodden shelter. The world twinkled with starry dew, the morning mist still blanketing the earth. Black Wind nuzzled Mulan's neck, and she saw an area of the thatched roof that was somewhat dry. *She did say she left the house for man or beast,* Mulan thought as she tore off an armful of grass. She made a sizable pile, which Black Wind immediately began to eat. She jumped on top of a large stone to reach for more, but a scatter of red in the distance caught her eye. Mulan cocked her head at the scarlet dots on the faraway trees. *Cherries?* Mulan wondered. No, it couldn't be; it was the wrong season. Curious, she hurried to the trees, leaving Black Wind to graze.

How the dates had managed to survive the storm as well as greedy birds was a wonder, but there they were — the small crimson fruit, some already wrinkled from ripeness, dangling beneath yellowing leaves. Mulan grinned, pulling herself up onto the branches. She searched out a smooth fruit and popped it in her mouth. She crunched at its sweetness and then spat out the pit, watching it fall to the ground like a copper coin. She felt suddenly rich and, making a basket with the skirt of her robe, began seizing handfuls of dates. *These will keep for a long time. Some of them are almost dried already,* she thought. *Along with the rice from the house, this means we won't be hungry. It's so lucky.* Mulan stopped picking dates. Was it luck? It seemed it could not be another coincidence. *Another Immortal must be helping us,* Mulan thought.

And then, almost as if on cue, a tinkling laugh sounded below her.

Chapter 19

The Peach

"Y OU'RE LIKE a little monkey up there," a silvery voice below teased.

Mulan looked down, and there was Daji in all her splendor and beauty. Again, her hair and robes flowed and floated around her, sparkling with more brilliance than the morning dew. Mulan shifted uncomfortably, suddenly itchy in the old borrowed robes. Her legs dangled, and she felt like a tattered peasant shedding dirt. She opened her mouth to try to form a greeting, but her words seemed to have abandoned her. Why did she have such a hard time speaking when Daji was near?

"I'm glad you found the date tree," Daji said, reaching to pick one, her sleeve waving about her like a billowing cloud.

"Did . . . did you bring it here?" Mulan stammered. "I mean . . . did you make it so I could find food?"

Daji gave another tinkling laugh. "I'm sure the Rabbit told you that there are some things best left unknown," she said, her face dimpling with a coquettish smile.

"Yes," Mulan said, her words coming out as slowly as if they were bathed in thick syrup, "but he thinks another Immortal is helping us. Is it you?"

"Another Immortal . . . ?" Daji repeated. Beside Mulan, a small brown bird landed and began to peck at the fruit, cocking its head at the two of them between bites. "But of course," Daji said. "I told you, I'm here to help."

"The Rabbit is trying . . ." Mulan felt her mouth go dry and was unable to continue.

"I'm here to help you," Daji said. "Not the Rabbit."

"But the Rabbit needs the —" Mulan tried again.

"The Rabbit doesn't know what he is doing, fussing about with his medicines and herbs," Daji said, waving her hand as if to brush him away. "Those plants won't work."

"They won't?" Mulan gasped. "But —"

"Mulan," Daji interrupted, smiling sweetly, "I'm here for you."

The wind blew gently, making the leaves and branches sway. The cool air filled Mulan's open mouth, pressing her words down into her throat.

"Everyone wants to save your sister, I know," Daji said. "You, the Rabbit, your mother and your father — they would do anything to make sure she survives. And of course they would. She is the perfect daughter — graceful, accomplished, and poised. Everything you are not."

Mulan flushed. She stared down at the dates in her lap and saw that in her climb, she had made a dark dirt smudge on her skirt. Even if she washed it, the skirt would be forever stained.

"But you can be," Daji said. "I can help you. If you do as I say, you can save your sister and be anything you wish to be."

Mulan raised her head. Daji stretched her arm out as if beckoning while the sun and the morning mist created a shimmering halo of divine light around her. She looked like a painting of a benevolent goddess welcoming a worshipper.

"Yes, you," Daji said to Mulan's questioning eyes. "You could be just as charming, just as lovely — more so, even."

A breeze brushed over Mulan's face, as soft as a tender kiss.

"Think about it, Mulan," Daji continued, her voice coaxing. "No longer careless and improper, always charging recklessly like an ox. No longer accidentally breaking bowls and statues. Your mother, no longer ashamed of you. Your father, no longer in despair over you. Instead, Mulan, you could be the pride of your family."

Mulan felt Daji's words curve up toward her, a stretching vine with tendrils of yearning. The bird hopped closer to her, a piece of date clutched in its beak. Could Mulan truly bring pride to her family?

"Yes," Daji said, answering Mulan's silent question. "You could be as beautiful and as graceful as the magnolia flower you are named for, and save your sister, too. But it is not the Rabbit's plants that can do it."

Mulan leaned forward and a handful of dates spilled out from her lap, thumping on the ground like heavy raindrops.

Daji gave her silvery laugh and, with a lithe movement, plucked one of the fallen dates off the ground.

"When you get to the Queen Mother's garden," Daji said as she placed the date in Mulan's lap, "don't waste your time with the Rabbit's little herbs. What you want is the peach."

"The peach?" Mulan asked, the words popping out from her.

"Yes," Daji said. "A bite of the Queen Mother's peach will save your sister and give you all you ever wished." She reached up to grasp Mulan's chin in her hand. "You must pick the peach from the Queen Mother's garden."

"The peach," Mulan said, finding that she could only repeat the words dumbly.

Daji smiled again. "Remember," she said, releasing Mulan's face, "it's the peach you want."

Daji withdrew her hand, and Mulan saw that the tips of Daji's long, slim fingers were tinged bloodred from the fruit. But before Mulan could even react, the bird gave a quavering trill and flew in front of Mulan's face and up into the air. Mulan's head jerked, and for just a moment, she gaped up at the small bird fading into the sky. When she looked back down, Daji was gone.

CHAPTER 20

The Red Fox

"SHE HAS still not tasted the honey!" Daji said in exasperation. The sharp beak of her bird shape had already melted away, and though she stood tall and beautiful again, her face was scowling. "What is wrong with this girl?"

Xianniang stretched herself into human form, her feathers disappearing into the smooth silk of her robes.

"And did you hear her?" Daji continued. "She said the Rabbit thinks another Immortal is helping them. Why? Who could it be?"

"I don't know, Mistress," Xianniang said, her bland voice belying her interest. For it was intriguing. *Was* there someone helping this girl? Was that why she had been able to defy Daji and her honey so far?

"At least now she knows about the peach," Daji said, waving her hand as if trying to brush away her annoyance. "She will not be able to resist that."

The peach. Xianniang remembered the peach, too. How it hung from the branch, rose-tinged, as if brushed with the light of the sunset. When she had reached for it, she had told herself it was for Bouyue. One bite would save him from the illness that was plaguing their village, something that all the herbs the Rabbit was collecting could not promise. It would save him and make her a hero, all the contempt for her transforming into admiration and acceptance.

She hadn't realized that as soon as her fingers touched the soft velvet skin of that peach — as soon as the sweet, luscious smell drifted into her nose — she, just like Daji said, had not been able to resist. Without even thinking, she had brought the peach to her face and taken a bite.

That one sumptuous, exquisite bite had destroyed everything.

"But it would be best if they never reached the garden at all," Daji said, tapping her slender finger on her cherry-red lips. Her white teeth glinted. "I shall have to be more *forceful*."

"More forceful?" Xianniang said, only the slightest question in her voice.

"Yes," Daji said, slowly. She flicked her sleeve with an imperious motion. A smile was forming on her face, a smile that Xianniang had seen many times before and knew meant mischief. "I think I shall rouse the bees."

CHAPTER 21

The Strange Cloud

THE RABBIT and Mulan were soon traveling again, the land slowly fading from green to brown. Mulan was grateful for the bag of food that bounced against her leg, but her thoughts seemed to bump uncomfortably inside her head with the same rhythm. *Your mother, no longer ashamed of you,* Daji had said. *Your father, no longer in despair over you. You could be the pride of your family.* How had she known? It was as if Daji had seen Ma's and Ba's disappointed faces and grieved eyes and had heard the whispers of Mulan's own heart during the darkness of the night. Had Daji come to help her? Then Mulan flushed. Was she so hopeless that she needed an Immortal? Mulan shook her head, trying to push the thoughts away.

When she had returned to the house with the dates, she had found, again, that she could not bring herself to tell the Rabbit about Daji. The flask of honey, which Mulan guiltily returned to her sleeve, also remained unmentioned.

It was strangely easy to keep secrets from the Rabbit. While he answered questions, he rarely asked them, and she noticed that he seemed to be spending more and more time sleeping. She often heard his snoring in her ear as they rode Black Wind, and he had recently taken to quickly retiring to bed after they had eaten in the evening.

So this time, it was Mulan who first noticed the danger. Underneath the Rabbit's sighing sounds of sleep, Mulan heard a distant rumble. *Not another storm,* Mulan thought, and began scanning the horizon for shelter. The empty grassland stretched far into the sky, the vivid blue making the grey-browns of the earth seem more faded in comparison.

As the humming grew louder, Mulan glanced behind her. And then, stopping Black Wind, she stared.

Yes, there was a cloud in back of them. But what kind of cloud was it? It was the strangest cloud Mulan had ever seen.

It seemed to be made of flickering shadows of tiny leaves, thin and filmy. It glittered and rippled, and the earth trembled with its buzzing.

Mulan nudged the Rabbit, who snorted awake.

"Hmm?" the Rabbit mumbled.

"Look," Mulan said, pointing. "What is that?"

The Rabbit's eyes widened. "GO!" he ordered, suddenly completely awake. "NOW!"

CHAPTER 22

The Bees

"GO! GO!" the Rabbit yelled louder than she had ever heard him speak before. Black Wind gave a loud neigh, and Mulan saw the whites of his eyes bulging and his nostrils flaring. Needing no more encouragement, Black Wind turned and flew into a gallop, the wind slapping Mulan's face.

"What is it?!" Mulan shouted to the Rabbit, Black Wind's crashing hooves and the hissing sky all but deafening her.

"Bees," the Rabbit said into her ear.

"Bees?!" Mulan made a quizzical face.

"They're swarming," the Rabbit said, "and they're swarming for us."

Mulan looked behind her again and then felt as if she had sucked in a breath of cold air. The rising and falling cloud *was* made of bees! Thousands and thousands of insect wings were swelling toward them, thousands and thousands of pinprick eyes glinting. The air trembled with a sibilating wrath, and Mulan pinned herself to Black Wind's neck, urging him even faster as he hurtled across the ground.

But the bees were relentless. They focused on the figures on the horse, gathering and bursting toward them like a shooting arrow. The buzzing was no longer an ominous murmur, but a rasping, grating shriek. Mulan looked desperately at the open plain ahead of them. There was no place to hide, no place to take cover. They could only run.

Mulan glanced over her shoulder and the terror squeezed in her chest, becoming a hot coal in her stomach. For the massive cluster of stinging insects was streaming toward them like an unstoppable, furious wave. There was no escape. Panic pushed Black Wind to a frenzy, and they raced frantically forward, pounding against the throbbing, empty earth.

"Mulan." The Rabbit spoke urgently in her ear. He wrestled his leg free from the wrap and let it dangle. "Pull the hair from my leg and throw it at the bees."

"What?" she gasped.

"Do it!" the Rabbit ordered.

The air vibrated with buzzing and Mulan felt as if her own blood were sizzling. With Black Wind's galloping drumming in her ears, Mulan reached with one arm to grasp at the Rabbit's leg and pull at the fur. To her surprise, the hair slid out easily, like newly sprouted grass, but she could feel it harden in her hand.

Then, in one fluid, forceful motion, she yanked Black Wind around, his mane whipping, as she turned to face the mob of raging bees. A deep, guttural roar burst from her throat as she felt a volcano of power erupt inside of her. With a strength she didn't know she had, she threw the Rabbit's hair at the swarm — her own hair and sleeve whirling and billowing like the tails of a wild kite. The thin hairs catapulted from her hand, flashing as they turned into thousands and thousands of sharp metal needles.

The needles soared at the mass of bees with a whistling keening, a high-pitched scream cutting through the rasping buzz of the sky. The tiny blades found their mark, and there was a swift, strange spitting noise, like a muffled popping of a thousand firecrackers.

And then . . . were the bees exploding? Each one seemed to be bursting into a blaze, but they were flames unlike any Mulan had ever seen before. The brilliant colors of a rainbow — purple, blue, gold — bloomed out from the insects. Their droning hum vanished, and the world was silenced to only the sound of Mulan's panting breath.

She sat frozen, her arm still suspended in the air, as she gawked. Butterflies! All the bees had turned into butterflies!

For a moment, they hovered. Their fragile wings flapped a trembling, multicolored cloud around Mulan as she continued to gape like a confused chicken. "Uh . . ." Mulan said, her head turning back and forth in confusion. She raised her hand in a tentative gesture. "Shoo?"

It was more a question then a command, but the butterflies immediately scattered. They flew up into the clear blue sky, adorning the heavens like fluttering flowers.

Mulan slipped off the horse in a daze. She stared up in disbelief at the withdrawing wave of butterflies, following them blindly across the field. Each butterfly was so delicate that even a gentle breeze blew it off course, yet it had only been a breath of time since they had been a vicious, killing swarm. It had only been moments before that she had been fleeing them for her life.

Black Wind nuzzled Mulan's shoulder and she gently

patted his face. The Rabbit thrust his head over the other side of Mulan's neck, his nose twitching as he peered up at the departing insects. The vivid butterflies became specks of color in the sky as the Rabbit's pink, naked leg hung below Mulan's elbow.

"Well done," the Rabbit said, as she placed him on the ground. And, suddenly, Mulan found herself smiling with the warm glow of pride.

CHAPTER 23

The Rabbit's Leg

THEY WATCHED until the last of the butterflies disappeared and the sky, clear and still, reached unblemished to the Heavens. "That's finished," the Rabbit said, with a satisfied grunt. "If only freeing all her servants were so easy."

Mulan nodded, but she barely heard him. She was too distracted by his leg. With the hair missing, the Rabbit's bare leg was pale pink, like the skin of a newborn baby. It would have been a funny sight, this soft, naked leg poking out from all of the Rabbit's dignified silver hair, except for the four stab wounds that marred the smooth skin. The scars were deep pink — like stains from a fruit — but a syrup-like amber liquid trickled from them.

Mulan could not stop staring. Even as she shuffled back to Black Wind, her eyes kept returning to the Rabbit's leg. The puncture marks. The seeping, golden-colored ooze. The Rabbit's wounds were just like Xiu's! There were four of them and larger, but they were the same kind of marks, the same kind of blistering. Xiu was dying of poison . . . did that mean . . . ? *Being an Immortal only means you are immune to sickness and aging,* the Rabbit had said. *We can be killed by blade or poison.*

"OW!" Mulan yelped. A sharp, stabbing pain burst from her toe, and she hopped and squawked as if being burned by a hot coal. She dropped to the faded grass and grabbed at the silver glinting from her foot. As she yanked it out, the stinging stopped. Between her fingers was a delicate needle, obviously a stray that had missed a bee. She shook her head in chagrin. She was always such a clumsy egg, like the time she'd been playing with the boys and kicked the ball so hard that it flew past them and broke the shrine statue . . . again.

Black Wind whinnied as if laughing, and the Rabbit watched with amusement.

"The mighty warrior, Mulan," the Rabbit said, in a tone of mock pageantry, "felled by a needle."

Mulan snickered. "More like the great weakling," she said, and then, as his words took shape in her mind, she began to hoot with laughter. "Me, a mighty warrior!"

The Rabbit only smiled, but his eyes twinkled as if he were silently laughing at a private joke. Mulan shook her head again and grimaced at the needle, even though the disgust was more for herself.

"Don't worry," the Rabbit said, with another smile. "It won't kill you."

Mulan poked the needle into the earth and then looked at the Rabbit. "But will the White Fox kill you?" she asked.

The Rabbit looked up in surprise. He met Mulan's worried eyes, and then slowly began to hop over to her.

Mulan nodded toward his wounded leg as he hopped. "Those are just like Xiu's," she said almost accusingly, as if he had argued with her. "You've been poisoned by the White Fox, too, haven't you?"

The Rabbit sat down next to her, the crisp grass making a crunching noise despite being withered.

"Yes," he said. "The White Fox injured me with *hupo* poison."

"Are you dying from it, as well?" Mulan demanded.

"Yes," the Rabbit said simply.

Of course he was, Mulan realized. He was always so tired and sleepy as they traveled. Now, as she looked at him, she could see he was smaller than when they had first met. Smaller, paler, and slower.

"It's not a coincidence that it is now that we are running into trouble on our journey," the Rabbit said. "My power has been diminishing. I can no longer shield us from the White Fox."

"You think she sent the bees?" Mulan asked.

"Of course," the Rabbit said, "and the storm, too. As I said, my powers are no longer strong enough to protect or assist us."

So he had been affecting things, Mulan thought, remembering the days of easy riding and fair weather.

"How much time . . . will you be able . . . ?" Mulan stumbled, as there didn't seem to be a proper way to ask your companion when he would die.

"I am stronger than your sister," the Rabbit said, "but I took in more poison. It seems I have until the new moon as well. The White Fox is poetically skilled with her poison."

"But if you can make the medicine for Xiu," Mulan said, jumping up, "you can make it for yourself as well. You can save Xiu and yourself."

"Yes," the Rabbit said. "I admit, that thought did cross my mind."

"Then we should keep going," Mulan said. She whistled for Black Wind, who had wandered off for fresher pastures. "You need that flower from the Queen Mother's garden, too."

"The flower from the Queen Mother's garden and the grass from Green Island," the Rabbit reminded her. "Your sister and I need both."

Mulan nodded as she hoisted the Rabbit into the carrier on her back. She was eager to continue, but a pang of uneasiness filled her. *Those plants won't work,* Daji had said. What if Daji was right?

CHAPTER 24

The Red Fox

"HOW DARE they?" Daji sputtered, her eyes blazing with fury. "The Rabbit and . . . that . . . that . . . girl . . . ! I cannot believe that little human-faced, beast-hearted witch!"

Xianniang said nothing, knowing better than to point out the self-blindness of Daji's insult.

"They destroyed them all!" Daji fumed. "All my bees! All of them!"

"The bees were not really destroyed," Xianniang pointed

out, and then immediately regretted it. That was not something Daji would want clarified.

"They are completely useless to me now!" Daji stormed. "They might as well have been destroyed! I can't believe it! My bees! I cultivated them for centuries!"

Longer than you cultivated me, Xianniang thought. She suspected that her own destruction would cause Daji less anger than that of the bees.

"The Rabbit must not be as sick as I thought he was." Daji continued to seethe. "He must be healthy for his power to still be so strong. . . ."

"Perhaps it was the girl?" Xianniang said.

"Nonsense!" Daji scoffed. "Do not talk foolishness, Xianniang."

Xianniang said no more; she did not agree. She saw the girl differently than Daji. This girl was not heedless, Xianniang had realized. The girl was like Bouyue, never noticing the dirt on his fingers but clearly seeing that Xianniang's bowl held only plain rice. And yes, the girl was clumsy, but Xianniang could see it was because she did not know yet how to control her great strength.

But Daji saw the girl only as awkward and unkempt — truly as opposite the refined, exquisite Daji as possible. Daji could never imagine that a girl so unlike herself could have any worth. Unless it was serving her, of course.

Was that how you thought of me? Xianniang wondered. How well Daji had been able to hide it! Daji had seemed so kind, so caring. But probably, Xianniang realized, the weakness had been her own. She had always longed for someone to show her such affection, to tell her she was not unwanted. In truth, Daji's gentle words had held as much power over her as the poison.

Of course, Daji's words were far from gentle now.

"But the girl will regret it, too!" Daji was snarling. "I will make sure she never gets to the garden! She and her sister can die a dog's death! Get me a flat stone!"

Xianniang did not bother to ask the size of the stone to fetch. She knew what Daji was planning, and while this did not make her hesitate, it did cause an odd feeling of curiosity. Daji was truly infuriated with this girl.

The stone Xianniang fetched was sizable and fairly smooth. It was also quite heavy, and Xianniang staggered as she placed it upright against the boulder where Daji was waiting impatiently. As soon as the stone was leaning securely, Daji flicked her sleeve and turned into the White Fox.

A sharp claw flashed from her paw, and with a *skkriiiiiik* that made Xianniang shiver, the White Fox scratched a straight line across the stone. Then the White Fox leaned in close and breathed upon the stone — a hot, burning breath that made the stone glow red. When she pulled away, the stone returned to its dull grey color, but the scratch was now a black scar that ran all the way through it.

The White Fox raised her head, surveying her work with satisfaction, and then, with a quick gesture, pushed the stone to the ground. It fell with clattering thunder, and a cracking noise filled the air like lightning. The sky gasped and groaned as if the earth had been stabbed.

Xianniang peeked over the White Fox's nine tails, each swaying with the arrogance of a peacock feather. Yes, the stone had split in two. The black line across the stone was now broken, a sharp wedge of space separating the pieces. Xianniang's eyes followed the head of the White Fox, her nose pointing to the horizon like an arrow. It was done.

But would it stop the girl?

CHAPTER 25

The Canyon

AFTER THE BEES, Mulan felt as though anything might happen to them as they journeyed. She half expected wild monkeys to attack or a hurricane to blow upon them. But as the days passed, she began to be lulled by the monotony, and she found herself thinking about Xiu and her parents, safe but frozen in the village. Would they understand why she had again acted so improperly? "A daughter brings honor through care of her husband and family," Ma had said.

"What man will marry a girl who flits around on rooftops, chasing chickens?"

Or goes on journeys with talking rabbits, Mulan thought wryly. But the words had cut into her, sharp slices that went straight into her heart. Xiu had grabbed her hand then, and her soft, warm touch offered comfort and love. Mulan began to feel the tears burn in her eyes. Improper or not, she had to save Xiu. She blinked the tears away and glared at the land now filled with dull greys and browns, with only glimpses of color from evergreens to assure them that the world was not completely dead.

"We aren't far now," the Rabbit said. Above, the sky was beginning to darken, and fish-shaped clouds were tinged golden as the sun began to dip. "This road leads straight to the City of Rushing Water."

Mulan felt relief flood through her. That morning, Mulan had woken to find a sheet of silvery frost glittering around them. She wasn't sure if it was because of their campfire, the warming drink the Rabbit had made her long ago, or the Rabbit's remaining powers, but she was grateful they hadn't frozen to death in their sleep. She was hoping for a real bed under a roof soon.

"Hopefully," the Rabbit said, "we'll find my friend quickly."

"Where in the city does he live?" Mulan asked.

"Oh," the Rabbit said, "he doesn't live there."

"He doesn't?" Mulan asked. "Then how do you know he will be there?"

The Rabbit paused. "I don't," he admitted.

Mulan almost halted Black Wind as she peered at the Rabbit over her shoulder.

"What?" she asked. "You don't know if he'll be there? How will we find him?"

"If he's there, we'll find him," the Rabbit assured her. "Lu Ting-Pin is always where the festivities are. We just have to find the biggest crowd of people, and we'll find him."

"Lu Ting-Pin?" Mulan faltered. "Isn't he one of the Mighty Eight Immortals?"

"He used to be one," the Rabbit said.

"Used to be?" Mulan questioned. "How can he —"

Black Wind gave a loud snort and Mulan looked back in front of her. Then, she gawked, and all other thoughts fell away.

For the earth before them gaped wide open, as if monstrous hands had torn the land apart. They stopped a safe distance away from the edge, but Mulan could see they were on a towering cliff. The road on the other side looked hazy, veiled by the great breadth of the chasm. Mulan quickly scanned the skyline and, as the sun sank deeper, realized the gorge stretched out endlessly.

"Let me down," the Rabbit said, wiggling from Mulan's back. After she had freed him, he stood at the edge and shook his head. "The White Fox," he spat, as if he were cursing.

Of course, Mulan thought. *She did this.* But how could she be so powerful? The White Fox seemed to be able to turn Heaven and Earth upside down.

"She has learned the landscape illusion, finally," the Rabbit said. "She was always a master of transforming her own appearance. I suppose it was only a matter of time."

"It's an illusion?" Mulan asked. "It's not real?"

The Rabbit shrugged, and Black Wind gave another snort. Mulan bent down and grabbed a stone from the ground, tossed it into the gorge, and watched as it bounced off the edge and slowly disappeared into the shadows. She looked at the Rabbit.

"Let's just say," the Rabbit said, "that it is real enough."

"Can we go around?" Mulan asked.

The Rabbit shook his head. "We'll have to jump," he said.

CHAPTER 26

Leaps of Trust

"JUMP? ACROSS the canyon?" Mulan almost choked. "Are you joking?"

The Rabbit shook his head again.

"There's no way we can jump that far!" Mulan protested. "It's impossible."

The Rabbit gave a small chuckle. "You should know by now that when you travel with an Immortal, nothing is impossible."

"Yes, but . . ." Mulan looked out at the vast gash of missing land between them and the road. It was true that since she'd left home, everything had felt like an unreal dream, but to jump across this never-ending gulf? How could she do that?

"You'll just have to trust," the Rabbit said.

"Trust you?" Mulan said.

"Yes, me," the Rabbit said, "but also yourself."

Mulan looked again at the wide abyss, the bottom shrouded by black shadows.

"I'll go first," the Rabbit said.

"We aren't going together?" Mulan asked. "Black Wind isn't going to carry us?"

"We would weigh him down. He's already carrying all the bags," the Rabbit said. "We should be able to carry ourselves."

"But . . ." Mulan started, then realized there was nothing to say. "Will . . . how do I get Black Wind to jump?"

"He knows," the Rabbit said, and he arched his head to Black Wind, his ears swaying. Black Wind whinnied. "You might want to take a running start like him. That might help."

Then the Rabbit hopped to the cusp of the cliff as casually as if he were sauntering down a country path. There, he stopped, and then, as if skipping over a puddle, he jumped from the edge.

Mulan gasped as the Rabbit flew through the air, a shooting star at dusk. He grew smaller and smaller, a silver ball, then finally, a pale dot on the road across the canyon. The light-colored, distant speck hopped up and down, and Mulan could imagine the Rabbit calling to her, urging her to come. The Rabbit had made it across.

Black Wind nickered and Mulan reached up to embrace his head. "Well, he did it," Mulan said to the horse. She made sure all the bags and the saddle were secure and then patted his neck. "What have the two of you been talking about without telling me?"

Black Wind whinnied again and nuzzled her neck. Mulan released him and he gave a small snort. Then he trotted around and behind her in a wide arch, lengthening the distance between him and the cliff.

Only when he had reached his desired span did he begin to run. Mulan felt the ground tremble as he galloped, dust billowing behind him.

Then he was past her and Mulan saw only haze as she coughed though his ballooning cloud. The grit had just begun to settle when she saw Black Wind give a mighty leap off the edge of the cliff. Mulan felt as if she were still breathing earth as she glued her eyes onto Black Wind's lunging shape, hurtling through the pink-washed sky. Then, as lightly as a black butterfly, he landed on the other side. Mulan sighed with relief.

She swallowed. Now it was her turn.

"For an illusion, this canyon sure seems real," Mulan said

to the empty landscape. "I hope the Rabbit is right." *The Rabbit doesn't know what he is doing,* Daji had said. But there he was, far away, across the gorge — a small hopping spot next to the toy horse that was Black Wind. *You'll just have to trust,* the Rabbit had said. He hadn't asked her or tried to convince her, she realized. He had just trusted her.

Mulan looked at the canyon in front of her and took a deep breath. She began to run. She sped across the earth, faster and faster, her thudding feet matching the rhythm of her pounding heart. Her hair whipped behind her, the burning in her legs and lungs bringing her blood to a boil. Closer, closer, she pushed herself forward even while the gaping chasm seemed to grow bigger and wider, a mouth opening to swallow her. Closer. Closer. Almost there. And . . . there it was!

Mulan slammed her foot on the edge of the cliff and thrust herself forward with all her might. "AAAAHHHHHH!" Her own wild scream rang in her ears as she squeezed her eyes shut. She flung her arms into the open air as if hoping to grab onto the clouds as she fell.

But she wasn't falling. Mulan opened her eyes. She was vaulting through the air, the wind shoving her across the gulf. The small shapes of Black Wind and the Rabbit grew larger and distinct. She began to see Black Wind's mane and flaring nostrils and the Rabbit's pointed ears and pink leg. Was she flying? The gentle pink of the sky had heightened, filling the sky with vivid, glorious color. As she strained forward, pressing her arm toward her companions, her hair and clothes streamed behind her, rippling like a proud banner carried to battle. Mulan wanted to laugh — she felt poised, powerful, and graceful.

Everything you are not. Daji's words suddenly came back to her, and all at once Mulan felt the weight of the flask of honey in her sleeve. A ribbon of bloodred light streaked across the sky as the sun dropped below the horizon, and Mulan's arm lowered with her doubt. The Rabbit's eyes widened and he waved his front paws while Black Wind threw his head back and snorted a warning, but it was too late. Mulan was falling.

Her arms and legs flailed and she plunged downward, plummeting past the Rabbit and Black Wind. As they stared helplessly, a squeak of terror flew from her lips, echoing up to them as she disappeared into the darkness of the abyss.

CHAPTER 27

Night

MULAN TUMBLED downward, flapping her arms frantically like an overgrown chicken. She grabbed at the side of the cliff in vain, her fierce clutching merely causing a cascade of falling rocks and disintegrating dirt.

Then, magically, miraculously, her arm flew onto something solid. She grasped it desperately, digging her fingers into dusty stone as her legs bounced against the rocks.

Her feet dangling, she gasped to see that she was clinging

to a ledge jutting from the side of the cliff. She flung her other arm onto it. She grunted, and, forcing herself to ignore the fire burning in her arms and lungs, she slowly and painfully dragged herself onto the precipice — one elbow, then the other, and then the rest of her, scraping and scratching.

When she finally felt solid ground underneath her, she simply lay there panting, her face buried in the dry dirt and stone. Every part of her body stung and ached, and for several long moments all she could do was listen to the pounding of her heart and marvel at its beat. At last, however, she dared to raise her head and sit up. Where had she landed?

Night had fallen, and everything around her seemed little more than different layers of darkness. She brushed off the pebbles and dust freckling her face and saw by the shadows that the ledge she was on seemed strong and sizable. Nevertheless, she decided it was best to be cautious, so, while still in a sitting position, she shuffled backward away from the edge.

But as she gingerly eased backward, something poked her back. Mulan yelped and almost jumped. She swung her head around and was surprised to see, in the dim light, the branch of a tree. She touched it to make sure, the rough bark reassuring her. It was a small tree, twisted and crooked, no doubt because of its inhospitable home — but it comforted her. Mulan pushed back to sit under it and found that now she could see the night sky. The bare branches of the tree silhouetted against the moon made it look like half of a sliced apple.

Mulan sat up. Half-moon? That meant half their time was gone! That gave them perhaps nine, ten days left? They hadn't even gotten to the City of Rushing Water, much less Green Island or the Queen Mother's garden! Were they going to run out of time to save Xiu? What was she doing here, sitting idly on a ledge?

But just as quickly as Mulan had sat up, she slumped back down. What could she do? How could she reach the Rabbit or Black Wind? The Rabbit didn't know where she was; he probably thought she was dead at the bottom of the ravine.

It would be a mistake to bring a mortal, the Rabbit had said. Mulan suddenly felt as if she were plunging over the cliff's edge again. He probably regretted it even more now, especially since she had turned out to be a mortal this inept. No matter how she tried, she never could get anything right. She remembered how, as a child, she had tried to glue back together the village shrine statue she had broken. No matter how strong she made the glue and however long she held the pieces, the wing of the stone phoenix fell off again. Yes, no doubt, the Rabbit was ruing the fact that he'd gotten stuck with such a mortal.

But he couldn't go without her. *The only way to save your sister is to have you come with me.* Would the Rabbit think she was dead? And if he did, would he just give up? Or would he try to continue without her even though he was weak and dying and probably wouldn't make it?

Tears began to burn in her eyes, and Mulan, always without a handkerchief, brought her sleeve to her face. As she did so, she felt the weight of the flask of honey.

Daji! Mulan thought. Hope streamed into her, like a shaft of light in the darkness. If Daji was the Immortal helping them, she could help! *If you need me, just call for me and I will come,* she had said. "Well," Mulan said to the darkness, "I need her now."

She straightened her clothes the best she could and combed her hair with her fingers. Then she sat up straight and cleared her throat. Feeling like a plaintive child, Mulan called out into the darkness. "Daji?"

Silence.

Maybe she needed to call louder. Mulan took a breath. "Daji!" she called in a stronger voice. "Daji! Please help me!"

Silence.

Mulan called a third time and then a fourth. She whispered and then yelled. She waited and then tried again. Silence. Not even the wind answered her. The half-empty moon gazed down upon her forlornly, as if mourning its missing part.

She's not going to come, Mulan realized. Despair washed over her, an ice-cold misery that turned her heart pale and ashen.

When she closed her eyes, she saw Xiu lying in bed as still as death, her mother weeping, and her father so grief-sick that he could not stand. She had failed — failed to cross the canyon, failed to help the Rabbit, and failed to save Xiu. She had acted recklessly and improperly for nothing. She was a disgrace to her ancestors. Mulan hugged her knees and leaned her head against the rough bark of the tree, and when the tears fell, she didn't even bother to wipe them away.

CHAPTER 28

Morning

"GET BACK here!" Mulan yelled. The speckled grey chicken clucked at her but kept running away. A thick morning fog was blanketing the earth and the sky, but the chicken was like a beacon, distinct and clear. Mulan raced after it, across a hazy field and under a big tree covered in clouds of mist like snow. She had to catch that runaway hen! She had told Ma and Ba that she would be responsible, that she could be dutiful like Xiu.

"Bad chicken!" Mulan scolded as the chicken jumped to the top of an old house. "Bad! Bad!" Using the window ledge, Mulan climbed up onto the roof. She looked down and gulped. Somehow, the ground below had suddenly become far away, as if she were standing over a huge abyss, endless and black. The chicken clucked at her.

"Come here, chicken!" Mulan said, her voice now coaxing. She reached into her bag and pulled out a red date, but it was sticky and covered with honey. She placed it on the ridge of the roof in front of her.

The chicken cocked its head and then slowly ambled toward her. It pecked at the date greedily. But as the chicken swallowed, Mulan saw it had turned the same color as the fruit, a deep crimson. Then it turned to Mulan and began to fly up at her. Mulan raised her arms to catch it, as if in a joyful embrace of homecoming. But as the chicken jumped into the air, it transformed into a fox! The fox's teeth were bared, sharp and white, its eyes gleaming with menace as Mulan stood frozen in shock. As the red fox opened its jaw to tear into her, it pushed her from the roof and, suddenly, they were both falling . . . falling . . . Mulan screamed awake.

Mulan blinked into the sun. How long had she slept? Every part of her body ached or stung, the dull pains reminding her of where she was. Mulan grimaced, shaking away the odd dreams of the night, and stretched her legs onto the cold stone ledge.

She looked out across the gorge and, in spite of everything, found herself marveling. The morning mist created a sea of clouds between the two cliffs, the sharpness of their peaks softened by shaggy evergreens. How far she had jumped! She stared at the distant bluff, slightly in awe.

"Mulan! Mulan!" Like a song from the Heavens, a faint voice was calling above. The Rabbit!

"I'm here!" Mulan yelled, leaping up like a frog trying to jump out of a well. She craned her neck upward, but only saw the steep wall of stone. And yet the calls grew louder and Mulan felt a flush of hope fill her, as if she had just swallowed warm rice porridge on a cold morning.

And her hope was not misplaced, because moments later, Mulan was showered by a scattering of dirt and stones. As she spat the earth from her mouth, she was greeted by the silhouette of two pointed ears poking over top of the cliff.

"There you are," the Rabbit said. The oblong shadow of Black Wind's nose joined him and snorted. Mulan was so grateful to see them that she couldn't even smile. How foolish she had been the night before, thinking he would have left her for dead. As she saw his ears sway against the bright patch of sky, she felt ashamed. The Rabbit would never have abandoned her.

"How are you doing?" the Rabbit called. "Sleep well?"

Mulan broke into laughter. The Rabbit was unflappable. After a harrowing jump and a night of despair, with a precipitous cliff between them, he was conversing as if they were having a pleasant chat over breakfast.

"Good thinking to get to the ledge," the Rabbit continued. "That was helpful."

"But the ledge just happened to be there . . ." Mulan said, smiling as she shook her head, too giddy to feel anything but amusement at the Rabbit's odd observations. "It was all luck that it was there and I was able to grab it."

The Rabbit made a noncommittal noise of agreement. The shadow of his head cocked to one side, one ear flopping over, and Mulan could imagine his nose twitching.

"Hmm," he said. "I wonder what the best way is to get you up here."

Mulan's smile disappeared, her heart suddenly as heavy as an iron pillar. How would she ever reach them? From her view, the Rabbit looked as far away as the moon, and the sheer cliff was crumbling with little to grab on to. She stared at the distant bluff through the limbs of the scraggly tree, its branches grasping at the sky like yearning fingers.

"Could you get a rope?" Mulan faltered.

"No need," the Rabbit said. He reached over the side of the cliff with his front leg, and to Mulan's amazement, it began to stretch. It grew longer and longer, extending down farther and farther. In the time it would take to drink a cup of tea, the Rabbit's paw had appeared in front of her, close enough to feed her with chopsticks. Mulan gaped at it, then up at the Rabbit at the top of the cliff, and then at his leg, spanning the distance like a bridge.

"What are you waiting for?" the Rabbit called from above.

Mulan tried to close her open mouth. *You'd think by now I'd stop being so surprised,* she thought. Maybe it was because the Rabbit always did his magic so nonchalantly, without any expectation of awe. Somehow, it made it all the more astonishing.

She grasped the Rabbit's paw with both hands and felt herself being jerked upward. She rose slowly, like a spider retracting a strand of its web. Mulan glanced below and saw the deep, endless abyss, the bottom disappearing into blackness. She wrapped her arms around the Rabbit's paw and grasped even tighter, which evoked a faint "Oof!" from the Rabbit above.

But he continued to draw her up, his leg getting shorter as she got closer to him. The vague horse and rabbit shapes grew clearer and more distinct, Mulan could now see the calm, placid expression on the Rabbit's face and Black Wind's nostrils flaring.

Then, in the space of a breath, Mulan was being hauled over the edge. Her legs bounced as she jostled over, causing a cascade of dirt and stones. She let go of the Rabbit's paw and scrambled onto the ground, the yellowing grass clasped between her fingers feeling as soft as the finest silk threads. The horizon swelled in front of her, the blue sky meeting the earth in a long line broken only by the figures of Black Wind and the Rabbit, who stood expectantly. She looked up at both of them and grinned.

"I'm so happy to see you," Mulan said fervently.

CHAPTER 29

The Rabbit's Past Mistake

MULAN SAT up, the euphoria of escaping the cliff dissipating as thoughts of their undertaking returned. Black Wind's warm nose pushed against her neck and the Rabbit hopped over to her, his paw back to its normal size without a hint of its miraculous reaching abilities.

There seemed so much more for her to say — how thankful she was that he'd saved her, how she hoped they could keep going and worried that they were running out of time, and mostly how sorry she was that she had failed in her jump.

Mulan suddenly flushed with shame, feeling as if she had drunk too-hot tea. What did the Rabbit think now? Was he annoyed about how right he had been about having to bring a mortal with him? Was he thinking that she was so unworthy and useless that they should just give up?

When Mulan finally dared to meet the Rabbit's eyes, she saw he was looking at her with his usual amused expression, but also with a certain tenderness.

"I'm sorry," Mulan said. The words were so bare and bald, yet they were all she could utter.

"What for?" the Rabbit said.

"For . . . for . . ." — Mulan hesitated — "being mortal."

The Rabbit laughed. "That's not something to apologize for," he said.

"No . . . I mean, you said it would be a mistake to take a mortal with you," Mulan said, trying to explain. "I'm sorry you were right."

The Rabbit's laughter immediately stopped and instead his face took on a pained expression.

"No, it is I who owe you an apology," the Rabbit said. "When I said that I was thinking of someone else I took on a journey, and it was not because she was mortal that it was a mistake."

"You journeyed with someone else? Who?" Mulan asked.

He looked at her with a sadness she had never seen before. "There is much to her story that I cannot tell," the Rabbit said, his ear drooping, "but I can say who she was."

The Unwanted Girl

When this field was covered by the sea and immortal beasts like dragons and phoenixes could roam the Earth without disguise, there was a girl who knew her mother did not want her. She did not know of the times her mother had tried to abandon her as a baby only for her to be brought back miraculously by beasts or woodcutters, but she knew that her mother felt only resentment toward her. She felt it in her mother's stinging slaps that left her face red for days, she felt it in the mostly empty bowl of rice she was always served last, but most of all she felt it from her mother's eyes, always bitter and cold. Every time her mother looked at her, the girl felt as if she were being pelted with hard, black stones.

Anyone who met the family could tell that this girl, of all the children in that large family, bore the brunt of her mother's anger and annoyance. The neighboring families assumed it was because the Unwanted Girl was the eldest and her mother held her responsible for the younger children's missteps. But it was not just her mother's lack of affection that made life hard for her. The truth was, there was something about the girl that was odd.

And she knew this as well. When her mother had sent her out in the freezing winter to find fresh bamboo shoots, the girl, after shedding tears in the snow, had inexplicably been able to find some growing. When the Unwanted Girl had fallen into a stampede of oxen, she was able to dodge the hundreds of crashing hooves and survive unscathed. And when a vicious wild beast threatened their livestock, the Unwanted Girl had rushed out, barehanded, and ordered the beast away. It had obeyed.

None of these things endeared her to anyone. Most people regarded her with suspicion and kept away. It seemed the Unwanted Girl could never do anything right, could never be accepted, and could never belong.

Most children would let such a plight destroy them; but the Unwanted Girl did not. She suffered greatly, of course, but she also had a spirit of iron, one that did not break easily.

And it was that spirit Lord Rabbit saw. When a sickness came over the Unwanted Girl's village, her family prayed and begged the Moon Lady to send them the healer Lord Rabbit. Their prayers were answered, for soon a silver rabbit dressed in the clothing of a fine lord came riding in on a yellow tiger. Lord Rabbit was quickly able to cure all in the girl's family, herself included, except for her youngest brother. When Lord Rabbit saw him, he shook his head.

"This medicine will not be strong enough," Lord Rabbit said. "He is too young and needs a different medicine, one that I do not have."

"Can you get it?" the mother asked tearfully, her hands stroking the boy's soft, plump burning cheeks.

Lord Rabbit hesitated. "The medicine requires many ingredients," he said. "Even with the tiger, I will have to travel to many places to get everything, and it may be too late."

"Please try," the mother begged.

"And even then, the medicine still may not work," Lord Rabbit warned. "His chi is already very weak. This type of sickness is difficult on such a small child."

"I'll give anything you wish! You must save him!"

Lord Rabbit bowed. "I will try," he said.

The Unwanted Girl followed him as he left, as if pulled by a thread. As he mounted the Yellow Tiger, she couldn't help calling out to him.

"Please!" she said. "Let me come! I can help! I know I can."

Lord Rabbit looked into her eyes and saw her powerful spirit, her strength and tenacity, but he also saw how she swallowed her tears alone at night, whispering to the moon her longing for a person to care for her or a place to belong. He did not think she could help him, but could he help her?

Slowly, he nodded, and the Unwanted Girl leapt onto the tiger's back behind him. They traveled great distances, stopping often. And, on one of their stops, the Unwanted Girl met the White Fox.

No doubt it was because the girl was traveling with Lord Rabbit that the White Fox became interested. Lord Rabbit had never traveled with a mortal before, and it piqued her interest. Perhaps at first, the White Fox just thought to cause some annoyance for her old foe by manipulating the girl, but she soon discovered that the Unwanted Girl could be very useful to her. With Lord Rabbit unaware, the White Fox was able to slowly gain mastery over her.

It was at their last destination that the White Fox finally revealed her control. The Unwanted Girl and Lord Rabbit had traveled to the Queen Mother's Garden of Splendors for the last herbs, and in the radiant palace of jade, Lord Rabbit pleaded to the Queen Mother herself for permission to pick the herbs.

"You do know that I am very careful whom I allow into my garden," the Queen Mother said, looking down at them as her attendants gently waved their feather-tipped fans above her. "Visitors tend to make a mess of the place. The last time I let someone in, they left flower blossoms everywhere! And before that, there was the monkey who—"

"The Moon Lady will vouch for my honesty and trust-worthiness," Lord Rabbit said humbly, his paws clasped to his chest as he bowed his head in reverence. "I will use extreme care in the garden."

"—ate all my Fruits of Longevity! He will now live for over six hundred thousand years! The insolence of it all!" the Queen Mother huffed, continuing as if Lord Rabbit had not spoken. She glared at him and at the bowed head of the girl next to him. "Those fruits are not to be touched. They are finally ripening again, and I will not allow them to be disturbed."

"Your Heavenly Highness," Lord Rabbit said, "I will touch nothing except the herb I need. We wish only to cure a child with *Qi-Ruohua* sickness."

"Both of you?" the Queen Mother asked, and Lord Rabbit saw that she was looking at the Unwanted Girl.

"Yes," the girl said, raising her head for the first time. "I wish to save my brother."

She could not meet the Queen Mother's eyes, but the sincerity in her voice was true and guileless.

"Yes," the Queen Mother said, studying the top of the Unwanted Girl's head, which she had already lowered again. "But can you save yourself?"

"Your Heavenly Highness?" Lord Rabbit was confused, as well as worried about the Unwanted Girl's brother. Their time to save him would soon end, and every moment was precious.

"I suppose I must allow the thread to be chosen," the Queen Mother said, more to herself than to them. Lord Rabbit cocked his head quizzically, but the Queen Mother just shook her head.

"Very well," she said. "You may pick the herb. But only that."

"Thank you!" Lord Rabbit said, bending his head to the ground in gratitude. "Thank you!"

"Remember, do not touch the fruit," the Queen Mother said with an odd gravity that further baffled Lord Rabbit. "I say this more for you than for me. If you touch the fruit, my annoyance will only be the beginning of your suffering."

So, with those strange words echoing in their ears, the Unwanted Girl and Lord Rabbit entered the Garden of Splendors. Lord Rabbit soon located the herb they were looking for, but when he turned to show the Unwanted Girl, she was gone. Where was she? Suddenly, a cold dread rushed over him, and he began racing through the garden.

When he found her, she was exactly where he hoped she would not be—in front of the Fruits of Longevity. Her hand slowly moved a fruit away from her face, its golden juice dripping from her mouth and fingers. And at the same time, a horrible screeching noise filled the air.

A force like a whirlwind swirled around the tree, plucking both Lord Rabbit and the girl from the earth. The herbs flew from his paw, the fruit bounced away from the Unwanted Girl, and a thunderous roar filled their ears. "You were warned!" the wind hissed as it threw them high into the sky, out of the garden, and over the golden walls of the Queen Mother's palace.

They fell for quite a while, and only by Lord Rabbit's power were they able to land softly. But though they were unhurt, all was lost. They had lost the medicine, and they had run out of time. Her brother would die.

But the Unwanted Girl's fate was worse.

For when Lord Rabbit and the girl had been flung from the garden and they both lay on the ground, gasping from their escape, a white shape came into view in the distance. The White Fox had been waiting for them. She was smiling.

Wordlessly, the Unwanted Girl rose and walked toward her. With every step she took, the girl began to transform, and when she finally joined the White Fox at the edge of the clearing, Lord Rabbit saw clearly what had happened. The White Fox now had a servant, one doomed to follow and obey her for as long as she lived. The Unwanted Girl had become the Red Fox.

CHAPTER 30

The Scent in the Air

MULAN WAS haunted by the Rabbit's story. Even after she had eaten, even after they had found the road again, even as they traveled toward the City of Rushing Water through wooded areas and hilly lands, Mulan could not help thinking of it. No wonder the Rabbit hadn't wanted her to come; it was almost as if they were reliving the same story now. The sick sibling, the search for the medicines . . . but it wasn't the same. This was different, right? Mulan shivered, thinking of the Unwanted Girl's fate.

Evening was arriving, and the sun sent streaks of crimson light into the darkening sky as it set. Mulan slowed Black Wind, looking for a good place to camp for the night.

"Tomorrow!" the Rabbit said.

Mulan turned to look at him, his nose twitching in the air, smelling the sky.

"What's tomorrow?" Mulan asked.

"Tomorrow we will be at the City of Rushing Water," the Rabbit said. "I can smell the river."

Mulan sniffed but smelled only the fir trees that now lined their path. "Should we just keep going, then?"

The Rabbit shook his head. "Best if we camp for the night and leave early. It's hard to tell how much longer it will take, and" — the Rabbit hesitated as if embarrassed — "I'm tired."

Of course he was, Mulan thought as she guided Black Wind to a small clearing off the path. The Rabbit had jumped across a cliff the night before and miraculously rescued her that morning. As she lifted him off her back, she suddenly realized how much lighter he was. She could feel his body tremble with every beat of his heart, feel his bones through his fine fur. He was dying, too, Mulan remembered, the gravity of his death causing a sudden ache. But she said nothing as she set him down on the ground.

They quickly set up camp; dry brush for the fire was

easy to find thanks to the surrounding pines. But as Mulan munched on her dinner of dates and rice, the Rabbit twisted in his blanket like a kitten and promptly fell asleep.

Mulan sat as the fire crackled, Black Wind silently grazing in the shadows. The Rabbit looked so small and frail as he slept, it was hard to believe how powerful he was. Though, *My power has been diminishing,* he had said. Mulan swallowed, looking again at the wheezing rabbit, his eyes tightly shut like a blind baby's.

Was Xiu weakening like this, too? With every shallow breath Xiu took, was her life draining from her? If only the spider had bitten her instead of Xiu! *You are too strong for your own good,* Ma had said, and she was right. Why else was Mulan always breaking teacups and shrine statues? It probably would have been good for her to lose a bit of her chi. Maybe it would have helped her be less bold, less rough. Maybe it would have made her gentler and more graceful and a pride to their family. Maybe it would have made her more like Xiu.

A soft breeze blew across Mulan's face with the scent of sweet honey. Mulan straightened and glanced around. A golden light shimmered in the distance, and she heard a faint sound beckoning her, the lilting song of a swallow. *Daji.*

CHAPTER 31

The White Fox

WITHOUT REALIZING it, Mulan found herself walking toward the glow, the waft of fragrant air pulling her as if she were a kite reeled in by a string. Her feet padded softly on the path of fallen pine needles, their yellow color gently illuminated. Mulan followed it into a thicket of trees lit with lanterns, and there Daji was waiting, just as she had been the first time they'd met.

"Hello again!" Daji smiled as if welcoming her to a party.

She was as beautiful as ever, her lotus-petal face so radiant and lovely that she seemed to be made of white jade.

Mulan stood by the threshold and felt the familiar, infuriating speechlessness fix upon her lips. She nodded a greeting.

"How are you?" Daji asked, concern growing on her face. She beckoned Mulan over to her and Mulan came slowly, as if walking upon ice. "Oh, Mulan, you look terrible. Look at you, so filthy and ragged. You could be a beggar child."

Instinctively, Mulan's hand flew to straighten her hair, but Daji caught it in hers.

"You've been so uncared for," Daji said, clasping her hand. "Has the Rabbit been ignoring you?"

Mulan shook her head vigorously. Perhaps she could not squeeze words from her lips, but she could at least make herself understood.

"Of course he has," Daji said. She pulled Mulan to a covered table. Daji plucked off the draped cloth and wrapped it around Mulan's shoulders. The rich fabric was warm and soft. Mulan couldn't help letting the lavish folds envelop her, the silk sumptuous as it brushed against her hands.

Daji took a napkin from the table. She caught Mulan's chin with her slender fingers, and then, as if Mulan were a small child, rubbed her face clean.

"Now you are ready to eat," Daji said as she finished. Mulan winced at the once dainty, now crumpled cloth, grimy and grey in Daji's snowy hands. "I have some treats for you."

Daji stepped aside, and suddenly Mulan was overwhelmed with the rich aroma of food. A pot of tea, the steam curving from its spout like a beckoning snake. A dish of deep crimson pork, glistening in dark, sweet sauce. A plate of lychees, luscious and large, delicate and glossy in golden syrup. The table was abundant with delectable luxuries that Mulan had only heard of in stories.

"Here," Daji said, placing a teacup in her hand. "You need some comfort after all the Rabbit's neglect."

Mulan felt the heat of the tea through the cup and brought it close to her face. As she looked into her cup, the amber liquid reflected her image, and she felt a small shock. Was that her? The tea's surface showed her a lovely milk-white face, arrayed in fine silk. The girl was completely unrecognizable except for the eyes. The eyes were her own; they stared back at her, troubled and worried.

"The Rabbit didn't neglect me," Mulan said, her words like ripping paper. "You did."

"Me?" Mulan could see that Daji was truly startled, as if Mulan's voice were thunder from an unexpected storm.

"I called for you," Mulan said, pushing her words out like boulders from a well. "On the ledge. On the cliff. I needed help."

"Oh, Mulan, I cannot just come whenever you want," Daji said, the charming expression on her face suddenly frozen. "And look at you now. You are fine."

Mulan frowned. The teacup suddenly felt small in her hands, fragile and flimsy.

"Why don't you eat?" Daji soothed. "I think you'll feel better after you eat something."

Daji lifted the plate of lychees with her ivory hands and offered them to Mulan. She picked up one of the fruits with her fingers, creating tiny glistening threads as the honey pulled away from the plate. Mulan froze. Honey. The swarm of bees. *She brought the Scholar a plate of honeyed plums,* the Rabbit had said. *He had eaten a great deal of her poison.*

Mulan dropped the lychee as if it were on fire. The silken wrap fell to the ground, exposing all her stained clothing, her scratched arms and dirt-caked shoes. "You . . ." Mulan choked. "You . . ."

"What is it, Mulan?" Daji said, a careful look of concern glued onto her face. "What's wrong?"

Mulan clutched the teacup with both hands, pressing it tighter and tighter as she felt her words and thoughts collide.

The delicate cup begin to crack, warm drops bleeding onto her fingers. Was Daji . . . was she . . . ?

In a swift motion, Mulan threw the tea at Daji. The liquid flew into the air, scattering like rain. Daji shrieked, raising her arm and whirling wildly to shield herself from the shower. But as she turned, Mulan saw what she was looking for. A fox's tail.

The teacup broke into sharp pieces in Mulan's hand. "You are not an Immortal helping us!" Mulan shouted, her voice raw and ugly. "You are the White Fox!"

Daji froze, her exquisite face suddenly pinching into hideousness. "Yes," she hissed, "you stupid, annoying girl! Why can't you do anything right?"

"Go away!" Mulan said, grinding the shards of porcelain to dust and throwing it as a cloud to the earth. "I never want to see you again!"

"Oh, you will see me again," Daji sneered, and Mulan couldn't imagine how she had ever thought Daji was beautiful. "And you'll be sorry, too."

With that, there was a loud clap in the air. Daji vanished in a flurry of white, and then an eagle darted up from her place into the black sky. Mulan, trembling, stared at the white shape piercing the sky and then back at the empty space in front of her.

There was a sudden rustling in the trees behind her. Mulan,

bracing for an attack, spun and scanned the night gloom. Two eyes glimmered at her and Mulan saw the dim silhouette of pointed ears. The Red Fox. The Unwanted Girl.

"Hello?" Mulan whispered.

The eagle screeched above, a sharp, harsh sound of fury that split the sky. The fox-shaped shadow shuddered and then disappeared into the small silhouette of a bird. The bird shot up into the sky and Mulan watched it fly after the eagle, melting into the blackness of the night.

CHAPTER 32

The Honey

IN THE morning, the trees sifted the radiant light pouring from the sun. Mulan, however, did not need the sun to wake her. She had barely slept, troubled by the experiences of the night. When she had left the thicket (along with Daji's finery and delicacies), the lanterns had extinguished, and Mulan had stumbled back to the camp, scratching and bruising herself even further. Yet, despite her exhaustion, she tossed and turned the remainder of the night, the image of Daji's face twisted in anger returning each time she closed her eyes.

The new golden light reminded her of something she needed to do. She pushed herself up and quietly tiptoed away from the sleeping horse and rabbit. Then she took the bottle of honey out from her sleeve. It was smooth and fine-grained, its creamy color the same white jade as Daji's skin. Mulan shuddered.

Mulan uncapped the bottle. She gently pulled the stone top off, slightly afraid something sinister would come slithering out. Nothing. Mulan peered in, but could only see blackness through its narrow neck. Bringing the flask close to her face also brought the aroma of honey. It was a thick sweet scent — rich and heavy. As she breathed in the fragrance, Mulan felt again the luxurious silk cloth, the warm tea, and Daji's smooth fingers pressing against her hand.

A sudden rush of wind flew across Mulan's face, pushing away the honey's fragrance and, instead, filling her nose with bracing, cold air. Mulan shook herself, gasping as if she had been submerged in water. She looked at the bottle in her hand, dread filling her. She needed to be rid of it.

Keeping the bottle an arm's length away, Mulan turned it over. A viscous golden stream slowly oozed from the bottle's neck, glistening and shining. She watched it stretch from the bottle, a rope of liquid sunlight falling leisurely.

But when the honey touched the ground there was a hissing sound, like sizzling drops of water on a heated cooking pan. Mulan jerked in surprise, pulling the flask back slightly. The sibilant sound continued, and Mulan saw that the honey had burned a dark line onto the earth. Her eyes widened in horror. The syrup continued to fall and burn, smoldering into a sooty shape on the ground. The honey *was* poison. Daji had planned to destroy her from the beginning. Madly, wildly, she began shaking the flask empty, the burning marks spotting like black drops of blood.

When no more syrup dripped from the bottle, Mulan stared at the ground, the black splotches surrounding her. What would have happened if she had opened that jar earlier? What would have happened if she had eaten the honey? Mulan shivered.

Another cool breeze brushed her face, and there was a soft thumping noise behind her. When Mulan turned around she saw the Rabbit looking at her. How long had he been watching? She felt the shame fall on her like a heavy boulder. What was he thinking? Did he wonder why she had a bottle of poison? Could he tell she had been with the White Fox? Would he ever trust her again?

The Rabbit's head cocked to one side and his nose twitched

as his eyes went from the bottle in Mulan's hand to the scorched earth in front of her and then to her face. He looked up into her eyes, and his brow furrowed as if he was confused.

"Your face is clean," he said.

CHAPTER 33

The Evil Emperor

"YOU COULD not have told me anything while you possessed that honey," the Rabbit told Mulan. "While you held it, the White Fox was able to keep you from talking about her. It's an old trick — she was 'sticking your lips together' to keep you from speaking unless she wanted you to."

"That's why it was always so hard to talk when I was with her!" Mulan exclaimed. It had been a great relief to finally tell the Rabbit everything. As they ate their morning meal, Mulan described all her encounters with the White Fox — from receiving the honey to last night's turbulent scene. "But wasn't it poison?"

"It was definitely poison," the Rabbit said, crunching on a date. "If you had eaten it, yes, it would have killed you eventually. But before it did, not only would you not have been able to speak unless the White Fox wanted you to, you also would have had to do her bidding."

"Do you think that is what happened to the Unwanted Girl?" Mulan asked, aghast.

The Rabbit stopped midchew and his ears drooped. "I have no doubt," he said.

Mulan looked down in chagrin. A sadness always came over the Rabbit when she mentioned the Unwanted Girl, and, remembering those two glinting eyes staring at her in the darkness, she could understand why. How different would that girl's life have been if she had not become the Red Fox?

"And what about the peach that she wanted me to pick?" Mulan said. "Is that poison, too?"

"Oh, no," the Rabbit said. "That peach is the Queen Mother's prized Fruit of Longevity. If you eat it, it will fix your ailments and give you up to six thousand years of life — more or less."

"So Daji was right when she said the peach could save Xiu?" Mulan asked.

"The peach would keep Xiu alive," the Rabbit said slowly, and then looked directly into Mulan's eyes. "But at great cost."

The Rabbit's words fell like stones in water, and he did not offer more. But he didn't need to. Just from the way he spoke, Mulan's heart chilled.

"Daji had it all planned out, then," Mulan said.

"Yes." The Rabbit nodded absently. He stared out into the sky, lost in reverie. "Interesting that she still calls herself Daji. I misjudged her."

"What do you mean?" Mulan asked.

"She must have, in her own way, cared about the emperor," the Rabbit said. "I thought she only wanted to control him."

"She controlled the Emperor?" Mulan said, her eyes bulging.

"Not this one," the Rabbit said quickly. "The emperor of the last dynasty. She's the one who really caused its downfall."

"She caused its downfall?" Mulan asked. "How?"

The Story of Daji

The White Fox has used many names and taken many forms. Her favorite form is that of a beautiful woman.

As the centuries have passed, she has perfected her art and is able to make herself into a creature of such surpassing beauty and charm that few are able to resist her.

The last emperor of the previous dynasty, Emperor Zhou, was not one of those few. He succumbed to her immediately and with unmatched passion. As soon as he saw her, he made Daji his royal companion and lavished gifts upon her, sparing nothing to please her and indulge her whims.

The fastest horses were whipped to exhaustion weekly, racing back and forth from the southern part of the kingdom just to fetch fresh, ripe fruit for her. The fuel in the charcoal heaters was broken into pieces and mixed with costly honey to sweeten the smell that offended her delicate nose. And, because Daji enjoyed the sound of silk ripping, rooms were filled with the finest handwrought silk just for her to tear.

However, this was just a tiny drop of Daji's exorbitant demands. The peasants of four hundred villages were forced into slavery to build her an enormous jewel- and jade-studded palace with a resplendent garden, complete with a hand-dug lake of wine. Servants hung snacks of roasted meat from the branches along that lake just for Daji to pluck and eat while she passed the time upon her three-story boat of gold and marble. And one day, when a leaf fell from a tree in front of her, she insisted that it—and any other fallen leaves— be replaced on its branch by a leaf made of silk. She quickly bankrupted the kingdom.

But it was not just her whims and excess that brought about the downfall of Emperor Zhou; it was also her cruelty. Soon she grew bored of boating on wine and picking delicacies and searched for other entertainment. When she heard that a true sage would have seven holes in his heart, she had all the wisest men of the kingdom killed and their hearts brought to her so she could see. When she saw an ant accidentally cooked after it fell into a frying pan, she had the emperor devise a similar execution for his enemies, delighting in their torture. But she was at her most heartless when she developed the notion to see a battle. Not a theatrical fight, nor one with a few soldiers, no. Daji wanted to see a battle in a real war with hundreds of thousands of soldiers.

So, to please her, Emperor Zhou declared war on a neighboring kingdom. Even though the battle had already begun when she arrived, Emperor Zhou forced his men to stop combat to find a good vantage point for Daji. He commanded his soldiers to build a road up to a cliff's ledge, and only after Daji was lounging on that ledge in a rosewood chair, comfortably fanned by her hand-maid and dining on fruits, did he allow them to continue the fight. Daji watched the carnage below, thrilled, but eventually even the brutal butchery became tiresome to her and she wished to return home. So even though his soldiers were winning, the emperor halted his troops midbattle and retreated.

All were aghast at the meaningless death of so many men. So when a few days later, Daji declared she wanted to see another battle, only bigger and bloodier, the kingdom revolted. A new emperor was declared and troops of all regions rallied to follow him, not to march to battle, but to attack their own capital. The suffer-ing commoners amassed at the city gates, eager to join the rebelling soldiers. As they stormed the palace, the Imperial Guard turned to fight with them, only to see there was no opposition. All demanded the end of this callous reign of blood and extravagance. Trapped and without any supporters, Zhou was easily killed by the new emperor's son, and Daji, with the help of her hand-maid, hanged herself.

Or, at least, pretended to hang herself. A day later, when Daji's body was retrieved for burial, they found, instead of a body, a stalk of bamboo. The White Fox, leaving behind her usual trail of blood and destruction, had escaped again.

"Emperor Zhou! He was the evil emperor that nearly destroyed the empire!" Mulan said. "My father helped end his reign! I knew Emperor Zhou was bad, but I didn't know the White Fox was the cause of his wickedness."

"Emperor Zhou was more foolish than wicked," the Rabbit said. "Though he didn't have that much goodness, either. He truly worshipped Daji with the devotion given to a goddess. I suppose that is why she wants revenge."

"Revenge?" Mulan asked.

"Zhou was killed by our present emperor, establishing his father's — and now his own — dynasty," the Rabbit said. "The White Fox wants him to suffer."

"So that's why she wants to kill Xiu!" Mulan said, suddenly understanding. "The prophecy said Xiu is going to save the Emperor! The White Fox wants to make sure she doesn't."

"The White Fox wants nothing to stand in the way of her vengeance," the Rabbit said. "I'm sure she has a special death planned for our current emperor."

"But she couldn't kill him, could she?" Mulan asked,

suddenly envisioning Daji swooping upon the Emperor with a dagger. "I mean, she would be killed if she tried, right?"

"The White Fox has declared that no man can kill her," the Rabbit said. "And for more than ten thousand years, her claim has been true."

You will see me again, Daji had said. *And you'll be sorry, too.* Mulan shivered, knowing that this was true as well.

CHAPTER 34

The City of Rushing Water

"THE CITY of Rushing Water is not a large city, at least not now. Today, it's really just the size of a village, and a small one at that. The people there are not very well educated," the Rabbit said. "It's probably best that we pretend that I am . . ." — he hesitated here, and Mulan could imagine the Rabbit's disgusted face — "your pet."

Mulan grinned. It was safe to do so, as the Rabbit couldn't see her. He was, as usual, on her back, and she was starting to feel incomplete if she didn't have him there. The road they were riding on had widened and was lined with thick groves of trees. They were almost to the village.

"All right," Mulan agreed, trying to keep the snicker out of her voice. "They will probably just think that anyway."

"Yes," the Rabbit said, "but I will have to keep silent when we are in the presence of others. I will not be able to talk and should act as much as possible like a normal rabbit. In the city, you will have to make the decisions on your own."

Mulan felt the joviality leave her. "But what about your friend?" she asked. "How am I going to find him?"

"If I know Lu Ting-Pin," the Rabbit said, "he'll find us. If he's there, that is."

"What if he's not?" Mulan asked. The Rabbit was silent. He was quiet for so long that Mulan wondered if he had fallen asleep again. "Rabbit?"

"I don't know," the Rabbit said, finally.

Mulan felt as if her insides were turning to ice. "If he's not," Mulan said, forcing herself to speak, "how will we save Xiu?"

"I'm not sure," the Rabbit said. "Perhaps another way will show itself to us."

Now it was Mulan's turn to be silent. She was not comforted by the Rabbit's words. She thought of Daji and how she had mistakenly thought Daji was an Immortal who was helping them.

"Do you still think there is another Immortal helping us?" Mulan asked. "You thought so at the Butterfly Fairy's house. Maybe they could help."

"It's possible," the Rabbit said. "But it would be more helpful if Lu Ting-Pin is at the City of Rushing Water."

Black Wind's hooves clomped against the ground, a lonely sound in the emptiness. The road was broad enough for carts and horses to pass both ways, but the overgrowing brush and fallen branches that Black Wind continued to sidestep told of its lack of use. When one particularly large branch needed to be heaved out of the road, Mulan couldn't help complaining. "Does no one care for the roads here?" she said.

"Not anymore," the Rabbit said. "A long time ago, the City of Rushing Water was thriving. Boats often docked there, so it was a bustling port."

"What happened?" asked Mulan as she hoisted herself back onto Black Wind.

"It was always a fast-moving river," the Rabbit said. "That is why it was called Rushing Water, of course. But one day, the river turned wild."

"Wild?" Mulan said, "How can a river turn wild?"

"The fast-moving water became dangerous rapids," the Rabbit said, "and it began to flood without warning. Any boat that tries to sail the river now is smashed against the rocks and destroyed."

"What happened to the people?" Mulan asked.

"Well, most of the homes have been ruined by the floods," the Rabbit said. "Anyone who could left a while ago, and the area has become quite poor with few prospects."

"Oh," Mulan said, mentally adjusting her expectations. She hadn't realized it, but she had imagined Rushing Water as a grand city, with tiled roofs winging out like swallowtails and ornately carved wooden windows. It seemed like the place should be majestic if they were going to meet Lu Ting-Pin, one of the Mighty Eight Immortals. *He used to be one,* the Rabbit had said.

"Rabbit, why . . . ?" Mulan started, then stopped, her question evaporating. Because in the distance, the city had come into view. Or at least the city wall had. Looming before them was a long grey stone wall, stained from weather and age. Worn pillars lined the way to the gate, and the road was paved with broken, crumbling bricks of past prosperity.

Black Wind trotted dutifully, his thudding hooves making an uneven melody on the broken road. The gate jutted up from the wall like a turret, with two curved roofs, the corners reaching skyward, layered on top. The large archway entry was echoed by the smaller one above it — a second-floor sentry lookout, Mulan supposed. But it was empty now. Perhaps the sentry had joined the gathering at the gate's opening. For in front of them, through the curved mouth of the gate, they could see a huge crowd of people that stood inside the city's entrance, watching Mulan's approach.

"Rabbit," Mulan whispered, slowing Black Wind, "I think they are waiting for us."

He peeked over her shoulder. "I think you are right," he said.

"What do you think is happening?" Mulan asked.

"I don't know," the Rabbit said before ducking back into the pouch. "But you will not be helped if you are seen talking to me."

"Rabbit!" Mulan hissed. He did not answer, and as Black Wind continued forward, she knew he would not speak again. She felt her heart thud with Black Wind's every step as the hundreds of eyes stared at her. None of the people waved or beckoned. None smiled or nodded. They all just watched her grimly, as if she were marching to her death.

Mulan gulped. She was almost at the gate now. "Hi!" she called, trying to sound pleasant and lighthearted. "Hello!"

But her friendly greeting might as well have been a battle

cry, for as soon as she was through the gate, the people surrounded her with an undercurrent of menacing grumbling.
She tried to shy away from the sharp ends of bamboo spears
pointed at her. One man, who wore leather armor and seemed
like an official soldier, reached up and gripped her arm.

"You're coming with me," he growled.

CHAPTER 35

The River King's Bride

"ALL RIGHT! I'm coming!" Mulan protested as the brandished spears waved at her and the man's hand tightened on her arm. She slid off the horse and found herself swept up by the mob, Black Wind's reins ripped from her hands.

"Black Wind! My horse!" Mulan cried out, trying to reach back for him. But the crowd ignored her plea and pushed her. Instead, they muttered to themselves — a low growl from starving wolves. Mulan caught some of the grunts swirling around her as she moved forward helplessly. "It's her." "Just like she said."

"What do you want from me?" Mulan asked, looking around desperately. "Where are you taking me?"

But no one answered or looked directly at her; all were dour and glum, as if determined to finish an unpleasant task. Even the official-looking soldier with the leather armor and metal spear marched her along without meeting her eyes. As he stared ahead stone-faced, she realized his expression reminded her of her own when she was sent to kill a chicken for dinner. Mulan shivered.

As they trudged through the unkempt streets and past ramshackle buildings with tattered paper windows and rotting wooden beams, she kept trying for an explanation. But it was to no avail. None answered her. Soon Mulan could see they were headed for the river. Another crowd, a larger one, waited for them there. The second crowd made a path for her, gawking wide-eyed. "But she's just a young girl," Mulan heard a voice say. "Shh!" someone else hissed. "Do you want them to take our daughter instead?"

Mulan could now see that she was headed toward a landing by the river, its water dark and turbid. The waves struck the ancient dock with angry blows, as if punishing it for past misdeeds. That crumbling and creaking platform was almost like a stage, rising slightly above the throngs of people with a large, odd-looking rock — a hulking, twisted white shape that seemed to be cringing from the water — as its usher. Through the weather-carved holes of this misshapen rock, Mulan could see two people waiting for her.

One was a short, rather rotund man. Mulan guessed that he was the magistrate, or at least some sort of official, from the black silk hat that stuck up from his head like a rectangle fan. His fur collar signified his comparative wealth, as did his plump, well-fed face.

His well-off appearance struck a strange contrast to the other figure on the landing. For next to him stood a malevolent hag. She was wrinkled and bent, her white hair hanging around her warty face in grimy clumps and her pale rags drooping to the ground like dirty puddles. But it was her eyes that made her menacing. She glared at Mulan with such viciousness that Mulan flinched.

Mulan felt herself pushed past the strange boulder and onto the landing in front of the Magistrate and the Hag. At a loss, Mulan bowed politely. The Magistrate gaped at her awkwardly, his soft face wearing an uncomfortable expression.

"It was just as she said," the soldier in the leather armor barked. "A girl on a black horse, riding through the gates."

"Ahh," the Magistrate said, tapping his fingers together.

His raised eyebrows came down slowly. "Well, I guess the River King," he said as he bit his lip, "shall have his bride, then."

A roaring murmur crossed the crowd, and Mulan had to speak loudly to make herself heard.

"What?" she said. "What are you talking about? What is all of this about?"

"You!" screeched the Hag, pointing a gnarled finger at Mulan. "You are the River King's bride. Without you, he will continue to flood the city and anger the waters. You must join him at the bottom of the river!"

"What?" Mulan gasped. Her thoughts were crashing in her head like the wild waves of the river before her. If she went to the bottom of the river, she would drown! What madness was this?

"This is ridiculous!" Mulan burst out. "I am no one's bride!"

The Magistrate's eyes bulged slightly, perhaps in surprise at Mulan's outspoken manner, an uncommon trait in most girls. But he pasted on as pleasant a face as possible.

"I am afraid you are," he said, his voice as smooth as oil. He looked at the mass of people fixated upon them. "This, uh . . ." He looked at the Hag, who scowled back at him before he continued. "This honored elder, here, has been able to determine what has caused the disturbance in our river," he said. "It seems the River King lost his mate and has been unhappy ever since. He has been longing for a new wife."

Mulan stared at him in disbelief. Honored elder? She turned to look at the old Hag, who returned her gaze with a sly smile. Mulan felt her insides turn to ice. That smile. It was familiar. This face was wrinkled and spotted with ugly, hairy boils, but it was the same smile she had seen on a face as beautiful as a fairy's.

"While such an honor would be great for any girl in our city" — the Magistrate spoke these last words loudly and slowly, giving the crowd in front of him a baleful look — "the, uh, honored elder was able to determine that his destined bride would ride into the city on a black horse. You came riding in today on a black horse, so, uh . . . you . . . uh . . . are the . . . uh . . . chosen bride," he finished pitifully.

"No, no!" Mulan said, desperately. "That . . . that . . . woman is after me. Don't you see? She's just trying to trick you into getting rid of me!"

The Hag cackled. "Now, don't be nervous, dear," she said wickedly. "You're going to be a queen."

"Don't listen to her!" Mulan pleaded to the crowd. "If you throw me in that river, you'll be killing me!"

A wave of discomfort moved through the watching throng.

"People of the city!" the Hag shrieked. "Do you want the

floods to continue? Do you like having hungry children? Do you like having your homes crumble on top of you as you sleep? Do you like having no future?"

The mass grumbled. "No!" a voice grunted, and the sound was echoed and repeated, becoming a babel of resentful discord.

"If you don't," the Hag said, her screech piercing into every ear, "then you must give the River King his bride!"

The cacophony of the crowd grew to a furor and the mob surged forward. Mulan saw the thousands of determined eyes and glittering teeth swelling toward her. She opened her mouth to scream. But before a sound could come out of her mouth, she felt the Rabbit's head rub against her shoulder.

"Wait! Wait!" Mulan yelled as loud as she could, throat raw with her effort. "I'll go! I'll go! Just wait!"

The Magistrate held up his hands, holding the mob back. They halted but did not pull back. Mulan could feel that their mad desperation was past reason, and she saw the Hag's sneer of satisfaction. There was no hope for her. She would not escape the furious river, but perhaps the Rabbit could.

"I'll go," Mulan said again, gulping. She tugged the pouch around toward her chest and then pulled at the cloth to reveal the Rabbit. "But you must promise not to hurt my pet rabbit."

"Pet rabbit?" A voice from the back of the crowd boomed

above all others, silencing all sound. A man came into view. He was tall, with a lengthy black beard, and while he wore a scholar's robe, a long sword was strapped to his back. He led a dark horse. Black Wind!

But even the relief of seeing Black Wind again did not lessen the wonder of the newcomer. There was something formidable about him. Perhaps it was the way he held himself, as if the air somehow weighed less upon him. Or perhaps it was the way he moved, like a mighty dragon about to leap into the sky. Whatever it was, all felt his power and were awed. Noiselessly, the crowd parted to make a pathway for him, and the sound of his footsteps echoed as he walked up to Mulan.

"Pet rabbit?" the man said again, his eyes twinkling even as his voice thundered. "If that rabbit is a pet, then I am not Lu Ting-Pin!"

CHAPTER 36

Lu Ting-Pin

LU TING-PIN! The Rabbit rolled his eyes at the tall man and Mulan felt a rush of hope. She looked out at the crowd, many of them looking confused and whispering. Most didn't know who Lu Ting-Pin was, she realized. They probably thought he was some sort of aristocrat, or perhaps a government official.

Mulan couldn't tell if the Magistrate knew, but he definitely recognized Lu Ting-Pin as someone highly esteemed, for he bowed deeply.

Without waiting for the Magistrate to rise, Lu Ting-Pin addressed him.

"What is going on here?" he demanded.

"Master Lu," the Magistrate said, in an ingratiating tone that made Mulan feel as if she had just eaten spoiled rice porridge, "we are conducting, uh . . . a . . . a ceremony to placate and honor the River King."

"A ceremony?" Lu Ting-Pin snorted. "This looks more like an angry mob! Is this the way a civilized town is supposed to behave?"

"This is no business of yours, Lu Ting-Pin!" the Hag broke in. Lu Ting-Pin's arrival seemed to have shocked her into silence, but she found her voice now. "The River King demands his bride! You are not wanted here!"

"A bride?" Lu Ting-Pin brushed aside the Hag's objections as if he hadn't heard them. "How do we know the River King wants a bride?"

"This . . . um . . . woman," the Magistrate said, indicating the Hag. "She informed us that the River King contacted her with his wishes."

"Did she?" Lu Ting-Pin said, arching an eyebrow. He looked at the Hag, who glared at him. "And you spoke with the River King yourself?"

"Of course," the Hag snarled. "He told me that he would

BEFORE THE SWORD

never stop flooding the river unless he had a new wife. So I notified the Magistrate immediately."

"Who, of course, told these townspeople," Lu Ting-Pin said, looking out at the sea of staring eyes, "and, no doubt, lined his pockets with bribes from fearful parents."

The Magistrate started, making a choked noise of surprise and guilt. An undercurrent of grumbling clamored through the crowd.

"And once he couldn't squeeze any more from them," Lu Ting-Pin continued, "you were able to divine a bride of destiny, am I correct?"

"I asked the River King to tell me which woman he wished," the Hag said, her chin rising in defiance. "And he told me she would ride into town on a black horse, and there she is!" The Hag's voice rose to an enraged screech and she pointed at Mulan. "That is the River King's bride! She must go to the bottom of the river, now!"

"This is the River King's bride?" Lu Ting-Pin said, his calm, unhurried manner like water upon the fire the Hag tried to stoke. He turned to Mulan and looked at her carefully, then turned back to the Hag, shaking his head. "This cannot be his bride. She is too young! She is not yet of marrying age."

"When they marry matters not!" the Hag snapped. "He wants his betrothed with him below!"

"That makes no sense," Lu Ting-Pin said. "If the poor River King has been in anguish over loneliness, why would he choose a bride he must wait to marry? There must be some mistake."

"There's no mistake!" the Hag ranted. "We must send this girl into the river!"

"Come, come," Lu Ting-Pin said, again in his untroubled way. He turned to the Magistrate and looked at him directly. "We don't want send the River King the wrong bride, do we? That's apt to make him even angrier."

The Magistrate shifted uncomfortably, his face growing flushed as Lu Ting-Pin continued to fix his gaze upon him. "No, no," the Magistrate mumbled, "we don't want to anger the River King."

"I think we should make sure we know what the River King wants," Lu Ting-Pin continued. He glanced over to the Hag. "Why don't you go down and ask him?"

"What?" the Hag sputtered. "Me? Go down?"

"Yes," Lu Ting-Pin said nonchalantly. "You need to find out exactly what the River King wants."

"I . . . I . . . I am not going to the bottom of the river!" the Hag said, her eyes narrowing with seething anger. "Not me!"

"But of course, you," Lu Ting-Pin said. "You are the River King's emissary. You already know him so well." He turned again to the Magistrate. "Don't you think?"

The Magistrate's face was now shiny with perspiration, completely flustered by Lu Ting-Pin's revelations and the townspeople's angry, suspicious eyes. "Um, yes," the Magistrate said, wiping his forehead and looking back and forth from the man to the Hag. "Perhaps it's best if she . . . uh . . . you . . . go see the River King."

A roar of agreement rose from the crowd as all finally grasped some of the truth. "He's right. Why would the River King want this girl?" one person grumbled. "He could have his choice of goddesses and fairies."

"I bet the River King didn't ask for a bride at all!" accused another. "You just made the whole thing up so you could get more money out of us!"

"If anyone's going to the bottom of the river," someone yelled, "it should be you!"

And with that shout, years of pent-up resentment and bitterness seemed to burst from the crowd. They surged forward, an unstoppable cresting wave of fury. The Hag's eyes widened, and with a shriek of wrath, she stepped back and jumped into the river. The Magistrate stared openmouthed at the empty air where the Hag used to be and then back at the surging mob. He yelped, then bolted away like a runaway pig.

The crowd swarmed after him. Lu Ting-Pin put one arm around Mulan's shoulders and the other around Black Wind, and the teeming hordes passed them by as if they were rocks in a rush of water. Mulan heard their frenzied howls and crashing feet, their clenched fists and gnashing teeth, but the rampage was a blur around her.

For while everyone else was looking elsewhere, Mulan's eyes were fixed upon the Hag. So when the Hag disappeared into the river, no one but Mulan saw the white fox tail poking out from the waves, nor did anyone but Mulan see the miraculous transformation of that tail into a fish's.

CHAPTER 37

The Wooden Sword

SOON, LU TING-PIN, Mulan, and the Rabbit were alone. They could hear faint howling echoes as the town's magistrate received justice from the townspeople, but the Magistrate must have been quite a good runner, for the pandemonium was a great distance away.

"Tuzi! My old friend!" Lu Ting-Pin boomed, his face splitting into a wide grin. "What are you doing here?"

"Hello, Yan," the Rabbit said, pushing his head and paws

out of the pouch. "What do you think I am doing here? I'm looking for you."

"Trouble, then?" Lu Ting-Pin said, sitting down next to the odd-shaped boulder, the shadows of its crags and hollows making the rock look like a deformed companion. He motioned for Mulan to sit down, which, after giving Black Wind a reassuring pat, she was only too happy to do. While Lu Ting-Pin and the Rabbit were greeting each other as if they had happened to meet in a teahouse, Mulan's knees were shaking. Had she almost just been thrown into the river? She felt more dazed than when she had fallen off the roof as a child. Mulan took a deep breath and shook her head in disbelief.

Lu Ting-Pin studied her, his keen eyes scanning her face. "I see you chose your companion here for battle. Her destiny of — "

"Mulan is with me by chance," the Rabbit interrupted hurriedly, "and the only destiny we need to concern ourselves with is that of her sister."

The Rabbit wiggled out of the pouch and onto Mulan's lap. Lu Ting-Pin's eyes widened as he saw the Rabbit's bare, injured leg.

"And yours!" Lu Ting-Pin gasped. "Tuzi! This is a mortal injury."

"I know," the Rabbit said. "Mulan's sister suffers from the same. We need to get to the Queen Mother's garden by the new moon. Can you take us?"

"Of course!" Lu Ting-Pin stood as if to make ready immediately.

"Wait," the Rabbit said, "there's more. We need to stop at Green Island as well. And our adversary is the White Fox."

"Ah," Lu Ting-Pin sat down again. "The White Fox. And she is still with — "

"Yes," the Rabbit said. Mulan looked at them both curiously.

Lu Ting-Pin's jaw clenched. "It's good," he said. "In fact, it is perfect." He stood and pulled the sword from his back, the red sash swirling from its handle. As he held it in his hands, Mulan was startled to see that the sword was carved of wood, not forged of metal. But Lu Ting-Pin did not notice her look of surprise, for he was gazing at his sword with a somber, prayerful look. "She will be the one to finish my penance," he said.

"You only have one more?" the Rabbit asked. "Nine thousand nine hundred ninety-nine already?"

"Yes," Lu Ting-Pin answered. He was still looking at the sword solemnly, but Mulan could see the hint of a satisfied smile tug at the corner of his mouth. She shrugged. Maybe the Rabbit would explain these cryptic exchanges to her later.

Lu Ting-Pin looked up from his sword. "So, we should not wait any longer," he said, and then glanced down at the Rabbit. "In fact, my friend, with the amount of chi you are losing from that wound, I think we should leave immediately."

The Rabbit nodded. Mulan stood up, carrying the Rabbit in her arms.

"We can pick up supplies at Green Island," Lu Ting-Pin said. He looked at the Rabbit and Mulan and tapped his fingers against his chin, mouthing numbers as he measured their weight in his mind. "We'll need a large rock or boulder to help keep the boat stable."

"And don't forget the horse," the Rabbit said. Mulan looked back and forth between them in confusion. What boat? And what about Black Wind?

"Ah, yes," Lu Ting-Pin said, gazing at Black Wind. Then he looked at Mulan. "He'll have to return home. A sea voyage to Kunlun Mountain is not the place for a horse."

Mulan put the arm not holding the Rabbit around Black Wind. "Home?" she asked. "By himself? How will he get there?"

"He knows the way," Lu Ting-Pin said. He placed the wooden sword under his arm and pulled a red thread from the sash attached to the handle. He handed it to Mulan. "Tie this onto your horse and he'll get home safely."

Mulan lowered the Rabbit to the ground and took the thread, watching it sway in the air as she walked to Black Wind. She placed the thread around Black Wind's neck, expecting it to be too short, but the string magically elongated and she was able to tie it securely. The horse nickered and nuzzled her ear as she patted his muzzle.

"Don't forget the saddlebags," said the Rabbit, who was standing by her feet. Black Wind neighed and lowered his head down to the Rabbit, who reached up to tap his nose.

"He'll be all right?" Mulan asked the Rabbit as she gave the horse one last hug. It would be hard to leave Black Wind behind.

"Yes," the Rabbit said, and Black Wind neighed again as she picked up the saddlebags. "He will be fine."

"He has much more cause to worry about us than we do about him," Lu Ting-Pin said, surveying the riverbank carefully. "Now, which rock should we use?" he mused. "It should be fairly large . . ."

"Why don't we just use that one?" Mulan said, nodding her head toward the strange-shaped boulder he had sat next to. She had noticed that rock the moment she was brought to the river, with its top-heavy, crouching shape and weather-aged perforations. It was misshapen and slightly monstrous looking, but as Mulan looked at it longer, there was something sadly beautiful about it as well.

Lu Ting-Pin hesitated and then cocked his head at the Rabbit, who shrugged in return. "Interesting choice," he said. "But a good one. I think it's just about the right size and weight for the boat."

"Uh, good," Mulan said. However, now it was her turn to hesitate. She glanced up and down the empty river. "But, uh, Master Lu? What boat are you talking about?"

Lu Ting-Pin looked around to make sure no stray townspeople were about and then grinned at her. "This one," he said.

And, in a swift, fluid motion, he whipped the sword out from under his arm and hurled it at the river. The sword spun in the sky, faster and faster, and then arched downward like a diving crane. As it hit the water, giant splashes flew into the air, showering all of them with droplets. Mulan wiped the water from her eyes, gawking, and then wiped her eyes again.

For instead of a sword floating in the water, as she expected, there was now a wooden boat.

CHAPTER 38

The Red Fox

SHE WAS dripping and bedraggled as she crawled out of the river, the water darkening her crimson fur to a murky brown. When she finally pulled herself onto the bank, she lifted her head and then spat out the white fish she had been holding in her mouth. The fish leapt upward and a clapping sound filled the air as the fish transformed into a lovely, graceful woman.

"Lu Ting-Pin!" Daji said the name viciously, as if she were cursing. "How dare he!"

She remained a wet fox panting on the ground.

"Xianniang!" Daji barked, not bothering to speak the rest of her order.

With a shudder, the fox transformed into a woman. Her clothes and hair were wet and she lay on her back, panting.

"Get up!" Daji said impatiently. "You have work to do."

Xianniang pushed herself up, still slightly breathless. "What do you want me to do now?" she said, trying to keep her petulant feelings from her voice. She did not succeed, for Daji snapped back with anger.

"You ungrateful mixed egg!" Daji said. "Don't you forget what you owe me! Everything you have is because of me!"

That was true, Xianniang knew. With the skills Daji had taught her, she could fit in anywhere. She had the power to be anyone and anything. Except for herself.

For when she was herself, she had nothing. She belonged nowhere and was not only unwanted but rejected by all. Her exile was also because of Daji.

She remembered, even if Daji did not, all the eyes upon her in horror. She remembered the clenching teeth, the wave of hands gripping their swords surrounding her. Daji had made her escape, but she had been left to face the whispers. "Witch," they had hissed. "Witch."

"Xianniang!" Daji snapped, as if ready to box her ears.

"Yes, Mistress," she said humbly, forcing herself from her reverie.

"Make me a fire from wet wood," Daji ordered. "Now."

She nodded and scurried away like a mouse to gather the wood. But the memories kept returning. As she held a freshly cut bamboo stalk in her hand, she could see the one from so long ago — that long bamboo stalk falling in a sweeping arch from the coffin. And she could still feel the harsh hands of the Emperor's soldiers clamping upon her as he barked, "What witchcraft is this? Your mistress still lives, doesn't she?"

Xianniang piled the wood neatly and then, using a trick Daji taught her, glowered at the hill of wood until a small flame began to flicker in its center. As the first stick began to hiss, Xianniang realized that she had hoped, all those years ago, to remain in the kingdom as herself — without Daji.

"Hurry," Daji said impatiently. "I need smoke."

As if prompted, a snake of dark smoke glided from the burning wood.

"More," Daji commanded. "More!"

The smoke thickened in obedience, swelling into a rising grey cloud that made Xianniang cough. It hung above them, ready to smother the earth.

"Good," Daji said. "I'll show them that the ocean is no place to be."

No place to be. Xianniang shivered, still in a fog of memories. "There is no place for witches in this kingdom!" the chancellor had declared. And they had clustered around her, swords pointing, teeth bared and faces full of malice.

What made it different from Daji's venom? Xianniang watched as Daji's teeth jutted out in glinting spikes, her face stretching as she transformed back into the White Fox. Daji glared with that same hostility, but, Xianniang realized, at least it did not have the revulsion the soldiers' faces had. They had looked at her in disgust, as if she had been a poisonous wart that needed to be cut off.

The White Fox raised her nose toward the gloomy cloud and pursed her lips as if about to bestow a kiss. A gentle breeze blew from her mouth, but the cloud glided quickly away, as though it were trying to flee.

A pleased sound rumbled from the White Fox. Xianniang silently transformed into her Red Fox shape to join her. Xianniang had accepted the truth long ago. Why was she bothering to think about that now? There was no place for her in the kingdom; there was no place for her anywhere, except where she no longer wished to be — by Daji's side.

CHAPTER 39

Sailing with the Odd-Shaped Rock

MULAN HAD just settled the strange rock in the boat's stern as they began to float down the river. Black Wind gave a whinny of farewell from the riverbank, and she watched him turn and walk away, growing smaller and smaller as the distance between them grew. Lu Ting-Pin finished raising the sail, the unfurling red silk suspiciously similar to the sash that had been tied to his sword, then joined her.

It was a wooden, flat-bottomed boat with a single sail and a cloth-covered shelter. But though humble in size and shape, the warm wood was polished and glossy and the sail was a vivid crimson, making the boat a striking figure on the water. Still, Mulan had felt doubtful about its traveling the sea. Lu Ting-Pin had seen her face and grinned. "Don't worry," he said. "It may be small, but it will ride through the waves."

"I'm sure," the Rabbit had replied dryly, "as long as you don't get distracted by any old ocean friends."

"No worries," Lu Ting-Pin had said, giving Mulan a wink. "We're too busy for visiting right now."

Mulan had not understood the wink, nor much of their conversation, but Lu Ting-Pin was right about the boat. Because now, as she stood at the bow, she could see it was sailing through the water as easily and as quickly as a grand ship, its pointed hull slicing into the sky.

"So tell me," Lu Ting-Pin said to Mulan, removing the bottle gourd from his belt and gesturing to the boat's storage with his chin, "why did you choose that stone?"

Mulan shrugged. "I don't know," she said. "I guess because it is so odd looking."

"You know, the townspeople don't like that rock," Lu Ting-Pin told her. "They think it's bad luck."

"They do?" Mulan glanced at the boat's stern and frowned. Perhaps the stone had not been a good choice. She looked at Lu Ting-Pin, but he did not seem concerned. She walked over to them and asked the Rabbit, who had been resting by Lu Ting-Pin, "What do you think?"

The Rabbit shifted uncomfortably and Lu Ting-Pin answered for him. "Immortals don't like to tell what they know," he said, smiling. "Because they don't like to admit that not only do they not know everything, but that things can change."

"The Rabbit tells me things," Mulan protested. "He has told me stories of almost everything."

"He?" Lu Ting-Pin's eyebrow rose and he shot a quizzical look at the Rabbit. "Male today?"

"She met me as a male healer," the Rabbit answered, "so I decided to just keep it that way for now."

"What?" Mulan said. "The Rabbit is not male?"

"Oh, he is," Lu Ting-Pin said, "but not always. The Rabbit can change into any kind of being, from a noble healer to an old peasant woman."

"Not anymore," the Rabbit said glumly.

Lu Ting-Pin nodded gravely. "Soon, though," he said, taking a sip from his gourd. "Take heart, Tuzi. The new moon is not far away."

"It's not?" Mulan straightened, alarmed. The long days of travel had lulled the urgency from her, and now a sudden fear filled her. "How much time do we have?"

"Next week is the new moon. We should just about make it," Lu Ting-Pin said with what Mulan realized was his usual confidence. He patted the handle of the yuloh that arched above his head as he sat, the other end disappearing into the water. "As long as this stays intact," he said, winking at Mulan.

"Did you enchant it?" Mulan asked, leaning in to inspect it. To her, the long wooden yuloh looked like the ordinary kind of oar attached to the back of the boat, though this was the first time she had been on a boat, so she couldn't be sure.

"The best I could." Lu Ting-Pin shrugged. "I'm still rather limited. But it should be enough."

"As long as no one gets in our way," the Rabbit said darkly. "Don't forget the White Fox."

"Nothing we can't handle," Lu Ting-Pin said, waving his hand as if to brush the White Fox away. "The two of us together are as good as a full-power Immortal, and Mulan here is a might — "

"What did you say about Immortals not telling their knowledge?" the Rabbit interrupted loudly, looking at Lu Ting-Pin with a pointed stare. Lu Ting-Pin met the Rabbit's eyes, smiled sheepishly, and took a drink from his gourd. Mulan looked at back and forth between them.

"What are you talking about?" Mulan said, when it was obvious neither would volunteer the answer.

"Oh, nothing, nothing," Lu Ting-Pin said. He held his gourd out to her. "Have a drink?"

"Now you offer her wine?" the Rabbit objected. "Are you purposely trying to ruin her?"

Lu Ting-Pin threw his head back and laughed. "It's just tea," he said, chuckling. "My gourds aren't allowed to make wine yet, you know."

He handed the gourd to Mulan. She brought it to her mouth, the delicate aroma of tea wafting into her nose. She sipped the warm liquid, enjoying its fragrant flavor, before asking, "Why aren't you allowed to make wine?"

He took the gourd from her and passed it to the Rabbit, who with a bit of difficulty angled it to drink as well. "Oh, it's part of my punishment," Lu Ting-Pin said, watching the Rabbit with amusement.

"Your punishment?" Mulan said. "What are you being punished for?"

The Rabbit put the gourd down and looked at Lu Ting-Pin, whose face suddenly became somber.

"You didn't tell her?" Lu Ting-Pin said to the Rabbit.

"It is not my story to tell," he replied.

A gentle breeze blew over the boat, and as it traveled through the ship's hold, they could hear the Odd-Shaped Rock make a faint whistling noise.

"You don't have to tell me if you don't want to," Mulan said, feeling awkward. "It's fine."

"No, it's not a secret," Lu Ting-Pin said. He took his gourd from the Rabbit and drank again. He grimaced, shook his head at the bottle, and looked out over the water. "And we have time."

Lu Ting-Pin's Story

I once fell in love with a mortal woman. Her name was Yellow Peony, and even though she was as beautiful as the flower, it was the light in her eyes that transfixed me. When she smiled at me, her eyes seemed to hold all the innocence and hope of the world, and I could not look away.

While we both knew it was wrong, only I knew it was forbidden. Yet that did not stop me. With a single glance, I had already helplessly fallen, and broke the strict moral code of the Mighty Eight Immortals by doing so.

We married in secret and I used my powers to

conceal our relationship, deceiving all that came upon us. But we could not hide forever. My seven fellow Mighty Immortals had already become suspicious of me, as my many lies claiming I was with someone else or in other places had become unbelievable. But it was the lake I had conjured that was my true downfall.

For around the home I had made with Yellow Peony, I placed a lake. It was a lovely lake with jade-green water and orange fish flickering through the gentle waves. But I had not placed it there for beauty. I had placed it there so that none could pass our home. I had thought, naively as well as wrongly, to keep Yellow Peony like a treasure from the world—hidden in a house in the middle of a lake, where only I could fly to her.

But a new and unusual body of water is not something the Immortals would miss. Finally, during one of my questionable disappearances, my seven associates decided to search for me. As they flew in the air, they noticed the lake—the lake they had never seen before and that seemed to have appeared from nowhere. Immediately, they went to investigate, and promptly, my deceptions were revealed.

My seven fellow Mighty Immortals were outraged, but it was their disappointment that truly vanquished me. Their judgment upon me was swift and painful. They circled around me, all with their powerful talismans flashing a lightning that seized and held me helplessly into the air. Many of my powers were painfully extracted from me, my penance was named, and I was forbidden to see Yellow Peony or interfere with her life ever again.

This last requirement was agonizing, yet I was forced to obey. And it was for the best, too. I had no right to interfere in her mortal life, I who had removed her from the world and treated her as if she were a flower or a pet. Yellow Peony was a woman with thoughts and a destiny of her own—a destiny I had injured with my selfishness.

Because over time, I slowly heard bits and pieces of what happened to her. She had our child, a girl, in disgrace, as all were aghast by our marriage. But soon after, the Immortals arranged for Yellow Peony to go to another town and create a different identity for herself. She was able to remarry (the Immortals quickly dissolved our marriage after the baby was born) and start a new family and life. However, Yellow Peony could not bear the sight of her eldest daughter, our child. The child she had with me was a constant reminder of my betrayal, our shameful relationship, and the dishonor it had brought her. The daughter bore the brunt of Yellow Peony's anger and resentment, an acrimony which should have been placed upon me.

And that is the most terrible of all my transgressions. My actions caused a mother to despise her own innocent child, and I shall always be ashamed. Because, even when I have completed my penance, it will never make up for the pain I have caused my poor daughter, who was so rejected that she became known as the Unwanted Girl.

CHAPTER 40

Fed
Fog

"THE UNWANTED Girl?" Mulan gasped. "Is she . . . is she the same . . ." Mulan stole a quick glance at the Rabbit and whispered, "Is she the same girl that became the Red Fox?"

"Ah." Lu Ting-Pin also looked at the Rabbit. "You told her that story?"

The Rabbit nodded, and a look of sadness passed between the two.

"I should not have interfered," the Rabbit said.

"You were only trying to help," Lu Ting-Pin said. "You wanted to give her a chance to find her way."

"And I led her to the wrong one," the Rabbit said, gloomily.

"Tuzi," Lu Ting-Pin said, "the blame is far from yours. Truly, the fault lies between me and the White Fox."

And at the mention of the White Fox, a strong wind blew, causing the sail to whip against the sky. An ominous darkness descended, and they stood, a sudden dread creeping upon all of them as the boat stopped moving. Mulan peered over the edge and saw that the water was still and smooth, as if the boat were sitting upon black lacquered wood. And when she looked up, she saw that a thick dark cloud enveloped them. A strange feeling of emptiness overwhelmed her: time, sound, and color had been sucked away. Everything — the sky, the sun, the earth — had disappeared into a haze of grey, swallowed by a demon of mist.

"Fog!" Mulan whispered with awe. Her neck ached of stiffness and Mulan realized that she did not know how long she had been staring. The blanket of sky covering them seemed to have held them still in both place and time. She placed her hand on her neck to rub away the stiffness and then grimaced. It was a vast understatement to call this merely fog, but she had no other word for it.

"The White Fox, again," the Rabbit said, with disgust. "Anything to try to slow us down."

Lu Ting-Pin whooped with laughter, his bellows even louder in that muffling cloak of mist. "Really?" he boomed, his voice breaking the heavy hush. "This old trick? Is this really the best she can do?"

"She's already made a storm," the Rabbit said. "And a swarm of bees and a canyon. She must be just about out, by now."

Lu Ting-Pin laughed again. "Even with all her centuries, she's still so uninspired! Spitting rain and blowing smoke!" he snorted. "Well, I can blow, too."

And with that, Lu Ting-Pin hopped onto the hull of the boat. He grabbed the mast with one hand and threw his other arm out into the fog. The sail remained still, but his sleeve billowed, flapping from the force of his energy. He opened his mouth and took a loud gulp of air. As he closed his mouth to hold in the sucked air, he looked down at Mulan and gave her a wink. Then, making a circle with his mouth, he blew.

A whistling sound trumpeted through the air. It echoed and roared, resonating like thunder from the heavens. The boat shook. Any awe Mulan felt for the created fog was now dwarfed by her wonder of Lu Ting-Pin. A gale of wind was gusting out of him, filling the sail and thinning the fog. The thick gloom that had enveloped them was ebbing away, and Mulan was beginning to see the sky again.

However, instead of the sun shining, a waning crescent moon hung in the sky. Somehow, time had passed and night had fallen.

CHAPTER 41

The Peach-Wood Sword

THE WANING moon's pale light made a path on the lapping, inky waves. Mulan glanced around in confusion. Not only was it now night, but the moon was much thinner than she remembered it. Also, they were on the open sea. How long had they been in that fog? She looked at both Lu Ting-Pin and the Rabbit, asking the questions with her eyes.

"It's an old trick, but effective," the Rabbit grumbled. "She slowed us down. We lost four days."

Four days! Mulan's eyes bulged. Had they been frozen in that fog for that long?

"We still have three days left," Lu Ting-Pin said reassuringly. "And I got us out to sea. So that makes up for some of it, right?"

The Rabbit grunted, but he nodded. He waved at them both and then slowly hopped into the boat's shelter, presumably to sleep.

Lu Ting-Pin watched him go. As the door shut, he shook his head.

"He's right," he said to Mulan. "She did slow us down, and we can't afford to lose any more time. The White Fox is nothing if not clever."

"How do you know the White Fox, Master Lu?" Mulan asked.

"Only by reputation," he said. "I have never met her."

"But . . ." Mulan started and stopped, unsure how to explain that Lu Ting-Pin had already met the White Fox as the Hag.

"But I am very eager to," Lu Ting-Pin continued, misunderstanding Mulan's stutters. He sat down and pulled his gourd off his belt. He took a long sip, and when he spoke again, all the lightness had disappeared from his voice. "I am very eager to meet the White Fox," he repeated. "So that I can kill her."

"Oh," Mulan squeaked. She stood awkwardly in front of him, her mouth gaping open. He gazed up at her and gave her a wry smile. He patted the floor next to him, beckoning for her to sit.

"Have you noticed anything unusual about my sword?" he asked, offering her the gourd as she sat down.

Mulan took a sip of tea. "Well, I've noticed that your sword can turn into a boat," she said, returning Lu Ting-Pin's wry smile. "And it's made of wood."

"Peach wood," Lu Ting-Pin specified, ignoring Mulan's first comment. "When my Immortal comrades cast their judgment on me, they took away my fly whisk so that I would no longer be able to fly great distances, and they turned my two-edged sword into one of peach wood. Can you guess why?"

Mulan shook her head.

"Because the wood of a peach tree," Lu Ting-Pin said, "has the special quality of being able to kill noxious beasts and demons. And killing demons is part of my punishment."

"It is?" Mulan said, sitting up. She felt the hot tea flow through to her toes and fingers, and they tingled as if covered with crawling centipedes.

"When this sword"—Lu Ting-Pin patted the wood floor they were sitting on—"destroys ten thousand demons, I will have completed my penance."

Mulan remembered the conversation he'd had with the Rabbit.

"And you've already killed nine thousand nine hundred ninety-nine, right?" she asked. "You only have one more demon left?"

"Yes," Lu Ting-Pin said, "and I want it to be the White Fox, the demon who now controls my daughter. If I kill the White Fox, my daughter will no longer have to be her servant."

"I thought no man could kill the White Fox," Mulan said, faintly.

"Just because it hasn't happened yet," Lu Ting-Pin said, "doesn't mean that is true."

"Do you think you and your daughter could . . ." Mulan trailed off.

"No." Lu Ting-Pin shook his head. "It is too late for us. But perhaps I can grant her freedom. That is the only gift I can give her."

The water washed against the boat in gentle waves, but Mulan could only see the emptiness of the ocean. Lu Ting-Pin offered his gourd again, and as the warmth of the tea filled her, she could not help thinking of her family, frozen in her faraway home. How long ago it was, all of them together sipping tea while Ba told stories of great battles! Or Ma waiting to fry the breakfast dough when Mulan was late so it would be fresh and crispy. And combing Xiu's hair, as silky and smooth as the sky above her.

Mulan looked up to the sliver of the moon, its light small against the sky and sea of blackness. Suddenly, she felt a rush of worry.

"How long will it take to get to Green Island?" Mulan asked, gulping. "And the Queen Mother's garden?"

"These days, to get to the Queen Mother's garden with a stop at Green Island usually takes me about seven or eight days," Lu Ting-Pin said slowly.

"Seven or eight days!" Mulan gasped. "But . . . but Master Lu, now we have only three days left until the new moon!"

Lu Ting-Pin nodded and gazed up at the diminishing moon with a frown.

"Will . . . will we make it?" Mulan asked. She hoped he would smile as he had before, with jovial reassurance. But he did not. Instead, he glanced up at the yuloh, the handle curving above them like a branch of a tree.

"I hope so," he said. "We shall see."

CHAPTER 42

The Island That Was Not Green

THE MORNING came gently, a soft light that danced delicately on the ocean waves and then sprinkled itself onto the boat. The wind that blew was warm now, like the steam from cooked porridge. The comfortable breeze, as well as the luxury of a roof to hide the dawn, had made Mulan oversleep. So when she came out from the shelter, she found the Rabbit and Lu Ting-Pin already awake. Lu Ting-Pin turned to her and smiled.

"Just in time!" he greeted her. There was an air of expectancy as spoke, as if he were about to unveil a gift. "Tuzi and I were able to hurry the boat a bit while you were sleeping, and look what we found!"

Proudly, he waved one hand toward the ocean, using his other arm to usher her toward the front of the boat. As Mulan peered out, she saw an odd shape in the distance, a bump in the straight, sparkling horizon of sea. It looked like a gigantic worn turtle shell caked with mud.

"Is it an island?" Mulan asked.

"Of course it's an island," Lu Ting-Pin scoffed. "It's Green Island!"

"But . . . but . . ." Mulan said in surprise, "it's not . . ."

"Green," the Rabbit finished for her gloomily. "Apparently the Dragon Beard Grass that once grew so abundantly on the island does so no longer."

"There must be some growing on there somewhere," Lu Ting-Pin said. "Maybe it's just not as plentiful as it used to be."

"Perhaps," the Rabbit said, but he did not sound hopeful.

"We'll stop for supplies," Lu Ting-Pin said with his usual confidence. "And hunt under every rock and bush for the grass. We'll find it."

❉

But they did not. As soon as they had docked the boat and had a quick meal from a street peddler of tea eggs and smelly tofu, they hastened to the sloping countryside. There, the Rabbit claimed, lush blankets of Dragon Beard Grass had previously covered the land all the way out to sea. But as they climbed the hills, they did not see even one blade of grass.

"What should it look like?" Mulan asked as she stumbled over crumbling dirt. She stood at the top of a hill, perhaps the highest point on the island. She could see their boat, its bright red sail an easy marker, and beyond it a cavern with what looked like a statue at its opening. "Besides green, I mean."

"It is fine and wavy," the Rabbit said, nosing under a stone, "and can grow quite long. And if you pull it out of the ground, you will see the roots are bright red."

"Red?" Mulan asked.

"You might as well tell her the story," Lu Ting-Pin said. He sat down, wiping his brow. The sun was blazing down upon them, and Mulan had already rolled up the sleeves of her robe. The Rabbit sat back on his haunches and sighed.

"I guess it wouldn't hurt," he said.

The Story of Dragon Beard Grass

Once, many centuries ago, an Immortal lived on this island. He spent his time in the hills collecting herbs and plants, and creating medicines. He helped many on the island, so the people began to revere him. Every day, someone from the island village would come to see him for medicine, help, or advice. It seemed that no problem, large or small, could not be solved by him. Even though he was bent and aged, he seemed so wise and powerful that many began to believe he was a dragon spirit in human form. But even those who did not believe it joined the others in calling the Immortal "Old Dragon."

One spring day, the Old Dragon told his visitors that he would be leaving the island. The news quickly spread across the island, and soon all clustered around the Immortal.

"Are you really going?" they asked. "Are you leaving the island?"

The Old Dragon looked at the crowd before him. "Yes, my friends," he said, nodding. "I am leaving."

"Why?" the villagers asked, many in tears. "Don't leave us!"

"I am needed elsewhere," the Old Dragon said. And with a wave of his hand, a shimmering cloud appeared at his feet. He stepped upon it as the villagers gaped in wonder. "I have enjoyed my time with you. This island has a spirit of peace; make sure you cherish it."

The cloud began to rise, carrying the Old Dragon up into the sky with it. He leaned over to call down to villagers. "Farewell, my friends!"

The people, now recovered from their awe, began to cry. "Don't leave us!" they begged. "Don't leave us!"

They wailed and howled, and the most desperate of them reached out to grab the Old Dragon to try to keep him from leaving. However, all they could grasp was his beard, hanging over the edge of the cloud. And to their surprise, when they pulled upon his beard, its hairs slipped from his chin as easily as young weeds from a garden. When they saw clumps of the Old Dragon's beard in their hands, the ends trickling with tiny drops of red blood, they were horrified and quickly released the hairs, brushing their hands in the wind.

So the people of the island stood helpless as the Old Dragon ascended into the sky and disappeared. But though grief-stricken, they vowed to always heed his words to honor the peaceful spirit of their island. For they realized that in his departure, he had left one last gift to help remind them. The hairs of his beard, which they had so dramatically pulled and released, were carried by the wind all over the island. These hairs took root in the rich soil created by the peaceful heart of the island and began to grow. Soon, the island was carpeted with the lush green Dragon's Beard grass and was called Green Island.

"So the grass was the Immortal's hair?" Mulan said, captivated. "And the roots of the grass are red because of his blood?"

The Rabbit nodded.

"Ah, Tuzi has all the stories," Lu Ting-Pin said proudly, "even the ones he doesn't know he has."

"What does that mean?" Mulan said, confused.

The Rabbit shuffled uneasily. "That's hard to explain," he said, but he met Mulan's expectant eyes and sighed.

"Mulan's no rice bucket. She's smart enough to understand," Lu Ting-Pin said. "Though I suppose it is even difficult for Immortals."

The Rabbit sighed again and looked at Mulan. "Remember how I told you the White Fox found an oracle bone?" he said to her. "An old bone, burned?"

She nodded.

"That was one of my bones," the Rabbit said. "When I shed my mortal body and exchanged my bones, well . . . those old bones still have the stories."

"All the stories! The stories of the past and the future — they're all inside the Rabbit," Lu Ting-Pin said. "They are written in his bones."

"But while they are in me," the Rabbit said, "I don't really know them all. Sometimes when I tell a story of the past, it is the first time I have heard it myself."

"So you know everything," Mulan said, still confused. "Except you don't?"

"I told you she would understand," Lu Ting-Pin said, overlooking Mulan's face of utter bewilderment. "Now, Tuzi, do you have any idea where we should look next for this blamed grass?"

Mulan stepped forward as the Rabbit and Lu Ting-Pin continued their conversation. She gazed again over the island, brown and rocky, that dark cave opening she had seen before like a blot of black ink on the landscape. It was nothing like the abundant green island that the Rabbit had described in his story. The grass had stopped growing on the island. Was it the dirt? This dry, crumbling dirt was not the *rich soil created by the peaceful heart of the island* the Rabbit had described, either.

It looked like the peaceful heart of the island had stopped making that special soil for some reason. Why? The light shape in front of the faraway cave glinted at her, like a star trying to catch her attention. Had something happened to the spirit of the island?

Chapter 43

The Bakery

T HEY ENTERED Green Island's main village tired and discouraged. They had searched the hills and the countryside, and most of the rocky shoreline as well. They had not yet inspected the cliffs beyond the docks, but Mulan had been able to get a better look at the cave she had seen from the top of the hill. And as she had guessed, there was a statue at its entrance — weathered, barely recognizable, but of a man Mulan suspected was a long-forgotten island hero.

None of that helped their present plight, of course. Their

extensive hunt had not uncovered a single spike of the Dragon Beard Grass. In fact, except for some scraggly evergreens, there was very little growing anywhere on the island. Green Island was far from green, and by the time they had dragged themselves through the village gate, Mulan felt the name was mockery.

The sky had been darkening, so Lu Ting-Pin suggested they go to town and ask the advice of some locals he knew. "And they will probably give us something to eat," he added, slightly greedily. "They own a bakery."

The Rabbit had given Lu Ting-Pin a wry look, but it was that comment that was causing Mulan to brighten now. They were trudging down the narrow, stone-paved street, made even narrower by the peddlers and craftsmen selling sticks of candied fruit, giving haircuts, and sharpening knives. As they weaved in and around throngs of people and carts, a rich, delectable aroma began to fill Mulan's nose. Her mouth watered, the scent of warm, sweet-savory meat and pastries tantalizing her. She hoped the smell was coming from Lu Ting-Pin's friends' bakery.

Lu Ting-Pin quickened his pace, perhaps also enticed by the aroma. Mulan, who was carrying the Rabbit, had to hop and scamper about to keep up with his lengthening strides. But it was worth it, for Lu Ting-Pin was entering the store she was hoping he would — the bakery spilling the delicious scent of pork buns.

Lu Ting-Pin waited impatiently for a customer to finish picking up his bags at the sales counter. As soon as he left, he smiled at the young woman behind the pastry displays.

"Hello, Li Jing!" Lu Ting-Pin boomed. "Do you know who I am?"

The woman cocked her head and studied him. "Is it . . ." She hesitated. "Is it Master Yan?"

"Of course!" Lu Ting-Pin said, beaming. "Is your father in the back?"

She nodded, then squeaked and clapped her hands in excitement. Mulan realized that Li Jing was really a girl, only a handful of years older than herself. "Ba is going to be so excited!" Li Jing said, her smile as wide as his. She moved to open the doors at her side, but Lu Ting-Pin held up his hand.

"First," Lu Ting-Pin said, "let me introduce you to Mulan . . . my, uh, niece. And her pet rabbit. Perhaps you could give them something to eat?"

Mulan felt the Rabbit shift on her back at those words, and she grinned broadly at the older girl across the counter. Li Jing smiled back, and Mulan instantly felt a sense of friendship.

"Of course!" Li Jing said, and she hurried out from behind the counter. "Come! Come!"

"I'll go see your father," Lu Ting-Pin said. He pushed past them through the swinging doors, his robes rippling behind him.

Li Jing led Mulan to one of the small tables at the side of the store. As Mulan sat down, Li Jing scurried around the shop, turning the sign on the door to CLOSED and then visiting various shelves. She returned balancing two trays — one piled high with aromatic buns and pastries, and the other holding tea. To Mulan's envy, Li Jing gracefully placed the trays on the table without even a rattle of the teapot. How Mulan wished she could be like that! Once, she had accidentally hit the table as she ran into the house, and the family's prized teacup flew up into the air. Mulan had flung herself down, skidded across the floor, and narrowly caught the cup in her outstretched hand. Even though she had saved the cup, Ma had still been horrified.

Li Jing took an empty bowl from the tea tray and put it on the ground. "Which do you think your rabbit would like?" she asked. "Red bean buns? Pineapple cake?"

"I'm sure he'll like anything," Mulan said, quickly placing the Rabbit on the floor, her eyes slightly bulging at the assortment of snacks in front of her. She could barely keep herself from grabbing and devouring the entire pile. However, when Li Jing handed her a cloth to clean her hands, Mulan found herself blushing. She grimaced at the brown stains she left on the cloth and felt ashamed as she looked at Li Jing's smoothly wound hair and spotless, softly clinging robes.

But Li Jing did not seem to notice and only pushed the plate toward her. With great will, Mulan took only one of the pork buns whose inviting aroma had been teasing her since she entered the village. Her eyes closed as she bit into it. Warm steam misted her face, and as the full flavors of the luscious, sweet pork melted into her mouth, she groaned involuntarily.

"Good?" Li Jing asked, pleased.

Mulan, mouth full, could only nod enthusiastically.

"You can thank your uncle for that," Li Jing said, sitting down across from her. "He's the one that changed everything for our family."

"He did?" Mulan asked, in between bites. "How?"

"Well," Li Jing said, "the story goes like this . . ."

Lu Ting-Pin and the Sweet-Smelling Cakes

When my grandfather was a young man, he sold rice cakes from door to door, carrying his wares in a straw basket. He worked hard but made a very meager living, only enough to support himself and his elderly mother. Every morning, he rose before his mother woke to grind the rice to make his cakes, cook them, and then carry them to this village to sell. When he returned home every evening, he gave his mother whatever cakes he had not sold.

Some days he would have good business and the village would line up before him to buy his cakes. On those days, he always made sure that he set aside one cake for his mother.

The New Year was my grandfather's busiest time. That was when all the villagers wanted cakes, for, of course, having a cake on the New Year meant one would get a promotion. My grandfather always carried an extra basket of cakes when he went to town then.

One New Year was especially busy. My grandfather sold all his cakes before evening, except for the one he put aside for his mother. He had to turn away customers as he made his way out of the village. Before he left, however, he was stopped by the mayor—the richest man in the district.

"Hey! Baker!" the mayor called out. "I need a cake for the New Year."

"I am so sorry," my grandfather said, bowing. "I promise to bring more tomorrow, but I have no more to sell today."

"Yes, you do," the mayor said, his keen eyes spotting the last cake in my grandfather's basket. "I'll take that one."

"I'm sorry," my grandfather said again, "that one is not for sale."

The mayor sputtered and tried to bargain, offering more and more money—as much money as my grandfather had made that entire day. But my grandfather still refused. Nothing would sway him to sell his last cake. Finally, very much annoyed, the mayor huffed away.

My grandfather continued on his journey home. But as he walked along the path, a ragged old man stepped in front of him.

"Please," the old man begged, "something to eat?"

My grandfather looked at the man, who was obviously suffering and in need. *I cannot turn him away,* my grandfather thought, and he pulled out some coins and offered them.

"No," the man said, "I cannot eat coins! Please, some food?"

My grandfather was at a loss. He could not give

away his mother's cake, nor could he leave this beggar to starve. Finally, he broke the cake in two and gave half to the beggar.

"Thank you!" the beggar said, grabbing the halved cake and disappearing into the shadows. "See you tomorrow."

My grandfather shook his head, confused, but finally continued home. The next day he returned to the village with two extra baskets of cakes. Business was brisk, yet the whole time my grandfather was selling, he kept thinking about the beggar. See you tomorrow, he had said. Was he planning to meet him again? Just in case, my grandfather decided to save not one cake, but two.

And he was glad he had. Because much like the day before, my grandfather's cakes sold out quickly and he left for home early. And, just like the day before, the beggar stopped him and asked for food. This time, my grandfather gave him a pastry without hesitation.

This continued for the fifteen days of the New Year. But then the New Year ended and none of the villagers were interested in purchasing my grandfather's cakes anymore. He trudged home sadly, his baskets full of unsold cakes. As he walked in the darkness, the beggar man stepped in front of him again.

"Why so glum, Baker?" the beggar asked.

"Oh, it is not as bad as your plight," my grandfather said, opening his basket. "Today, I have plenty for you to eat."

"Thank you," the beggar said, grabbing a pastry, "but tell me why you are so troubled."

"It's only that the New Year is over," my grandfather said, "and no one wants my cakes anymore. I worry that I will not be able to take care of my poor mother."

The beggar laughed. "Well, that is easily fixed," he said. He pulled at a pigskin bag tied around his waist and pulled out a small jade jar. He handed it to my grandfather. "Sprinkle a little of this in your flour every time you cook," he said, "and you'll find everyone will want your cakes."

My grandfather did as he was told. When he made his rice flour in the morning, he opened the jade jar and saw it contained a silvery-white powder. He took a pinch and sprinkled it in his flour. Then he made his cakes and put them in the baskets to steam. As they cooked, a magical, delicious aroma filled the air. It filled the house and caused his mother to waken. She rose out of bed, exclaiming, "What smells so good?"

And, just like the beggar said, my grandfather found

that everyone wanted his cakes again. The fragrant scent enticed even the stingiest, and, as during the New Year, my grandfather sold all his cakes—all except two, of course. My grandfather made sure to save one for his mother and one for the beggar.

But on his way home, my grandfather did not see the beggar. Instead, he saw a fine gentleman, standing and waiting for him.

"Hello, Baker!" the man said. "Troubles over? Told you it was a problem easily fixed."

My grandfather looked at the man carefully. This man was obviously wealthy and noble, but there was definitely a resemblance. "Are . . . were . . . you the beggar?" my grandfather gasped.

The man laughed. "You may call me Yan," he said.

❀

"And that was your uncle!" Li Jing finished. "He changed everything for us! After that, my grandfather never had any problems selling his cakes. He could stop selling door-to-door, and he opened this shop that my father runs now. People say he makes the best cakes on Green Island and beyond. I've always been taught to remember Master Yan as our great friend and benefactor."

Mulan smiled, glad that Lu Ting-Pin was responsible for this family's prosperity, as well as the divine quality of their cakes, though she suspected it was the latter that he had been most concerned with when he helped them.

"Can I ask you something?" Li Jing said. Mulan nodded and Li Jing continued in an eager, hushed voice, "Is your uncle an Immortal?"

Mulan stopped chewing, unsure how to answer. Lu Ting-Pin had once been one of the Eight Immortals — but what was he now that he was doing his penance? And would he want Li Jing's family to know? Finally, Mulan answered honestly, "I don't know."

Li Jing sighed. "We don't know either," she confessed. "But he must be very old, right? He knew my grandfather and my father. He only shows up every ten to twenty years or so, and each time he looks the same. I'm so glad I finally got to meet him!"

"You never met him before?" Mulan asked. The pile of cakes was almost gone, and she was slightly appalled at the amount she had consumed. She was glad Ma was not there to see her improper behavior.

"No . . ." Li Jing said thoughtfully. "But he looks exactly like he's been described to me. My father has told me everything about him, and once when I was a child he made a statue to show me."

"A statue?" Mulan said, sipping her tea, enjoying the fullness in her belly. "Did your father make that statue on the far side of the island?"

"No!" Li Jing laughed. "My father is a baker! He made one out of dough. He didn't make the Stone Statue!"

"Oh, of course," Mulan said, also laughing. "Who made the Stone Statue, then?"

Immediately, all the laughter drained from Li Jing and she turned sober. "We try not to talk about the Stone Statue," she said in a low voice. "It's bad luck."

"Why?" Mulan asked in an equally low tone.

"I don't know," Li Jing whispered, looking around. "The statue appeared before I was born—about twenty years ago. Some say it's a man who fell in love with a wicked fairy who got bored with him and turned him into a statue."

Mulan felt a strange excitement begin to bubble inside her. "How do—"

Li Jing stood up abruptly, biting her lip. "I should go check if my father needs me," she said. "I'll be right back."

As Li Jing walked away, Mulan felt as if fireworks were lighting inside her. A wicked fairy? Turning a man into a statue? Mulan looked down at the Rabbit, eager to see his reaction, only to be disappointed.

For the Rabbit, face in his bowl and nose covered with cake crumbs, was fast asleep.

CHAPTER 44

The Missing Grass

LU TING-PIN rushed to the table. "I found out more about the grass!" he said. Then he frowned and looked around. "Where's Tuzi?"

Mulan pointed down.

Lu Ting-Pin shook his head at the sleeping rabbit, knelt down, and poked him. "Wake up, Tuzi!" he said.

The Rabbit snorted awake, crumbs blowing from his nose. Mulan picked him up and placed him on her lap.

"I found out more about the grass," Lu Ting-Pin said

again. "Li Jing's father says that some sort of blight hit all the plants on the island about twenty years ago, and it has still not recovered."

"Twenty years?" the Rabbit said, his ears cocking. "How can a blight last that long?"

"It seems the soil of the island has completely changed," Lu Ting-Pin said. "It is no longer fertile, and very little grows on it. Luckily, this island has always relied mainly on fishing and trade, so they've managed."

"But for all the soil to change . . ." the Rabbit said, shaking his head. "That means the heart of the island is in turmoil."

Again, Mulan felt a strange excitement bubble in her as an unformed idea began to take root in her mind. *About twenty years ago, the soil changed. About twenty years ago, the Stone Statue appeared. Was there a connection? What if . . .*

"Then there's no chance of finding the Dragon Beard Grass here at all," the Rabbit said. Mulan's attention raced back to the conversation in alarm, her emerging thoughts temporarily forgotten.

"No," Lu Ting-Pin agreed, "we will not be able to find it here."

"We won't?" Mulan burst in, unable to keep quiet. "What will we do, then? Can we find it elsewhere?"

Lu Ting-Pin and the Rabbit looked at her gravely. Mulan looked at them, feeling as if all the cakes she had eaten had turned to stones. An image of Xiu lying in her bed as still as death swept over her.

She turned to the Rabbit almost accusingly. "You said we needed both plants for the cure. . . . You said . . ." Mulan broke off as the Rabbit's serene eyes met hers, and she remembered that it was not just Xiu who needed the cure. She gulped. "We need to find the grass."

The Rabbit did not answer but instead looked past Mulan out the window. Night had fallen and the sky was already black, the glowing lanterns lighting the streets. She followed his gaze upward and saw the sliver of the moon, like a worried eyebrow, hanging in the darkness.

Finally, the Rabbit looked at her. "We don't have the time to go elsewhere," he said. "We have only two days left to make it to the Queen Mother's garden before the new moon. We must leave tomorrow."

"Maybe the Queen Mother will have some," Lu Ting-Pin said hopefully. "It is the Garden of Splendors."

"Which is precisely why it wouldn't be there," the Rabbit said. "Dragon Beard Grass is much too humble and common to be grown in her garden."

"It's not that common now," Lu Ting-Pin pointed out.

The Rabbit sighed and nodded. He looked at Mulan. "It's our best chance," he told her.

But it was not a good one, and they all knew it.

CHAPTER 45

The Two Rocks

I T WAS decided they would take the supplies to the boat that night so they could leave as early as possible the next morning. "Li Jing's father will give us anything we need," Lu Ting-Pin said. "And we can spend the night here, too, with civilized luxuries — like clean clothes and a bath."

He had been looking at his own dirt-stained robes when he said that, but Mulan was secretly relieved. The idea of a bath was quite welcomed. And, she thought, it would be best to arrive at the Queen Mother's garden as presentable as possible.

So, in the darkness of night, they carried boxes and bins of food and water down to the dock. The Rabbit carried the lantern to light the way, with Lu Ting-Pin and Mulan stumbling behind. When they got to their boat, Lu Ting-Pin dropped his bundles with a loud thump.

"Our supplies should weigh the boat down enough," Lu Ting-Pin said. "We can get rid of that rock."

The rock! The Odd-Shaped Rock from the City of Rushing Water. As Lu Ting-Pin dragged it out of the boat in the flickering light of the lantern, Mulan thought she saw a strangely shaped figure in it. The twisted layers and the weathered hollows were like tattered clothing and long, disheveled hair. . . .

"Where should I put it?" Lu Ting-Pin asked. "I probably shouldn't just dump it into the sea."

"I know where," Mulan said, and she felt her idea fully root and form.

❀

They left the supplies in the boat, and Mulan, carrying both the Rabbit and the lantern, led Lu Ting-Pin, who huffed and puffed as he lugged the rock. She brought them to the far edge of the island, past the sand dunes to the rocky cliff.

"It's here, somewhere," Mulan said, swinging the lantern back and forth. The Rabbit had promptly fallen asleep once securely bundled in the carrier wrap; Mulan found his soft snores in her ear oddly comforting against the sound of the roaring sea in darkness.

"Wherever it is, I hope it's close," Lu Ting-Pin said, panting. "I'm not an Immortal right now, you know."

Mulan frowned and took a few more steps forward. Then she screamed. A ghastly pale ghost stood before her! Its face was a melted distortion, its hands outstretched as if pleading.

"What is it?" Lu Ting-Pin cried in alarm as the Rabbit snorted awake.

Mulan gulped and forced herself to bring the lantern closer. It was not a ghost. It was the Stone Statue, disfigured by weather and age and made unearthly by the flickering light of the lantern.

"Nothing," Mulan said. "I mean, it's what I was looking for."

Lu Ting-Pin came over. "Ahh," he said when saw the statue. "Now I understand."

The Rabbit peeked over Mulan's shoulder and gasped in surprise. "How did you know this was here?"

"I saw it from the hilltop," Mulan said. "And talked to Li Jing about it."

"Curious," Lu Ting-Pin said. "It seems quite a peculiar coincidence."

"We've had a couple of peculiar coincidences," the Rabbit said. He promptly told Lu Ting-Pin about the storm and the house they'd sheltered at. "It made me think perhaps some of your old friends might be helping us out."

Lu Ting-Pin thought for a moment and shook his head. "No," he said, "doesn't sound like them. They prefer big, grand miracles, and they like getting credit for them." Then he grinned sheepishly. "Like me."

The Rabbit hummed in agreement. "Yes, I suppose it's too subtle for the Mighty Immortals. I wonder who?"

"Why wouldn't whoever it is just let us know?" Mulan asked. She felt slightly resentful. Perhaps she wouldn't have been so easily deceived by Daji if the real Immortal had just shown themselves.

"It's curious," Lu Ting-Pin said. "It could be a test of some sort. Or maybe it's someone who is not supposed to help us."

"If it's someone who is not supposed to help us," Mulan asked, another idea coming to her, "could it be someone who is a servant — someone like the Red Fox?"

Both Lu Ting-Pin and the Rabbit looked at each other and then shook their heads.

"I only wish," Lu Ting-Pin said. "But to be able to tie threads of past and future would be beyond her scope, beyond that of even the White Fox. Even the Immortals would have to work together to do so."

"But a servant is a likely possibility," the Rabbit said. "Someone without authorization — someone very powerful but with a very low position . . ."

"Or someone very powerful with a very *high* position," Lu Ting-Pin added.

"Come now, Yan," the Rabbit chided, "only the Jade Emperor or the like would be bound by that."

"Why would the Jade Emperor not be allowed to help?" Mulan asked.

"He's bound by the Mandate of Heaven not to directly interfere with the fates of the people on Earth," Lu Ting-Pin said, showing signs of boredom. "Which I admit, I have never quite believed. I think he just claims that so he doesn't have to be bothered."

Before Mulan or the Rabbit could say another word, Lu Ting-Pin heaved the Odd-Shaped Rock in front of him. "Coincidence or not," he said, "we still have to decide about this. Where should I put it?"

Mulan nodded toward the statue. "I think it should go right next to it," she said. "Put them close together so they touch."

She and the Rabbit watched as Lu Ting-Pin dropped the

misshapen rock next to the deformed statue, pushing and shoving until the two stone creatures collided into each other as if in a fierce embrace. As Lu Ting-Pin stood up, Mulan watched anxiously.

"All good?" Lu Ting-Pin asked her.

"I guess," Mulan said doubtfully. She was beginning to feel as she had long ago after she had caught that flying teacup. She had dived and twisted with the dexterity of a cat, but when she finally held up the unbroken cup in exultation, Ma just shook her head with displeasure. Mulan's triumph had shriveled inside of her like a dried mushroom.

"Anything wrong?" the Rabbit asked in her ear.

Mulan looked at the two stones standing silent and unmoving in the light of the lantern, the constant sea rumbling behind them. "I thought something would happen," she admitted. "But they're still just two rocks."

Lu Ting-Pin put his arm on Mulan's shoulder. "Come," he said, "let's go. Sometimes miracles do not like to be watched."

So, with the light of their lantern bobbing away in the darkness, they left the Scholar and the Waiting Wife, and hoped that the wife was waiting no more.

CHAPTER 46

Green Island

T HE MORNING arrived slowly. Even with the luxury of a bath, clean clothes, and a bed in the baker's prosperous home, Mulan found little comfort in the night. There were only two days left before the new moon. Xiu and the Rabbit were getting weaker and weaker. They needed both plants to cure them. What if the Queen Mother's garden didn't have the Dragon Beard Grass? But even as Mulan asked herself the question, she knew the answer. If there was no Dragon

Beard Grass in the Queen Mother's garden, nothing could be done. Xiu and the Rabbit would die.

We should go as soon as possible, Mulan thought. She pulled the curtains back from her stately carved canopy bed (which filled almost the whole room) to wait for the night to thin. Slowly, the elaborate lattice carvings in front of her were silhouetted by grey and then silver as dawn began to filter through the paper-lined doors. Then, as the faraway squawking chorus of seabirds sounded through the quiet of dawn, Mulan pushed herself out of bed.

The night before, Li Jing's family had invited them to breakfast in their family quarters, but Lu Ting-Pin insisted that they meet in the bakery for their morning meal. "The shop is right next door," he had said, in an offhand manner that did not fool Mulan. She knew it was his stomach that was dictating their location. He continued with authority. "We'll meet there as soon as we get up."

So it was to the bakery that Mulan hesitantly crept now. Was she the only one awake? The morning sun streamed through the sky well, a purple-tinted rectangular patch of the heavens framed by the slats of the tiled roof. Mulan tiptoed across the courtyard of the house, past a small magnolia tree reaching up into the light with its budding branches. Gently, she pushed open the modest wooden doors of the shop, expecting an empty room.

But instead the store was full of light and activity. Li Jing's father, a round-faced man with a perpetual smile, nodded a greeting as he held up a large pan of steaming buns. An older woman, her slight figure belying her wide grin of welcome, was arranging cakes on a platter. Mulan guessed that this was Li Jing's mother, because she immediately called out, "Daughter! Mulan is awake!"

Li Jing seemed to pop out of nowhere, carrying a teapot. "Good morning! Good morning!" Li Jing said, beaming. "Come! Your uncle has already eaten a whole tray of cakes."

Li Jing led Mulan into the main room, to the table she had sat at the day before. Lu Ting-Pin and the Rabbit were already there, their mouths full as they gave her a morning greeting.

Mulan sat across from Lu Ting-Pin, and a plate of steamed buns and a cup of tea were promptly conjured up by Li Jing's considerable serving skill.

"His pork buns have gotten very good," Lu Ting-Pin said, breaking open a pastry and smelling it as if testing the scent. "His red bean cakes still need improvement, though."

Mulan bit into one of the cakes on her plate, and again, her eyes instinctively closed as the rich, velvety filling of the sweet bean paste coated the inside of her mouth. She licked her lips. "They taste good to me," she said.

There was a harrumphing noise from below the table. "If your character was as fastidious as your belly, you'd get in a lot less trouble," the Rabbit mumbled.

Lu Ting-Pin pretended annoyance. "Hush," he said, then added wickedly, "Pet rabbits shouldn't talk."

Mulan burst with a snort of laughter which grew into giggles as Lu Ting-Pin joined with his booming guffaws. Li Jing came in with another plate of cakes. "It's nice to see you so happy," she said, smiling. "Last night you all looked as if someone were dying."

Mulan felt the laughter drain from her, and all the cheer disappeared from the air. Li Jing frowned. "Did I say something wrong?" she asked.

Lu Ting-Pin pasted on a smile. "Of course not!" he said, patting Li Jing on the arm. "You just reminded us that we have an important journey ahead of us. But your father's cakes should give us the strength to get through. Do you think I could try some of those pineapple ones, too?"

Li Jing smiled proudly and trotted off. The new plate of cakes was as aromatic and as toothsome looking as the other, but Mulan had lost her appetite. She looked down at the

Rabbit, who was delicately nibbling on the filling of a lotus seed bun. She stood up.

"I think I'm going to go out," she said. "Maybe I'll check up on the boat."

Lu Ting-Pin nodded. "Good idea," he said. "We'll be off as soon as we're done here."

Mulan suspected that would not be soon, considering the number of cakes piled in front of him. She stepped out of the bakery and onto the street, the mist of morning still clinging to the grey-tiled roofs of the buildings lining it. She heard faint clatters and shouts from behind the closed wooden shutters of the shops and homes as the village slowly awakened. *This is just like morning in the courtyard at home,* Mulan thought, and she felt a sharp sting in her heart. She, too, should be behind wooden shutters with her family. She should be with Ma and Ba and Xiu cooking rice porridge and combing hair, yelling and laughing. But instead, she was walking alone, her footsteps making a hollow sound on the empty stone street. At the gate of the village, she looked out over the island — the silver haze of dawn softening the rocky, brown contours of the land — and started down toward the water.

However, it was not the boat that Mulan went to. As soon as it was in view, she turned and headed toward the far edge of the island. It was easier making her way now that there was light, and she soon saw what she had been looking for — the Stone Statue and the Odd-Shaped Rock.

But *was* it the Stone Statue and the Odd-Shaped Rock? As Mulan neared the two forms, she realized that they were not the same as when she had left them the night before. They were no longer stone — somehow they had both crumbled into piles of dust and dirt.

Mulan frowned in confusion. Slowly, she reached toward the large mounds. As soon as her fingers touched the tiny granules, the ocean roared out a wild gale of wind, blowing the dirt up and into Mulan's face. She coughed and blinked, brushing away the flying dust. But her hand slowed its movements as she noticed the breathtaking spectacle around her. A shaft of light from the morning sun beamed down upon the dust floating around her, making it glitter and glow. The shining particles hovered around her, and Mulan felt as if she were surrounded by millions of infinitesimal stars, twinkling with unearthly magic.

"Wow," Mulan breathed. But as she spoke, another blast of wind blew from the sea and the shimmering dust scattered. Mulan turned and watched as the glinting air gusted up behind her and over the cliffs. She looked back at where the Stone Statue and the Odd-Shaped Rock had stood. They were gone.

And yet — Mulan squinted. A thin layer of dust remained where the rocks had stood. Was there something green in there? She knelt and brushed the ground, the remaining dust whirling up into the air in sparkling puffs. Yes, there was something green! Fine green stalks as long as her fingers were sprouting from the ground. The stems were delicate and curved, waving with every rumble of the ocean.

Could it be? Mulan's fingers trembled as she gently pulled out one of the sprouts, revealing crimson roots like unraveled red silk threads. She quickly grabbed a handful more, jumped up, and began to run. She raced up and over the hills, her feet flying — not noticing that they no longer stumbled on crumbling earth. She stopped only once when she saw a tall, distant figure carrying a rabbit walking toward the docks. She waved and hollered and leapt forward, completely overlooking the shimmering light spreading over the island as the dust scattered and sprinkled.

"Rabbit! Master Lu!" Mulan shouted as she ran to them, one arm waving, hair flying and feet pounding. Lu Ting-Pin looked at her with slight alarm, and the Rabbit lifted his head with worry. Mulan grinned and flung her arm in front of them, her fist clutching the slender sprouts. She panted, "I have the Dragon Beard Grass!"

CHAPTER 47

The Red Fox

SHE WONDERED if this was what it would feel like to be dead. They had plunged into the deepest part of the sea, where all was blackness. She heard nothing. She saw nothing. It was simply a vast emptiness.

But then, in the midst of the blankness, there was a faint gleam. She knew the anglerfish was in front of her. The bulbous lure that sprouted and arched from its head was glowing with an eerie incandescence, yet it still hid the fish's monstrous, gaping mouth. Daji was signaling her.

Xianniang flashed back her own light, the more hushed illumination of the lantern fish she had transformed into. *Yes, I am following.*

They kept swimming. Daji had been annoyed that the fog she had created had not slowed the boat longer. "That Lu Ting-Pin!" Daji had cursed. "He has always been a nuisance!" But then she had stopped, and a smile began to curve her mouth. "He's not just a nuisance to me," she had said thoughtfully. "Perhaps we should let an old friend of his know that Lu Ting-Pin is going to be in the area."

Which was why they were now fish swimming into the inmost depths of the ocean. Deeper and darker, like two tiny stars falling in a midnight sky. Then, finally, one light stopped moving.

Xianniang flitted forward toward the anglerfish, still slightly taken aback by its grotesque appearance as their dim light brought the fish Daji had changed to into view. The anglerfish's small eyes squinted in its huge head — a head split by a cavernous mouth lined with translucent, needlelike teeth. It was not like Daji to transform into something so . . . so ugly.

However, Daji had her reasons. The anglerfish had stopped at what Xianniang had thought was finally the ocean floor. But it was not. It was, in fact, what Daji had been looking for.

The luminous lure, that fleshy orb that dangled from the

anglerfish's head like a fishing rod, now began to gleam with blue-green radiance. It grew stronger and brighter — far more powerful than any glow from a lantern fish — a beacon in the endless darkness. *Wake up,* the beam seemed to say. *Wake up.*

And with that light, there was a sudden tremble in the layers of black, and both fish felt themselves pushed backward from the force of moving water. Then, like a pair of moons suddenly emerging before them, two enormous eyes opened.

CHAPTER 48

Black Water

MULAN FELT as buoyant as their boat, skim-ming through the waves as easily as if sliding on ice. She leaned against the mast, letting the wind whip her hair and face. The light glinted off the sea — its wide expanse of deep blue stretching endlessly against the greener blue of the sky. Mulan touched the pouch tied to her waist that Lu Ting-Pin had given her. It was made of leaves that had been specially treated with yellow oil, and "completely waterproof," according to Lu Ting-Pin, so that the precious Dragon Beard

Grass would be protected. She checked the knot. Yes, that was secure, too.

Both Lu Ting-Pin and the Rabbit had been delighted when she had presented the grass. Lu Ting-Pin had burst out with his booming laugh of joy, and the Rabbit had smiled with such relief and gratitude that Mulan felt herself glow with pride. "A good omen to depart with," Lu Ting-Pin had said as they climbed onto the boat.

However, the best omen appeared after they had sailed away. They had been waving goodbye to Li Jing and her family when the whole of the island began to come into view. But this time, instead of looking like a jagged brown boulder in the sea, the island had softened. A gentle yellow-green was velveting the sharp peaks and spreading over the rocks to the sea. Green Island was green again. *The heart of the island is at peace,* Mulan thought with a smile, her own heart feeling as open as the boundless sea before her.

"Tomorrow!" Lu Ting-Pin called out.

"Tomorrow?" Mulan asked.

"Tomorrow we will be at Kunlun Mountain," Lu Ting-Pin said. "And the Queen Mother of the West's palace and garden."

"And not a day too soon," the Rabbit said, creeping out from the cabin to join them. Mulan was startled when she saw him. She hadn't noticed how weak he had gotten. His once lush and shimmering silver hair was now dull grey, the color of ash. He carried himself slowly and carefully, as if every limb was in pain. "Tomorrow night will be the new moon."

All the exuberance Mulan had been feeling drained away. That meant tomorrow was their last day. After that, the poison would reach Xiu's vitals. If they did not get the second plant by tomorrow night, it would be too late for her. And too late for the Rabbit.

Suddenly, the yearning to see Ma, Ba, and Xiu swelled up inside her. How Mulan wished she could just see all of them again! Even one of Ma's scoldings would be welcome now. She felt tears begin to burn in her eyes and turned toward the front of the boat, pretending to gaze at the water to hide them.

But even as she blinked away her tears, she felt as if a heavy shadow had come over them — the horizon darkening with her mood. Wait, had a dark shadow really fallen on them? Mulan blinked again and gazed up, fearful of another false fog. No, the sun still shone above them in the azure sky, streaked by white clouds. Mulan returned her gaze to the front of the boat, frowning. The boat continued to glide effortlessly through the water, but the ocean waves below their boat were no longer deep blue . . . they were now black. The water looked as if it had turned into ink.

"Rabbit! Lu Ting-Pin!" Mulan called. "Come look at this!"

Lu Ting-Pin trotted over blithely enough, but when he saw the inky sea he froze as if struck.

"Mulan," he said, clipped and serious. "Pick up Tuzi."

She rushed over to the Rabbit, who had been shuffling toward them, and quickly put him in her wrap carrier, shifting him to her front so he could see easily. A cold dread was creeping over her. She had never heard Lu Ting-Pin speak like that before — his voice harsh with alarm, without the softening of confidence or jest.

Lu Ting-Pin went to the oar and lifted it straight up so that it hung above him like the high branch of a tree. With Mulan staggering, the boat reeled and came to a full stop.

"What is it?" Mulan said, returning to the bow of the boat. Above the usual ocean rumble, they could hear a strange, ominous gurgling. Mulan leaned over to see below, and her eyes widened. The darkened water was churning with a murky, dusk-colored froth. The bubbles began to swell, larger and larger, multiplying and spreading as the stilled boat began to sway at a dangerous clip.

"Oh, no," the Rabbit said. His eyes, like Lu Ting-Pin's, were glued to the foaming dark water and round with horror.

"What?" Mulan asked again, louder and more urgently.

Then, suddenly, the sea tore into two. The boat lurched, an enormous blanket of water spurting up to touch the sun and then crash down, throwing the boat and its passengers like a toy. Mulan sputtered and blinked, waving her arms wildly as she was tossed from side to side. She was finally able to grasp the mast and clung to it as the water and waves plummeted upon them. The sky filled with a grotesque sucking sound that nauseated Mulan, leaving her gasping and blinded. She wiped the water from her eyes so she could see . . . and then wished she hadn't.

CHAPTER 49

The Sea Beast

FAR ABOVE MULAN, above all of them, was a monstrous mountain with bulging eyes. No, not a mountain, but some sort of horrific, gigantic sea creature with mottled, slimy skin and evil eyes protruding like boils. It waved one of its many limbs over them, its rows of bowl-shaped white suckers ready to squeeze them into a sludge. It gave a strange, eerie wail that echoed in the sky. Mulan cringed.

"Your old friend!" the Rabbit yelled to Lu Ting-Pin, who was hanging on to the side of the boat, one arm raised in a vain attempt to shield himself from the immense crashing wave. He rubbed his face against his shoulder and grimaced. The swaying tentacle narrowly missed the boat and smashed down into the water, sending up a fresh onslaught of water as they desperately clutched at the boat.

"Old foe, you mean!" Lu Ting-Pin yelled back as soon as he was able to breathe again. He mopped his face uselessly with his wet sleeve and scowled. "I should've killed this beast four centuries ago!"

"Well, you can do it now!" the Rabbit shouted, spitting out water.

Lu Ting-Pin pulled himself to his full height, and with a proud, graceful motion, swept his arm to his back to grasp . . . air. He groaned.

"What's wrong?" Mulan had to scream to be heard through the thunderous din of the provoked sea. Another tentacle was swinging above them, and this one looked as if its aim was on target for the boat.

"My sword! We're using my sword as this boat!" Lu Ting-Pin bellowed, looking around in confusion. "What am I supposed to fight with?"

"I don't know!" the Rabbit hollered back as he gazed upward. "But do something!"

The circular white suckers of the tentacles were coming

down upon them now, like a chain of full moons falling to earth. Lu Ting-Pin gaped at the destroying limb and then lifted his chin. Without another word, he sprang from boat, grabbed the tip of the tentacle, and forced it up and away from the boat.

Mulan gawked. "He can fly?" she gasped.

"Only short distances," the Rabbit said. "And he has some other limits, too."

But whatever those limits were, they did not seem to be stopping him now. Lu Ting-Pin was soaring like an arrow, his legs extended like a bolt of lightning that crashed into one of the creature's eyes. He bounced off as if the eye were a taut drum, but Lu Ting-Pin's feat was not in vain. The transparent staring eye suddenly filled with a milky liquid and turned opaque, and Mulan realized that the beast was now partially blinded.

This, of course, caused the creature to become even more enraged. Its other eye could still see, and with one of its many legs, it swatted at Lu Ting-Pin in the sky as if he were a pesky fly. The monster's other limbs thrashed in the water, tipping the boat in all directions.

Again, Mulan grabbed about madly as the assailing water and turbulence forced her across the boat. When her arms found the bottom of the yuloh, she clutched gratefully, but her tired arms screamed in pain.

"Lu Ting-Pin can't last much longer," the Rabbit said, his low tone barely audible among the din, "and neither can we."

He was right, Mulan realized. They were both gasping and drenched with water, and even if the boat refused to topple, they would be thrown out. Mulan looked at the yuloh, the handle arching above her head like a reaching arm. Lu Ting-Pin had enchanted it somehow to make the boat sail quickly, she remembered. She pressed her body against the oar and saw the boat shift with her direction. She began to steer it the best she could to the front of the sea creature. Then, just as she was directly before it, she saw the small figure of Lu Ting-Pin fall from the sky, taken down by a blow from the beast's tentacles.

Mulan looked up at the oar. *You are too strong for your own good!* Ma had scolded. But would that be strong enough? Mulan clenched her jaw, jumped up, and grabbed the handle, forcing it down. The boat lurched and the Rabbit stirred. If he made a sound, she could not hear him. She could hear nothing — not the crashing of waves, the shrieks of the sky, or even Ma's voice in her head. All she could hear was her blood in her ears, pounding and pushing, pushing so hard and so fast that she felt she might explode with the force within her. And it was with that force that she pushed the oar against the sea.

The boat staggered forward with such power that she was thrown again. It hurtled through the water, darting faster and faster, soaring through the waves so swiftly that even Mulan's wet, heavy clothing lifted and spread like eagle wings as she clung to the boat. Above her, Mulan saw the sea monster turn its great bulging eyes down toward the boat as if puzzled, lifting a tentacle to bat it away.

But too late! The pointed bow thrust into the creature with such force that the creature reeled backward, its eyes swelling in a silent scream. The boat bobbed up and down as the beast writhed in pain, and Mulan's arms could no longer hold. She was flung from the boat, flying and falling, shrieking as the cold, black water swallowed her.

CHAPTER 50

The Sword Boat

MULAN PUSHED herself up through the cold waves, choking and sputtering. Over the sound of her own wheezing, she thought she heard a faint voice above.

She looked up and saw Lu Ting-Pin swinging on one of the beast's struggling tentacles, his arm wrapped around it as if in a passionate embrace. "Mulan!" he called, throwing something toward her. "Here!"

Down fell Lu Ting-Pin's gourd, bobbing merrily next to her in the sea. Mulan seized it, putting it underneath the

Rabbit's chin as she clasped tightly. Wave after wave crashed over her, but with the gourd, she was able to rise up again, gasping.

The creature writhed and thrashed, the boat thrust into it like a spear. Lu Ting-Pin seemed to have recovered his bravado, for she could hear his laugh as he sprang through the air to the back of the boat. There, he gave it a mighty heave so the bow thrust deeper into the beast's body. He did this a second and a third time, each push causing the creature to flail madly and Mulan to cling frantically to the gourd as she plunged through the violent waves.

But when Lu Ting-Pin shoved the bow the fourth time, it pierced so deeply that the boat was almost completely engulfed by the beast's flesh. Suddenly, the tentacles stopped all movement as if frozen in ice. A dark liquid began to seep from the edges of the wedged boat, a thick purple blood that floated, making a brackish film on the waves. The sea creature had suffered its mortal wound.

The waves slowly calmed, but Mulan felt her weary arms begin to fail. She saw Ba's loving face in her mind and suddenly remembered when she had tried, ashamed and tearful, to glue the village shrine statue back together. "Your job is to bring honor to your family," Ba had said as he helped her hold the broken pieces. "Every day, you must rise up and continue."

Rise up and continue. Rise up and continue. Those words kept repeating over and over, up and down with the rhythm of the climbing and falling water. "I'm trying, Ba," Mulan whispered, but the constant gripping of the gourd, the repeated submerging and striking, had almost brought her to collapse. She felt more drowned than alive. The gourd was just beginning to slip away when she heard Lu Ting-Pin.

"Hold on a bit longer," he said. He seemed to be standing on the water.

"I don't know if I can," Mulan said faintly.

"Of course you can," he said, looking at her proudly. "You are a mighty warrior. You didn't slay that ugly brute for nothing just now, did you?"

"I only helped," Mulan croaked weakly, but she found that the corners of her mouth were slightly curving. Ba was a mighty warrior. She would try to be like him. Her arms tightened again around the gourd.

Lu Ting-Pin flashed her a grin and then hopped back to the boat protruding from the immobile sea beast, even more grotesque in death. Its speckled, turgid flesh was beginning to swell like a blown-up pig's bladder, and the stench of death wafted. Bracing his legs against the bloated body, Lu Ting-Pin grunted as he forced the boat out of the beast. The purple-blue blood now poured out from the gash, making large spreading pools of a nauseating syrup. Lu Ting-Pin leapt lightly through the air to the back of the boat, now pulled mostly out of the beast's flesh. The bow of the boat was stained in blood and the mast was broken, the torn sail flapping madly from its single attached rope. Lu Ting-Pin tugged again at the boat, this time jerking it free as the unruly sail swung from side to side.

As the boat came unstuck, an eerie gulping noise echoed across the waves. The monstrous sea creature began to lower in the water, the blood-coated water gurgling violet bubbles as it sank. Mulan gaped, her wide eyes returning the stare of the swollen, bulbous, unseeing eyes of the beast as the water slowly covered and hid them from view. Then, with a sound that was oddly like a rude burp, the dead beast was completely submerged and gone.

"Come on up!" Lu Ting-Pin said, his voice again coming from above and behind her. As she leaned back, she saw that he was standing on the boat. She looked at him helplessly, almost delirious with exhaustion. The sun made a halo of light around him as if granting him divinity, and his arms reached down to her, seeming to extend like the Rabbit's had when he had pulled her from the gorge. Dreamily, Mulan felt Lu Ting-Pin's hands grasp under her arms and pull her up onto the boat.

"You can rest," Lu Ting-Pin said to her. "We're fine, for now."

Half-heartedly, Mulan loosened the wrap holding the Rabbit and found him already asleep, his limp body rising and falling in unison with hers as they breathed. Her wet clothes were leaking small lakes of water that seemed to glue her to the ground, and with great effort, she raised her hand to feel the pouch at her hip. Yes, the Dragon Beard Grass was still there.

Then, with her final strength gone, Mulan's arms splayed to the floor from the weight of her sleeves. The boat rocked like a cradle. Wearily, Mulan closed her eyes, welcoming the still peacefulness of sleep.

CHAPTER 51

The Water of Kunlun Mountain

MULAN SNORTED awake, feeling as if she were being roused from a century of sleep. She forced her eyes open, painfully breaking the crust that had formed on them during her slumber. As she sat up, she rubbed her mouth with the back of her hand, slightly revolted to find she had been drooling.

Where was she? Oh, she was in the shelter of the boat. Lu Ting-Pin must have placed her and the Rabbit there; she vaguely remembered being carried.

Mulan looked at the Rabbit and she felt her heart pale, a sudden grief falling over her like rain from a clear sky. She knew he had not woken since their encounter with the sea beast, and she suspected that he would not until they had the medicine. For now he was just like Xiu, as still and as white as death. *But not dead,* Mulan thought, clenching her jaw defiantly. She and Lu Ting-Pin could still save them.

Quietly, she rummaged through the remaining supplies — everything rather soggy and slightly damaged — until she found the saddlebags that she had taken from Black Wind's back. Carefully, she opened the one she was looking for. Yes, Xiu's cloth rabbit was still there. Mulan reached for it and saw that, even though damp, it was uninjured. She hugged it close, seeing her gentle sister smiling at her as she closed her eyes.

She inched over to the Rabbit and pressed the toy close to him. Did she imagine it, or did his nose quiver? In the darkness, she couldn't quite tell, but at least with Xiu's toy next to him, he looked less lonesome.

"Mulan! Are you awake?" Lu Ting-Pin, probably hearing the movement, called to her. She ducked out of the shelter.

The light of day blinded her and she felt herself flinching from the brightness. As her eyes adjusted, she gasped.

Lu Ting-Pin had somehow managed to fix the mast, and it reached to the sky bandaged, the tattered sail tied to it with a series of questionable knots. But beyond the wounded boat, the sea was lapping in gentle waves and had taken an azure color. The water met the celadon sky with layers of soft, low-hanging clouds. And in that distant mist rose a majestic mountain island — green and gold, with numerous peaks that touched the heavens. The highest summit glinted with a sparkling light, as if it had a twinkling star as a beacon.

"Kunlun Mountain!" Lu Ting-Pin announced with a flourish, even though it was unnecessary. Mulan looked at him and saw that even though he was smiling and looking pleased with himself, his face was worn and the skin under his eyes looked as if it had been rubbed with soot. She realized it had been Lu Ting-Pin's exertions that had brought them to Kunlun Mountain in time, and that it had been no small feat.

"We made it!" Mulan said, her smile growing into a grin. She laughed. "We made it!"

Lu Ting-Pin joined her laughter, both of them giddy with triumph and hope. Their laughter — Lu Ting-Pin's deep bellows and Mulan's clear peals — made a joyous music that echoed in the delicate blue of the sky.

GRR — AAAH — OOOHMP! The boat made a deafening warning groan that was neither joyous nor musical. Mulan and Lu Ting-Pin looked at each other and then scanned the horizon. No other boat; no horrid sea creature. The water and sky were clear, with only the slightly tattered red sail marring the picturesque view.

The boat groaned again. Frowning, Lu Ting-Pin went to the back of the boat to check the yuloh.

Mulan walked toward the bow, just as concerned. Something was not right. She looked out again over the sea, searching for some sort of foe hiding in the water. But no, the waves were like crystal, and while she could see the flashing orange and yellow of playful fish, nothing seemed ominous. There was only the soft slapping of water up against the sides of the boat.

But wait, was the water rising? There was more water covering the side of the boat than a moment ago . . . and were the fish getting larger? No, the fish were getting closer! The water wasn't rising—the boat was sinking!

CHAPTER 52

An Immortal's Breath

"MASTER LU!" Mulan called, "Look at the water . . . and the boat. . . . I think we're sinking!"

"What?" he exclaimed and rushed over to where Mulan was standing. They both leaned over the edge, watching the water rise against the planks of the boat.

"Great Emperor of Jade!" Lu Ting-Pin said as if swearing. "What a fool I am! How did I forget?"

"Forget what?" Mulan asked, confused.

"The water surrounding Kunlun Mountain is different

from the rest of the sea!" Lu Ting-Pin exclaimed. "It's lighter!"

"Lighter?" Mulan said, still confused. "What do you mean?"

"It's . . . it's . . ." Lu Ting-Pin struggled to explain, his hands gesticulating in panic as well as frustration. "It's not as thick. . . . Things cannot float on it!"

"Things cannot float on it?" Mulan repeated.

"Nothing can float on it!" Lu Ting-Pin said. "Not ships, not gourds, not people! This water sinks everything!"

Mulan stared at the edge of the boat, now almost level with the water. She ran to the covered shelter, quickly put on the carrier, and gently eased the Rabbit into it. She touched the waterproof bag at her waist, checking its secure closing and attachments. Before running out, she saw Xiu's cloth toy lying on the ground. Quickly, Mulan grabbed it and shoved it in with the Rabbit.

Mulan dashed out from the shelter and was dismayed to see water already splashing over and onto the deck. Lu Ting-Pin stood with panicked eyes, pulling his hair in agitation.

"What should I do? What should I do?" he was muttering. "Can't swim . . . can't fly . . ."

"Wait," Mulan said. "What do you mean you can't fly? I thought you could just carry us over from here!"

Lu Ting-Pin shook his head wildly. "I can't fly carrying

mortal weight!" he said helplessly. "When the Immortals took away my fly whisk . . ."

Mulan did not bother to listen to the rest of Lu Ting-Pin's words. Obviously, these were the limitations the Rabbit had mentioned. The water was now up to her ankles and rising swiftly. She glanced around, hearing only her heartbeat and the sloshing of water. What should she do? *You can never give up, can you?* Ma had said. No, Mulan thought, she couldn't. The red sail flapped at her, and instinctively, Mulan jumped to the mast.

Her blood pulsating as if it were boiling, she gave a forceful jerk to the ropes attaching the sail to the stern. The already weak ropes wrenched free and flew to her. She grabbed their ends, twisting and knotting, her hands taking orders from some unknown part of her. Then she turned to the sail and, with both hands, gripped the red silk and — *RRRIIIIIPPP!!* — tore it from the mast.

Quickly, she fished out the ends she had just knotted together, which already lay in a knee-high bath of water. Shifting the carrier so that the Rabbit avoided the cords, she brought the large knot to her chest and grabbed the upper lines. She looked behind her. The sail was falling, but the gentle breeze had kept it from collapse. It was still open to the wind.

The water rose up her legs and Lu Ting-Pin stood in front of her, still frowning in bewilderment.

"Master Lu!" Mulan hissed. "Blow!"

"What?" he said, surprised.

The water was at her waist now, and she looked desperately at the sail behind her. "Just blow!" Mulan ordered, her voice like a falling boulder.

Lu Ting-Pin did as he was told. Just as when he had blown away the fog before, he gulped the air, filling his cheeks. Then his mouth split open and a great gale blasted forth. The wind resounded across the sea, thundering in Mulan's ears; her hair whipped back and she closed her eyes from the force of it.

And it filled the sail behind her. The red silk billowed out, and with a violent jerk, Mulan felt herself being thrown up into the air. Her breath was knocked from her, and only by luck was she able to grip the ropes in time before falling back. When she was finally able to open her eyes, she found herself gliding in the sky, her wet clothes flinging water droplets like flying rain. Down below, right over the top of the vast expanse of smooth green water, the small toy statue of Lu Ting-Pin stood looking up at her, his mouth still open and the back of his head touching the tip of the boat's disappearing mast.

CHAPTER 53

Ashore at the Isle of Kunlun Mountain

MULAN WATCHED as Lu Ting-Pin finally turned from watching her and bent down to seize something from the water. When he straightened, he was holding a sword, which he quickly slid onto his back. Then he raised his arm and leapt into the air.

He flew past her, shooting her a wink, while she grimaced. *Rise up and continue*, Ba had said. Well, she was rising, but Mulan's hands were burning and she could already feel the bruises on her chest and shoulders from the ropes. These pains were not improved when she felt another rough jerk. She craned her neck and saw, from the corner of her eye, the figure of Lu Ting-Pin pulling the sail.

The water sparkled as she skimmed above, glittering azure silk rolling out below her. The sea lightened to pale green and then to celadon, and while Mulan could not see behind her, she suspected they were close to shore. This proved correct as she felt the sail being pulled downward and jade rocks the color of moss in snow began to jut from the water.

The rocks became more abundant, as did the green color, for soon the ground below her was the vibrant shade of a kingfisher's wing. They were past the glittering sands, above the rocky cliffs. The land was coming closer to her now, and Mulan saw that the emerald iridescence was actually feathery grass that brushed against her feet as she descended. She dropped gently, the plumed grass softening her landing.

Mulan lay splayed in the grass, immobile with relief. The tufted grass turned from green to blue as it swayed beside her in the sun. She winced as she finally unclenched her fists, releasing the ropes — two raw, scarlet lines were etched painfully in her palms where the ropes had cut into her. Gingerly, she checked the Rabbit, carefully shifting him so that he lay on her heart and she could feel his faint breath. She touched the pouch at her waist and sighed with relief. That was safe, too.

The face of Lu Ting-Pin suddenly beamed down at her. Kneeling, he helped Mulan sit up and tilted his gourd to her mouth. There was water in the gourd now — cool, sweet water without even a hint of the briny sea. Mulan gulped it down.

Lu Ting-Pin made a *tsk*ing sound and, without a word, ripped a piece of fabric from the bottom of his robe. This he wrapped around Mulan's hands, the deep trenches caused by the ropes raw and bleeding. He repeated this with her other hand, and Mulan felt the burning pain dissipate to a dull, faint ache.

"That was a feat worthy of an Immortal," Lu Ting-Pin said to her, smiling. "I'm a bit jealous that I didn't get to do it myself."

Mulan shook her head, but her mouth curved. She took another sip of water as the immense expanse of sea glinted and the sand below her shimmered as if made from the dust of diamonds. She shook her head again. The water was calm and limpid and as lovely as a painting — yet it had almost just killed her.

But her curving mouth fell open when she turned around to see the place she had landed; she was not prepared for the beauty of the Isle of Kunlun Mountain.

Beyond the waving grasses were forests of curved and

twisted trees. A pearl-white mist floated in and among the top branches, creating a sea of clouds. And rising from that, reaching into the sapphire sky, was a series of craggy, rounded peaks of jasper. More trees dotted these cliffs, their gold, green, and red leaves harmonizing with the speckled stone. It was a glorious, ancient fairy-tale painting come to life, and Mulan caught her breath in amazement and awe. Lu Ting-Pin sneezed.

"It's the peacock grass," he said apologetically, rubbing his nose. "Immortal paradises and all their perfect purity always make me feel a bit ill."

Mulan could not help laughing. "Have you been here before?" she asked.

Lu Ting-Pin looked even more uncomfortable. "Once or twice," he said, looking up at the sky guiltily.

Mulan decided it would be best not to ask about his previous visits. She looked up at the sky, where the afternoon sun was just starting to tire and begin its slow journey to night. They had made it to the Isle of Kunlun Mountain, but now they needed to get to the Queen Mother's garden. Mulan looked at the Rabbit, curled up helplessly and mute in her pouch. He was not going to be able to offer any guidance. She sighed and gently pushed Xiu's stuffed toy to his nose.

She looked up at the tall peak, standing like a pillar of

Heaven. A light glinted and glittered from the top, and Mulan thought she could see the arched rooftops. "The palace must be up there," she said, "and the garden, too."

Lu Ting-Pin nodded.

"Well, how do we get there?" Mulan asked.

"We'll have to go see the Queen Mother," Lu Ting-Pin said reluctantly.

"We do?" Mulan looked at Lu Ting-Pin, who looked even more ill at ease than before. "How are we going to do that?"

"Oh," Lu Ting-Pin said faintly. His eyes were round, and he pointed behind Mulan. "They'll take us."

CHAPTER 54

Palace of Jade

MULAN WHIRLED around and saw that a line of guards stood behind her. Soundlessly, they spread out, and soon Mulan and Lu Ting-Pin were surrounded. One guard, who judging by the ornateness of his gold armor was of higher rank, stepped forward.

"We're here to take you to see the queen!" he barked.

"See," Lu Ting-Pin said, turning to Mulan with a tinge of his roguishness returning, "problem solved."

Mulan smiled at him weakly.

"We're ready whenever you are," Lu Ting-Pin said politely to the armed men. "Lead the way!"

They marched to a path of jade stones, which Mulan had not noticed hidden in the feathery grasses. This led them through a thicket of flowering trees, the soft breeze revealing the luminous centers of delicate pink blooms as pearls.

Except for the stomping of their boots, the guards were silent as they advanced. As Mulan stared at some coral-shaped mushrooms changing colors, Lu Ting-Pin nudged her.

"So, I think it might be better if you make the request to the Queen Mother," he said in a low tone. "She might not be happy to see me."

Mulan gazed at him sidelong. "Why?" she asked, in an equally soft voice. Over his shoulder she caught a glimpse of a spotted deer running, its crystal antlers sparkling. "What did you do?"

"Well, uh," Lu Ting-Pin said, giving Mulan a sheepish look, "she didn't appreciate the birthday present I brought for her husband."

"What did you give him?" Mulan whispered. Through the trees, in the distance, a white waterfall was cascading while multicolored birds with long swooping tails flew above.

"A porcelain bedpan," Lu Ting-Pin admitted.

Mulan almost stopped walking.

"You gave the Supreme August Jade Emperor a bedpan for his birthday?" Mulan hissed in disbelief, giving Lu Ting-Pin the full attention of her incredulous face.

"He was turning one hundred thousand!" Lu Ting-Pin said, defensively but with a mischievous curve to his mouth. "I thought it would be useful."

Mulan shook her head, suddenly understanding why the Rabbit always rolled his eyes at his good friend.

They were out of the flowering forest now and at a set of curving stairs, also made of jade — its vivid color blending into the peacock grass that seemed to grow everywhere. Mulan looked at the lush greenery and touched the pouch at her waist gratefully. She had not seen a blade of Dragon Beard Grass anywhere.

As they mounted the stairs, her eyes widened. They stretched all the way up the jasper mountain, thousands and thousands of steps reaching into the clouds. She whispered to Lu Ting-Pin in alarm, "We're going to be climbing the stairs for days!"

He shook his head. "They wouldn't make the Queen Mother wait that long," he said. "I'm sure there's some trick."

What the trick was, Mulan would never know, though each time they rounded the stairs, she noticed that they were much higher up than she expected. Around one bend, she was as high as if she were again flying on the sail, and around another, they were stepping through snow-white fog. When they cleared the mist and climbed the third curve, Mulan could only faintly see the tops of forest through the thin gaps in the rippling ocean of clouds below.

So, in what seemed the time it would take to finish a meal, the stairs — which were now white jade veined with green — had widened to a landing. This time when Mulan looked up, she flinched from the light reflecting from a towering wall of gold, no doubt the border of the Queen Mother's palace city.

The next landing stretched to a long ramp that led to an arched opening in the glinting gold wall. More armed guards stood at attention at the entry, nodding as they passed through. As they exited the dark tunnel, Lu Ting-Pin nudged her again. "Prepare yourself," he whispered. "The Queen Mother likes things bright and showy."

And he was right. Because as soon as they stepped out from the corridor, Mulan was forced to shield her eyes from the blinding brilliance she had entered.

Glistening before her was a nine-story palace of glossy jade. The eaves of the tiered, gold-tiled roofs were studded with blue gems, and the corners swooped upward like the wings of a flying phoenix. Gleaming cinnabar pillars held up the cresting verandas, with ornate, intricate designs decorating the wide beams between them. All the vivid colors glowed a radiant rainbow, and the clouds enveloping the palace were tinted ruby, amber, and turquoise from the reflected splendor. It was dazzling, magnificent, and also very intimidating.

"Are we going in there to meet the Queen Mother?" Mulan whispered to Lu Ting-Pin, with a slight panic.

Before he could answer, the blue-green jade doors of the palace opened. A cloud of song spread from the open doors and blue-clad maidens carrying rainbow banners, feathered parasols, and pheasant fans streamed out and down the polished stairs toward them.

"No," Lu Ting-Pin said, his eyes widening with something like horror and his face blanching. "It looks like the Queen Mother is coming out here to meet us."

CHAPTER 55

The Queen Mother of the West

MULAN THREW herself down in the humblest of kowtows, seeing only a blur of dazzling purple and gold as she dropped. Lu Ting-Pin knelt beside her, as did the rows of golden-armored soldiers.

The wind stopped its music and Mulan heard a rich, full voice say snappishly, "And what are you doing here, Lu Ting-Pin?"

Mulan cautiously lifted her head to peek at the Queen Mother of the West and almost gasped aloud. Without knowing it, Mulan had been expecting to see a dainty creature like Daji, but the Queen Mother was not like that at all.

She was beautiful, yes, but where Daji had been delicate and ethereal, the Queen Mother was strong and forceful. Lovely maidens surrounded her with pheasant fans, yet they all dimmed next to the resplendence of the Queen Mother. Her violet silk robes gleamed with gold and jewels, elaborately embroidered and ornamented. Upon her head was an exquisitely wrought gold crown, bursting with radiant light from the nine inset stars. Even so, all this brilliance could not overwhelm the Queen Mother — the fine white jade of her moon-shaped face belied the power of her black eyes, which flashed dangerously at Lu Ting-Pin.

Lu Ting-Pin gulped. "Your Heavenly Highness," he said, "I'm only tagging along. I'm trying to help my two friends here."

With that he pushed Mulan forward, who almost yelped in surprised.

"Hmm." Mulan could feel the Queen Mother's commanding gaze considering her. In a slightly less annoyed voice, the Queen Mother said, "And who are you?"

"Your Heavenly Highness," Mulan said, her voice sounding like a mouse's squeak in the immensity of the surroundings. Was she really speaking to the Queen Mother of the West, the queen of all the Immortals? It seemed a dream, but Mulan knew she could never imagine something so unbelievable. Her mouth was dry and she felt as if she were an ant meeting a dragon, but she knew she must continue. "I am just a mortal girl, but I seek a plant from your garden." Mulan carefully lifted her pouch to show the Rabbit, and was glad to see that her hands were not trembling like her knees. "The Rabbit and my sister need it to be cured of poison."

"What plant?" the Queen Mother asked, slightly suspiciously.

"The . . . the . . ." Mulan's mind raced as she quaked inwardly. What was the plant called again? So much had happened since the Rabbit had told her . . . it was a long name. . . . "The . . . um . . . Essence of Heavenly Majesty!" Mulan almost shouted, so thankful to have remembered.

"Ah," the Queen Mother said, looking at the Rabbit carefully. "*Hupo* poison."

Mulan nodded with relief, tiny drops of perspiration forming on her brow. One of the Queen Mother's attendants waved her pheasant fan, causing a gentle breeze.

"And why should I allow you to take this plant?" the Queen Mother said, now looking directly into Mulan's eyes. Mulan felt herself squirming from the force of the queen's gaze, but there was something in the look she was giving her. A bit like the Rabbit's — slightly amused — but also something else. Suddenly, Mulan realized the Queen Mother was testing her.

"What have you done to deserve it?" the Queen Mother went on, her eyes expectant. Mulan gaped back, at a loss. Again, the attendant waved her fan, and a tip of one of the pheasant feathers drifted down. Suddenly, the hovering feather trembled and began to flutter, and Mulan saw that it had transformed to a dull brown butterfly. It landed on the bottom hem of the Queen Mother's robe, precisely in front of Mulan. It opened its wings and, to Mulan's surprise, revealed a shimmering pattern of vivid blue and green — the color of the sea and grass of Green Island.

"The Butterfly Fairy," Mulan gasped, and she looked up and met the Queen Mother's watchful eyes again. But this time Mulan sensed a hint of pride. Suddenly, Mulan understood.

"You?" Mulan gasped. "You are the Immortal who helped us! You brought us to the Butterfly Fairy's house and put the Odd-Shaped Rock and the Stone Statue in my path. It was you!"

With that, the Queen Mother smiled at her with such a look of gratified satisfaction that there could be no doubt that Mulan was right. The blue-green butterfly flitted up and landed on the Queen Mother's shoulder, quivering. The queen's face softened as she turned her head toward it. "You were always one of my favorites," the queen said gently.

As Mulan watched, she suddenly felt a heart-wrenching pang. Ba often looked at her that way, with that same tender smile mixed with sorrow; and Mulan realized it was the pain of loving someone without being able to stop their suffering. To see the powerful Queen Mother of the West, the Queen of the Immortals, with that same grief was like seeing her illuminated with light. Mulan realized that, through all the grandeur and ceremony, the queen was a being of true compassion and kindness. How foolish she had been, thinking that Daji with her simpering manipulation was a deity! Now, in the presence of the Queen Mother, Mulan felt as if she were seeing a real peony for the first time after only looking at paper flowers.

"You have done me a favor," the Queen Mother said, turning back to Mulan. The veil of coldness had returned to her face, but Mulan was not deceived. "So I suppose it is only fair for me to return it. Though I will probably regret it, and I know the gardeners will be quite vexed, you may enter the garden."

Lu Ting-Pin's head popped up and he looked at Mulan with excitement.

"But," the Queen Mother said, holding up her finger, "you

may pick only one item. Nothing more. And only *you* can pick it," she said, looking over her nose at Lu Ting-Pin. "Not him."

"Can . . . may . . . he come to the garden with me?" Mulan asked.

The Queen Mother looked again at Lu Ting-Pin as if he smelled of dung. "Fine," she said, finally, flicking her sleeve. "I don't want him sullying up the palace, anyway. Pick your plant and then leave, and make sure you take this stupid egg with you."

"Oh, thank you, Queen Mother! Thank you!" Lu Ting-Pin burst out, throwing himself on the ground in humble gratitude — but not before Mulan caught a glimpse of a satisfied grin. The prankster had gotten away with another joke, she realized, and Mulan wished she could see the Rabbit roll his eyes.

CHAPTER 56

The Red Fox

THE SKY was a lovely azure blue, the same color of Emperor's robe when he made his offerings to the Heavens. The white clouds, shaped like soft, puffy steamed buns, floated gently across it. It would have been the ideal sky, one out of a painting or story, except for the two screeching birds skimming across it. Their dark silhouettes were like brown stinkbugs on a silken shirt, ruining the perfection and making one cringe.

However, no one saw them. Xianniang had lost sight of the boat long ago, but not before being impressed by the girl's ramming it into the sea creature. Daji, of course, was more furious than ever.

"Impossible!" Daji had sputtered after they'd watched the beast bubble down into the purple-black water. But for the first time, Daji was at a loss. Even though they could now see only the straight line of the sea, Daji glared at it with a cold look of venom. For once, a smile did not creep upon Daji's face, nor did her eyes light with wickedness. All of Daji's schemes and tricks had failed — failed as they had never had before.

"Their luck will break eventually," Daji said, finally, the bitterness seething in her voice. "If they make it to the garden, we will stop them there."

"Stop them?" Xianniang asked, trying to keep her questioning tone humble.

"We just need to make sure they do not pick anything before night falls," Daji said, her face as if carved in stone. "We will wait and watch."

"And if they find it?" Xianniang asked.

"Then we attack," Daji said. "And I will kill him."

"Kill him?" Xianniang asked, her surprise overcoming her pretended timidity. Daji had never planned to outright kill someone before — that was too crude, too messy. She usually preferred to let someone or something else strike the final, mortal blow.

"Lu Ting-Pin, of course!" Daji said, mistaking Xianniang's confusion. "Him and his silly sword! It's all his fault! That girl would be at the bottom of the sea by now if it weren't for him."

It was strange how Daji kept dismissing the girl, Xianniang thought. From the beginning, the girl had overcome every trick Daji had used, yet it was Lu Ting-Pin that Daji believed was responsible. Yes, he was an Immortal — or at least used to be — but the girl was not as powerless as Daji presumed.

But when Xianniang looked at Daji, she saw the immovable clench to Daji's jaw and the boundless fury in her eyes. Xianniang realized that Daji's wrath had passed reason. This was not about her beloved Emperor Zhou. This was about being thwarted, something Daji was not used to, and it created an insulted rage deeper in her than any passion caused by mere affection.

Daji had not lost any of that ire even when she transformed into an eagle. Her sharp, curved beak looked as if it could swallow the sun and her scolding shriek at Xianniang's lagging hawk shape was harsh enough to tear the sky. Xianniang pushed herself forward, trying not to let the fatigue of flying over the endless ocean slow her wings.

Finally, the Isle of Kunlun Mountain came into view. Xianniang knew it was a gorgeous paradise, but she was too weary to appreciate it — and she had long become numb to things with beautiful appearances.

Instead, she kept her eyes on the eagle in front of her. They circled around the island, and then the palace, until Daji found what she was looking for. The garden. The eagle swooped down, with the hawk following close behind. As they reached the treetops, both birds began to shrink. They almost seemed to shrivel into the air, their feathers and beaks melting away and the wings thinning and diminishing. If any Immortals on the island had happened to notice the two stray birds flying above, they would've shaken their heads in confusion at the birds' sudden disappearance and decided it was all imagined. No Immortal would have noticed two extra bees on the flowering bush.

But unlike the other bees in the garden that flitted from one flower to the next, these two bees sat quietly in the purple blossoms, settled for a long wait. Would the girl come? Xianniang wondered. That girl that Daji did not even call by her name. Mulan.

Would Mulan come?

CHAPTER 57

Garden of Splendors

THE GUARDS left Mulan (carrying the Rabbit) and Lu Ting-Pin at the gate of the garden, another arched entry of jade topped with sweeping, gold-tiled roof. The entire garden seemed to be enclosed, as a red wall of cinnabar stretched endlessly from either side of the gate.

"In we go," Lu Ting-Pin said cheerfully. He was in high spirits since he had received his unofficial pardon from the Queen Mother, and he almost skipped through the entry.

They passed through a small courtyard tiled with a luminous mosaic pattern of the smooth, rounded pebbles — no, not pebbles. The ground gently massaged her feet as she walked, and Mulan took a closer look to see they were pearls. Silvery grey pearls had been arranged with lighter ones to create a plum blossom motif on the ground.

But it was the moon gate across the courtyard that caught Mulan's breath. For it was through that round opening that she caught her first glimpse of the Queen Mother's garden. Cascading willows draped over a jade-green pond surrounded by jasper stones. Glistening lotus flowers rose through the wide, floating leaves, like shooting stars breaking though emerald and garnet clouds. Brilliant flowers dotted the greenery like scattered jewels, and multicolored birds with sweeping tails arrayed themselves on branches. The Queen Mother's garden was truly a garden of splendors.

Lu Ting-Pin sneezed.

"All this grandeur makes me feel like my blood is flowing backward," he complained as he ushered Mulan through the moon gate. "Let's find this plant and leave. What does this Essence of Heavenly Majesty look like?"

Mulan halted and stared at Lu Ting-Pin. "You don't know?" she gasped. "I thought you would!"

"Me?" Lu Ting-Pin looked back at her with equal surprise. "But I don't know about plants and herbs! That's Tuzi's specialty."

They both looked at the Rabbit, curled up around Xiu's toy like an infant, silent and still.

"Maybe we could ask the Queen Mother?" Mulan asked, gazing back through the moon gate toward the palace. But even as she said it, they both knew they could not. The queen had granted her one favor. She would do no more. Lu Ting-Pin and Mulan looked at each other helplessly.

"It's a flower, right?" Lu Ting-Pin asked Mulan. She closed her eyes. What had the Rabbit said? *To cure* hupo *poison, she needs to drink a decoction of Dragon Beard Grass and a freshly picked blossom of the Essence of Heavenly Majesty.*

"Yes," Mulan said, nodding, "and the Rabbit said it had to be freshly picked to work."

Lu Ting-Pin leaned in close to the Rabbit's ear. "Tuzi!" he said slowly, forming each word carefully. "The Essence of Heavenly Majesty! What does it look like?"

They both bent closer to the Rabbit, holding their breath as they hoped the Rabbit would give some sort of answer. He did not.

They straightened, staring silently at the Rabbit as if they could will him to speak. But the Rabbit's eyes and mouth stayed shut, his once gleaming fur now drab and dark in Lu Ting-Pin's shadow.

Mulan turned to look at him and realized with horror that the sun was now directly behind him, a soft pink tint washing over the sky. Soon it would be the night of the new moon.

CHAPTER 58

The Search

L U TING-PIN was also staring up at the lowering sun, his look of dismay unsoftened by the pink light. He met Mulan's eyes, their faces mirroring alarm.

"There must be something," Lu Ting-Pin said, stroking his beard furiously. "We just need to think!"

Essence of Heavenly Majesty. Essence of Heavenly Majesty. Mulan's mind raced. "Lu Ting-Pin!" she said. "The name! The name of the plant!"

"What about it?" Lu Ting-Pin said, his brow furrowing. "Other than its being ridiculously long? These royal gardeners . . ."

"It's a clue!" Mulan said. "They must have called it that because of the way it looks, right?"

"Yes, of course!" Lu Ting-Pin said, his face lighting up. "So, what color would Heavenly Majesty be? Gold?"

Mulan stared upward at the heavens. High above them, the amethyst sky had already darkened, deepening to violet. It was the same color as the Queen Mother's robes — a royal color. A majestic color. "Purple," Mulan said. "I think the flowers must be purple."

"Of course!" Lu Ting-Pin said. He jumped up and looked around. "Let's look for all the purple flowers and go from there. We don't have much time."

They headed in separate directions, Mulan walking briskly and Lu Ting-Pin hopping into the air in flight. As Mulan walked the winding paths, she became aghast at the vastness of the Queen Mother's garden. How would they find the flower they needed? Among the elegant trees and carefully placed stones, plants of all sizes received her. Some she knew, like the azalea bushes flowering pink and the cabbage-sized peonies of garnet and snow. However, others — flowers with petals

like flaming phoenix wings and multicolored blossoms of layered chrysanthemum, peony, and lotus petals — she could only
blink at. All were astonishing in beauty, but none, yet, were
purple.

Mulan felt her heart turn grey as the she followed the
curved path through a flower-shaped opening into another
courtyard. How futile this was! The garden was endless
and awash with plants; they would never be able to find the
Essence of Heavenly Majesty. Above, the sun began to protest
its departure, the gentle pink heightening and filling the sky
with vivid color. How could they have come so far, merely to
fail now?

She stepped into the new courtyard, then halted. Her
mouth gaped open and Mulan could only stare at what was
before her.

The courtyard, the ground paved again with a luminous
pearl mosaic, stretched out almost endlessly. It was completely
empty with the exception of a tree, exactly in the center. And
it was clear this was no ordinary tree.

It was ancient; one could tell by its permanently gnarled
and twisted limbs and its rugged bark, almost stonelike with
age. But glossy green leaves sprang from the branches, cush-
ioning the cascades of round, blushing fruit. Peaches.

Remember, it's the peach you want, Daji had said. Mulan

now knew better than to believe her, but she could not help being transfixed. A delicate aroma, fresh and sweet, tickled her nose. The peaches, velvety with rosy fuzz, glowed with a soft golden radiance, a flushed light that was more gentle and delicate than that of a lantern. They dangled temptingly, swaying toward her in the breeze, and Mulan knew that these were the queen's prized Fruits of Longevity.

The peach would keep Xiu alive, the Rabbit had said. Now that they couldn't find the flower, was this their only choice? When the Queen Mother had said Mulan could pick one thing, she had not forbidden the fruit as she had when the Rabbit had been with the Unwanted Girl. Mulan could pick the peach without punishment. Her arm rose and her hand reached for the fruit.

But at great cost, the Rabbit had also said. Mulan's hand stopped in midair, the tender flesh of the peach only a fingertip away. What cost? The Unwanted Girl had been thrown out of the garden, and the Rabbit had been unable to save her brother. But was the cost even higher? Maybe when the Unwanted Girl had eaten the Fruit of Longevity, she was saved from the poison of Daji's honey; yet she was also doomed to serve the White Fox for all six thousand years of her prolonged life. Was that what the White Fox had planned for Xiu? And for herself? *It's the peach you want,* Daji had said. But it wasn't what Mulan wanted. It was what Daji wanted. *Your job is to bring honor to your family,* Ba had said. Doing what Daji wanted could never be honorable. Mulan's arm dropped.

She turned away from the tree, trembling, not even noticing that she was going through the same flower gate opening that she had already entered. She could not pick the peach. Xiu would die. And — Mulan swallowed — so would the Rabbit.

Mulan peeked into the pouch and looked down at the frail creature. "Rabbit," she whispered. "I can't find the plant. Help me!"

The Rabbit remained silent and still.

Mulan straightened and saw the sun edging closer to the horizon, large and burning white, glaring with harsh brilliance. She closed her eyes to hide the view. A tear rolled down her cheek.

Suddenly, she felt the Rabbit stir. "Mulan," he mumbled, as something dropped to the ground. "For you." Mulan's eyes flew open as she looked to see what had fallen.

It was Xiu's stuffed toy.

CHAPTER 59

The Cloth Rabbit

"MULAN! MULAN!" Lu Ting-Pin's voice echoed toward her.

"I'm here!" she yelled back. She looked at the Rabbit, who was again mute and motionless in the carrier. She bent down to pick up Xiu's toy, which the Rabbit had pushed out. Why had he done that? Was it by accident? Or something more?

Lu Ting-Pin dropped down beside her, obviously having realized that flying over the winding garden paths was the faster choice. "I found two plants with purple flowers," he said breathlessly. "One has nine pointed petals, and the other is shaped like a horn with a star spreading from its center. Which is the Essence of Heavenly Majesty?"

Mulan was scarcely paying attention. Instead, she was staring at Xiu's cloth toy as if seeing it for the first time. She had clutched that worn silk hundreds of times, so many times that she had forgotten what it had once looked like. But years before, the toy rabbit had been reddish orange and neatly embroidered with the standard poison-fighting animals. Suddenly she remembered the Rabbit's medicine bag from so long ago, the one she had smelled to clear her stuffed nose. It had felt familiar then, and now she knew why. It was just like Xiu's toy. The same silk, the same design. The viper, spider, toad, centipede, and scorpion all embroidered around a floral design. Xiu's now-shabby animal was a dark copper color and the silk threads of the embroidery had all but worn away, with only a flower and the spider remaining. A white spider.

The stories of the past and the future — they're all inside the Rabbit. Even the ones he doesn't know he has. Mulan closed her eyes, remembering herself as a young girl and the old peasant who had given her the toy rabbit. The woman had been wrinkled with sun-darkened, dappled skin and, Mulan suddenly recalled, light amber eyes. *The Rabbit can change into any kind of being, from a noble healer to an old peasant woman.* Had the Rabbit been the peasant woman? Had the Rabbit given her this toy, knowing she would need it someday?

Mulan opened her eyes, the cloth rabbit still in her hands. Her finger traced the embroidered flower, its fraying lavender threads getting caught in the roughened skin of her fingers. She lifted her head and looked at Lu Ting-Pin.

"You said there was one with nine petals?" Mulan asked quickly. He nodded.

Mulan began to count the embroidered petals on Xiu's toy, her finger trembling. Seven, eight, nine. Nine tapered triangles.

"It's that one!" Mulan said, almost shouting with relief and excitement. "That's the Essence of Heavenly Majesty! That's the one we want!"

Lu Ting-Pin grabbed her wrist. "Come on," he said, "this way!"

They raced along the crooked walkways as the sun hovered above the line of the earth, the sky soaked in a ruby color as it tried to linger. *We must have the Essence of Heavenly Majesty in our hands by the night of the new moon,* the Rabbit had said. As they ran, Mulan gazed upward, where the sky was already tinged deep blue by night.

CHAPTER 60

Finding the Flower

"IT'S OVER HERE," Lu Ting-Pin called.

Mulan panted, tightening the pouch to steady the Rabbit, whom she had quickly shifted to her back. They had run over bridges, through courtyards, and past waterfalls. Mulan was slightly amazed at how much of the garden Lu Ting-Pin had been able to inspect. However, considering how quickly he was gliding through the garden as her feet pounded and she gasped for air, she realized that even if he was not quite an Immortal, he still had a distinct advantage.

Finally, Lu Ting-Pin led Mulan through a gourd-shaped doorway into an open courtyard that expanded to a rippling lake. A golden pavilion stood in front of them, gleaming in the falling light. But its beauty was unnoticed by both of them as they rushed toward the greenery beside it. There, under the protection of an elegant cypress tree and two flowering bushes, grew a small patch of flowers.

And just as they reached them, the garden illuminated. Round lanterns magically lit themselves and lines of bright silk moons suddenly hung in the air all around them. Mulan looked up and saw that the lower curve of the sun was now touching the horizon, fiery ribbons of orange and red streaking across the sky.

The setting sun cast a golden glow on the flowers, which stood proudly — their leaves sprouting from straight stems that led to their purple blooms. Those blooms were a pure, rich violet, and they opened to the heavens like stars, shining with the rosy light from the sun.

Mulan, wheezing, looked at the cloth toy and then back at the flowers. *You may pick only one item,* the Queen Mother had said. They couldn't make a mistake. A bee buzzed around Mulan's face and she frowned as she shooed it away. Yes, the embroidered flower on Xiu's toy and these flowers matched. This had to be the Essence of Heavenly Majesty.

"These are the ones!" Mulan said, too relieved to even feel joy. "We did it!"

As she crouched down to pick a blossom, the bee burst from one of the flowers and flew at her. Mulan swatted at it, the cloth bandages around her hands unwinding. Then another bee darted at her. In surprise, Mulan flapped both her hands wildly. Her manic waving pushed her off balance and she fell to the ground in an awkward sitting position, her arms flailing as she tried to avoid crushing the Rabbit.

But even as she sat with her legs sprawled, the bees continued to buzz angrily around her. Mulan flinched from them in confusion, waving her hands again to bat them away. Lu Ting-Pin came to help her, and as he placed his hand on her arm, the bees landed on either side of them.

A clapping noise filled the air, echoing into the sky. As both Lu Ting-Pin and Mulan glanced around in bewilderment, the bees transformed into the Red and White Foxes.

CHAPTER 61

Lotus Blossoms

BOTH FOXES hissed and immediately pounced. But Lu Ting-Pin was faster. In a swift, fluid motion, his sleeves billowing, he grabbed the sword from his back and thrust himself between Mulan and the White Fox.

With his other hand, he yanked the gourd from his belt and tossed it at the Red Fox. The gourd spiraled in the air, colliding with the Red Fox in midleap. The Red Fox fell to the ground, her legs splaying as the gourd lay on top of her. She struggled to rise, but the gourd pinned her to the earth and the Red Fox could only thrash and spit.

However, only Mulan saw this. Lu Ting-Pin kept his attention on the White Fox, whose sharp claws and cruel teeth glinted as she leapt at him. With his spare hand, Lu Ting-Pin seemed to gather air, and just as the White Fox's jaws were about to tear into his flesh, he threw the invisible chi at her. She flew backward, the power of Lu Ting-Pin's energy propelling her as she reeled. Screeching with anger, the White Fox spun around against the sky, raking into her own leg with her paw and ripping out her hairs. And when she landed, the White Fox became Daji, beautiful and vicious, holding a handful of flashing daggers.

Daji shrieked the feral scream of an animal. Malevolence burned in her eyes, making Mulan cringe. But Daji was blind to her, consumed with punishing Lu Ting-Pin. She turned toward him, a whirling flurry of silk and savagery, and hurled a deadly rain of glittering knives.

Lu Ting-Pin raised his sword and, with movements too fast for Mulan to see, deflected each dagger, making a metallic drumming that quickened to a rolling, pulsating beat. His sword slapped away each blade, and as the daggers bounced off, they transformed into lotus flowers that landed on the stones with a gentle thump.

The sight of these scattered flowers only enraged Daji more and she stormed at him again, a knife in each hand. Yet these, too, were knocked away. Daji tried again and again, but no matter how she twirled and twisted, each dagger she cast fell to the earth as a flower. Finally, when the ground was strewn with lotus blossoms, Daji was empty-handed and panting with fury.

"Are you finished?" Lu Ting-Pin asked coldly. Half the sun had dipped below the horizon, its golden radiance still controlling the sky.

Daji shrieked again, a piercing cry of wrath. In a mad frenzy, she flew at Lu Ting-Pin with her fists. With a look of disdain, he thrust forth his empty hand, and the unseen chi struck Daji with such force that she collapsed to the ground.

Daji rolled to her side, gasping, her arms outstretched. As she tried to press herself up, her arms fell back and her face sank to the earth, buried in lotus blossoms. Lu Ting-Pin walked to her, his sword brandished.

"White Fox Demon," Lu Ting-Pin said, "your time is over."

CHAPTER 62

No Man Can Kill the White Fox

LU TING-PIN pointed his sword at Daji's prostrate body, her slender shoulders trembling as she breathed. Her fingers pressed into the ground, and she lifted her head to look at Lu Ting-Pin.

But the face that looked at Lu Ting-Pin was not Daji's. Lu Ting-Pin froze.

Daji's new face was not the elegant beauty of before, but softly round with gentle eyes of innocence. The cherrylike lips on Daji's transformed face smiled, a sweet, shy smile. She propped herself up with her hands and gazed at Lu Ting-Pin.

"But would you kill me, Lu Ting-Pin?" the woman said, her voice now low and hesitant. "The one you called your delicate peony?"

Lu Ting-Pin blanched, his eyes widening. Behind the woman, the sun was a sinking, overturned bowl, spilling its last radiance into the darkening sky.

"You also called me your love," she continued. "But it was your love that made my family disown me. It was your love that forced me out of my village. It was your love that broke my heart."

Lu Ting-Pin remained motionless. He had paled to the same color as Daji's white robe, and the red tinge of the sky burned on his face.

"It was you who abandoned me and our child," the woman said, an edge to her soft voice. "It was you who made me dishonor my family, my ancestors. It was you who filled me with so much shame and resentment that it turned me against my own daughter."

Mulan looked at the Red Fox, still pinned under the gourd. The animal was no longer struggling. Instead her eyes were intently fixed upon Daji, round and wondering.

"And it was you who turned me into this," the woman said, her face now pinched and hardened. "You who turned me into a woman who doesn't want her own child. A woman who is bitter and angry. A woman who no longer sees innocence or hope."

The sword in Lu Ting-Pin's hand began to tremble, and Mulan could see his mouth fall open in his shadowed face as he struggled to breathe.

"So, who is the demon, Lu Ting-Pin?" the woman said, her voice harsh and grating. "Me, or the man who destroyed the woman he loved?"

Lu Ting-Pin gave a cry as if struck and fell to his knees. The peach-wood sword dropped to the ground beside him, clattering. Lu Ting-Pin bowed his head and covered his face with his hands, his figure a hunched silhouette against the last of the setting sun.

CHAPTER 63

The Ten Thousandth Demon
of the Peach-Wood Sword

A S LU TING-PIN sank into the shadows, the woman smiled. And with that look of evil satisfaction, her face transformed again, back to the beautiful, vicious face of Daji.

The last curve of the sun clung just above the horizon, clasping the sky with clinging fingers of orange and yellow light. The colors cast a halo around Daji as she stood triumphant. She glowed with unearthly splendor, her malice made even more dreadful by her beauty. Daji looked at Lu Ting-Pin's bent figure and her eyes glinted with exultation.

"No man can kill me," she gloated.

Her smile widened, her mouth stretching to show all of her teeth. To Mulan's horror, those teeth grew large and sharp and pointed as Daji transformed back into the White Fox.

Daji's evil smile was now the bared teeth of the White Fox. But the eyes were full of the same malicious glee as she looked at Lu Ting-Pin's slumped figure. She raised her claws, preparing to pounce.

Mulan caught her breath. The White Fox was going to kill Lu Ting-Pin!

"NO!" Mulan shouted. Her blood burned and vibrated as if a firecracker had exploded inside of her. She flew forward, seizing the peach-wood sword from the ground. She clutched the sword with both hands, brandishing it at the White Fox. The White Fox turned to Mulan in surprise and then hissed.

You dare? the White Fox's eyes said to Mulan, flashing with fury and arrogance. The White Fox bared her fangs and snarled. *You die.*

And then the White Fox leapt through the air at Mulan. A deadly arch of glinting claws and teeth, a malice of centuries soaked with the torture and disdain of innocents, an evil twisted in beauty and charm — all of it hurtling toward Mulan in a savage, murderous attack.

Mulan yelled, a guttural, ugly sound of desperation and defiance. Fire was crackling through her, her clenched hands pulsating with her boiling blood. The peach-wood sword swung through the air as Mulan, roaring with unknown power, drove it into the White Fox.

Celestial blue flames burst from the sword. Almost on its own, the sword slashed into the White Fox — as smoothly as if it were slicing snow. The cold flames flared into a giant blaze, swallowing the White Fox in a brilliance that made Mulan wince. Then an unearthly shriek shattered the Heavens, a piercing shard of sound that tore into the sky.

Mulan clung to the sword even as the icy flames hid her arm and the screech stabbed her ears with its fierce hatred. She could feel and taste the cruelty and bitterness of that scream, an inhuman sound of endless fury and violence that forced her to the ground.

But as Mulan collapsed to the earth (awkwardly, as she was trying to protect the Rabbit at the same time) the shriek withered to silence. The blue flames extinguished as if suddenly doused, and Mulan found herself splayed facedown, the hand of her outstretched arm still clutching the hilt of the sword.

Tightening her grip, Mulan looked desperately for the White Fox, preparing herself for another blow. But where was the White Fox? Had she disappeared? Mulan looked at the sword and saw that the blade now lay in a fox-shaped puddle of black ooze.

CHAPTER 64

Setting the Prophecy

MULAN QUICKLY pushed herself up and pulled the sword away from the black puddle. A strong, sickly-sweet smell wafted from the viscous liquid; Mulan cringed, recognizing the scent of Daji's poisonous honey. But then a strange scratching and buzzing filled the air, and the dark ooze began to tremble and quiver. A cracking sound came from the earth as if it were stretching after a long confinement, and then mounds of scorpions and spiders squirmed out of the murky pool, each crawling on top of the others in impatience.

More and more creatures — snakes and caterpillars, as well as the scorpions — slithered out as the inky slime grew smaller and smaller. Hundreds and thousands of noxious creatures formed and fled until, finally, the black puddle was no more.

Mulan was mesmerized as well as horrified. The sword must have killed the White Fox. And now . . . the White Fox . . . Daji . . . was turning into this scourge of vermin. Mulan felt her heart sicken with revulsion, but she could not stop staring. Only after the last of the poisonous pests scuttled under the piles of lotus blooms and then to the far corners of the garden (where they later caused a blight on one of the queen's prized azaleas) did Mulan turn away.

It was then that she felt the eyes of the Red Fox on her. The Red Fox, still pinned down by the gourd, full of suspicion and defiance, hissed.

Mulan looked into the Red Fox's eyes. She saw the fox's resentment and anger, her rage and fear, but Mulan also saw the Red Fox's pain. A heartache of centuries, of a child unwanted and unloved and then of a girl who did not fit in, could not find a place to belong, and was manipulated by Daji. A girl a bit like herself.

The sun had finally sunk behind the horizon, and shadows of night began swallowing the vivid light it had left behind.

Swiftly, Mulan bent and plucked a blossom of the Essence

of Heavenly Majesty. She held it up to the twilight, a delicate silhouette against the amethyst and orange, and looked at the Red Fox.

"I have the Essence of Heavenly Majesty," Mulan said to her. "The prophecy of the Hua sisters is now set and cannot be changed. Leave my sister in peace."

And with that, Mulan walked over to the Red Fox and kicked off the gourd. As it rolled away, the Red Fox jumped up and immediately crouched to attack. Mulan, one hand grasping the flower and the other the sword, pointed the weapon at the Red Fox.

"Leave my sister in peace," Mulan repeated.

The Red Fox gazed up at Mulan, and again, their eyes met. They looked at each other for a long moment, unsaid words passing between them.

Then a clapping sound echoed and the Red Fox disappeared into a blur of feathers that streaked into the sky, melting into the gloom of the oncoming night. The lanterns of the Garden of Splendor magically brightened, thousands of silk moons glowing to offset the emptiness of the heavens above. The Red Fox was gone.

Chapter 65

The Decoction

A S SHE GAZED at the blankness of the sky, Mulan felt a hand on her shoulder. She turned to see Lu Ting-Pin.

"She was right. No man could kill the White Fox," he said. His gourd was back on his belt and he was pale, obviously still shaken by his encounter with Daji, but he was smiling at her. "Only a girl could. And only a girl like you."

Mulan tried to smile back, but she was too startled by his words. A girl like her? And for a moment, a flame sparked inside her, casting light on a reflection of herself she had never seen before. Maybe she was not a girl who was too bold and stubborn and rough. Maybe, perhaps, she was, instead, a girl with great courage and determination and power. A girl who would bring honor to her family, but in a different way than expected.

The flame quickly flickered away, but she found she could meet Lu Ting-Pin's admiring eyes without discomfort. She handed him the sword, charred and blackened, her arms suddenly trembling with its weight. As he took the sword, the strips of cloth bandaged around her hands fell to the ground. Her hands were completely healed and unscarred.

Lu Ting-Pin plucked the cloth from the earth. "The Queen Mother wouldn't like it if we left garbage here," he said. "She's already going to be upset with all those bugs." He gave Mulan a wry grin but then glanced down at the sword, weighing it in his hand as if confused. He opened his mouth as if to speak, then closed it again, apparently unsure of what to say.

Meanwhile, Mulan found a stone bench — one that the queen no doubt used to enjoy views of the lake, though Mulan was oblivious to impressive views as well as to speechless Immortals. Instead, still clutching the Essence of Heavenly Majesty in one hand, she was shifting the carrier to the front and taking out the Rabbit. He was even smaller than before;

she could feel the brittleness of his bones through the thin fur as she lifted him — dull, matted fur the color of ash. His body no longer burned with heat. Instead it was cold and clammy. His eyes and mouth were now pale drawn lines, and he was as still as a stone.

Mulan looked up at Lu Ting-Pin with fearful eyes. "Is he . . ." Mulan started.

Instead of answering, Lu Ting-Pin pulled the gourd from his waist and sliced it with an elegant swoop of his sword. The gourd's top fell to ground, and what remained in Lu Ting-Pin's hand was the bowl-shaped bottom.

"The grass!" Lu Ting-Pin said, urgently, returning the sword to his back. "The flower!"

Mulan rummaged through the bag on her hip, and when she had both the flower and grass in her fingers, she saw that the gourd bowl had filled with hot water, steam rising from it like a cloud. She dropped the plants inside.

They dissolved and the water immediately changed color, becoming a silvery violet. A strong, crisp scent — like that of a cool morning in spring — puffed from the bowl onto their faces.

The Rabbit twitched. His eyes stayed closed but his mouth opened. Mulan hoisted him up, and Lu Ting-Pin tilted the bowl to the Rabbit's mouth. The shimmering water spilled into the Rabbit's mouth, dripping onto his chin and whiskers. They watched as the Rabbit gulped, the liquid dropping down his throat.

Nothing.

The Rabbit did not move again, nor did he make a sound. Mulan looked at Lu Ting-Pin helplessly. Had they been too late after all? The sky was still clinging to the remains of the sun, but the twilight deepened to dusk. Mulan's heart chilled and Lu Ting-Pin stroked his beard. But then . . .

"I'd get better faster," the Rabbit said, his voice faint and his eyes looking up at them expectantly, "if you'd give me some more."

CHAPTER 66

The Cloud

THE RABBIT made a miraculous recovery. After another sip of the liquid, his eyes brightened and he could sit up. After two more sips, he was able take the bowl on his own to drink. And after six sips, the Rabbit was fully restored and stood to his full length, his fur now lustrous, rippling with a luminous glow like a silver pearl.

"Well done," he said to Mulan, handing her the bowl. He said no words to her about the search for the flower or the White Fox, but when he met her eyes, Mulan flushed with pride, her heart nested in as much pleasure as if he had awarded her a prize.

The deep purple curtain of dusk was drawing over the sky, and the Rabbit frowned. "We should go," he said. "Your sister waits."

Mulan jumped up. Xiu! Ma and Ba! Home. The Rabbit's words were like the very last heft of the shovel while digging a well — her dull, constant pain cracking open to a rushing spring of yearning. It was time to go home.

"Need any help?" Lu Ting-Pin asked. He had changed, too, Mulan realized. The paleness had left him, and he seemed taller and more vivid. His hair was blacker and his eyes sparkled brighter. Even his robes were bluer — before they had been the dull color of open sea, and now they were the brilliant hue of the afternoon sky. However, the biggest change was the sword in his hand. While the Rabbit had been regaining his strength, Lu Ting-Pin had been wiping away the soot and grime from his blade. Now it gleamed, and it was the gleam of metal, not wood.

"That counted?" the Rabbit asked dryly.

"Apparently," Lu Ting-Pin said, grinning. "The terms of the punishment were that the sword needed to kill ten thousand demons. They forgot to specify that I had to be the one wielding it." He winked at Mulan.

The Rabbit rolled his eyes. Mulan smiled.

"So, let me," Lu Ting-Pin said. "It's been so long!"

"Fine," the Rabbit said. "But hurry up. Mulan wants to get home."

Lu Ting-Pin took the pouch Mulan had used to carry the grass and placed it on his belt. Though it had been empty, he took from it a small piece of paper and a paintbrush. He painted a cloud and showed it to Mulan with a smile. The Rabbit sighed.

Then, with a flick of the sleeve, he tossed it. The paper dissolved into the air before reaching the earth, becoming white smoke. The smoke grew thicker and fuller until it formed a huge, iridescent cloud, as large as a bed but shaped a bit like a steamed bun, hovering above the ground.

"Your chariot," Lu Ting-Pin said, gesturing at the cloud with a flourish. "This will whisk you back to your sister and family."

"You could have transformed one of these lotus flowers," the Rabbit grumbled. "One fewer for the queen's gardeners to pick up."

Lu Ting-Pin just waved him away with a grin. "Good to see Tuzi is back to his old form," he said to Mulan. Then his face softened. "But this is where we say goodbye."

"But your gourd!" Mulan said, holding up the bowl that was cupped in her hands.

"Oh, I'm glad to be rid of that one," Lu Ting-Pin said. "Now that my penance is over, I'm going to get a gourd that makes wine. Anyway, you need it."

Mulan looked at him, unable to put into words all that she wished to say. "Thank you, Master Lu," she said, finally.

"Ah, don't thank me! I thank you," Lu Ting-Pin said, putting his hands on her shoulders. "I thought it was strange that the Rabbit did not want me to tell you who you are. But I see now that you already know."

Mulan frowned in confusion, but before she could reply, the Rabbit was pulling her to the cloud.

"We must go," he said to her. "Come."

They stood in front of the cloud, shimmering with opalescent light.

"Farewell!" Lu Ting-Pin called, bowing. "The greatest joy in life is seeing a friend unexpectedly. I hope to have that joy with you soon."

The Rabbit nodded at Lu Ting-Pin nonchalantly, but Mulan saw the look of affection that passed between them as the corner of Rabbit's mouth curved. She bowed as low as she dared while holding the bowl of liquid, the water now the color of the sky at dusk. It was time to go. Mulan stepped one foot onto the cloud.

"Oh, wait," Mulan said, remembering the cloth rabbit she had left on the stone bench. "Xiu's toy!"

But it was too late. Because instead of stepping on a puffy, cushion-like surface as she expected, Mulan's foot went through the cloud. And as soon as her toe entered it, a mist rose over her, covering her so that all she could see was thick white fog, silencing all sound. Disoriented, Mulan brought her other foot down to steady herself, but to her dismay, there was no ground for her foot to find! Mulan wobbled precariously, unbalanced and dizzy. She was falling through the cloud.

CHAPTER 67

Home

MULAN'S FEET finally found the earth and she stumbled forward. She shook her head, trying to rebalance herself, and as she did, the fog of the cloud dissipated to reveal . . . a kettle?

Mulan blinked and then realized that the kettle was familiar. It was the same one she had used tens of hundreds of times. She was in the kitchen. Her kitchen. The jars of oil and soy sauce, the clay vats tied with cloth, the baskets hanging from the ceiling, and the bamboo tub — they were exactly as she had left them.

However, it looked different, too. Everything seemed crisper and thicker and more solid. It was as if the cloud had wiped away all the enchantment and magic that Mulan had been able to see.

But not *quite* all.

For as she looked down, she saw that she was still holding a bowl in her hands — an old earthenware bowl that she had used for years. But the liquid inside it was a shimmering, silvery violet — as if it were filled with a piece of the sky at dusk.

Then Mulan heard voices in the other room. Ma! Ba! Xiu.

Still clutching the bowl, she rushed through the door, bursting into the other room.

"Gently, Mulan," Ma admonished her. "You needn't barge in like an ox."

"But . . ." Mulan said, glancing all around. Her parents stood together as if in the middle of a serious conversation and looked at her curiously. Xiu was still and silent on the bed, and Old Auntie Ho leaned over her. Through the window, a purple gloom had covered the colorful remnants of the departed sun, lining the sky for night's entrance. Had she imagined it all? The Rabbit, Lu Ting-Pin, the White Fox? That steam that had hit her face . . . it seemed so long ago, but maybe the medicine was so powerful that it had dazed her and created a wild fantasy in her mind. She shook her head in confusion.

Next to the window, a tall man was tying a cloth toy to the leaning pole. He looked at Mulan.

"Just returning this," the Healer said. "It must have fallen off."

Mulan studied him. He was the same Healer she remembered, tall and aristocratic in his rich robes. His finely featured face did not give the smallest hint of miraculous secrets or Immortal powers, but she couldn't help staring at his amber eyes and his silver beard, as lush and soft as rabbit's fur.

"Mulan!" her mother was scolding, as Mulan realized she was gaping in a way that no well-behaved young girl should. Mulan dropped her head.

"Is the decoction ready?" the Healer asked, coming toward Mulan and taking the bowl. He inspected it and nodded. "Yes, this is right. Well done."

Mulan looked up at his last words, and when he smiled she could not help feeling disconcerted. That smile was so familiar. It was the Rabbit's smile.

The Healer brought the bowl to Xiu's bed and Auntie Ho shifted Xiu to a sitting position. Then, with her parents and Mulan crowding around and watching, the Healer eased the liquid through Xiu's lips.

They all waited. They waited in silence while the world outside the room continued. Mulan could hear a dog bark and whine. Sounds of boys playing ball, arguing and cheering, drifted through the window. The fire from the kitchen stove crackled and birds began their twilight songs. Ordinary, commonplace matters that Mulan had seen and heard every day of her life merged and mingled around her, making the marvels of her adventure even more unbelievable. *It could not have truly happened,* she thought. She was being foolish to think that it could have been real. As Xiu remained still, Mulan's heart stung from the thousand cuts of her breaking hopes. The blackness of night spilled into the sky.

But then, in the last remaining light of dusk, the blanket covering Xiu began to rise and fall. She was beginning to breathe regularly. Auntie Ho lit a lantern, and they could see that Xiu's ghostly white face was now tinged with warmth, returning to her rosy, healthy glow. A soft sigh escaped Xiu's mouth, and then, her eyes slowly fluttered open.

Ma and Ba threw themselves onto Xiu's bed, embracing her and weeping. Auntie Ho crushed Mulan in a joyous embrace. "It's a miracle!" Auntie Ho said, dancing. "A miracle!"

"Mulan?" Xiu's soft voice cut through rejoicing and she held out her arm to her older sister. "Is the spider gone?"

Mulan came over to the bed and clasped Xiu's hand. She placed her head on Xiu's shoulder, blinking away her tears. "You don't have to worry about that spider ever again," Mulan said, pressing Xiu's hand close. "I killed it."

CHAPTER 68

A Mighty Warrior

HAPPINESS SEEMED to burst from Mulan's home and throughout the entire tulou. After assuring herself of Xiu's recovery, Ma rushed at a frenzied pace to cook Xiu's favorite strengthening foods. This zealous energy was only added to by Auntie Ho, who delivered the good news like thunder — a loud, shouting proclamation to the other villagers. Almost at once, a stream of visitors came, clustering and bearing gifts.

And in the midst of the crowd and noise and cooking, the Healer silently slipped away, unnoticed by all.

All except for Mulan, of course, who saw his bright crimson cloak flap out the door. Quietly, she followed him. She passed through the tulou's round courtyard, nodding politely at villagers calling out celebratory greetings, avoiding statues and stepping over chickens, but never losing sight of that red robe. Finally, right outside the tulou, she caught him.

Night had finally conquered the sky, turning it to a black velvet scattered with starry diamonds. The many lanterns inside the tulou cast a golden glow that streamed from the doorway, gilding the Healer with its light. He stood as if waiting, and when Mulan reached him, she heard a whinny in the distance. Black Wind!

The horse galloped out to them, nickering. Black Wind nuzzled his nose into Mulan as she hugged him and watched the Healer carefully remove the red string from the horse's neck. So it had been real! She had not imagined it. She and the Rabbit had truly saved Xiu. Mulan felt as if she might burst, the questions and wonder overwhelming her.

However, as she met the amber eyes of the Healer, a strange tranquility washed over her and she found herself asking only, "Will I ever see you again?"

"Of course," he said, the amused look that so often adorned the Rabbit's face now on the Healer's. "Though you will probably never realize that it's me."

"Because you're always changing forms," Mulan said.

"Yes," the Healer said, "but also because the time you have with Immortals fade from your memory."

Mulan's face clouded. "So I won't remember you?" she asked, and a strange ache trickled onto her heart, as if cold drips from a melting icicle were falling upon it.

"You might," the Healer said, and there was a sadness on his face as well. "But only as part of a very strange dream."

Mulan released Black Wind and turned to the Healer. "But everything will be fine now, right?" Mulan asked. "The White Fox is gone and Xiu will live to grow up, save the Emperor, and bring honor to our family."

"You should know by now that Immortals do not like to tell what they know," the Rabbit said, giving her a grin much like Lu Ting-Pin's.

"But . . ." Mulan started and then stopped, thinking of all that the Rabbit knew and did not like to tell. "Lu Ting-Pin said you didn't want him to tell me who I was."

"And he also said that he realized he did not need to," the Healer said.

"I don't know what he meant," Mulan said. "Who am I?"

The Healer gave her a rueful smile. "Mulan," he said, finally, as he put his hands on her shoulders, "you are a mighty warrior."

"What?" Mulan said, incredulous. "I'm no warrior."

The Healer shook his head in disbelief. "You have thrown bladed needles, returned an island to green, flown on an Immortal's breath, slain the ten thousandth demon of a peachwood sword, and saved the lives of your sister and the Jade Rabbit," the Healer said. "What else could you be?"

"But that was . . ." Mulan sputtered. "That doesn't mean I . . . I'm just . . ."

The Healer brought his forehead to hers. "Of everything, this is what you must not forget," he said seriously. "You are a mighty warrior."

With that, he released her. Then he turned and walked away. Mulan, one arm around Black Wind, found herself staring at the lighted ground in front of them. The Healer's departing shadow was long and thin, but hers . . . hers, with its resolute stance and broad shoulders, looked strong and powerful. Perhaps it *could* be the shadow of a mighty warrior.

"Mulan! Mulan!" voices called, spilling out from the tulou. "Where are you?"

"Here!" Mulan called into the entrance. She looked back to the Healer, but he was gone. She squinted, and then she saw the pale shape of rabbit ears fading in the distance. Mulan smiled, knowing that the Healer, in the dark peace of night, had transformed back to the Jade Rabbit.

"Mulan!" the voices called again. "Your parents want you! Xiu wants you!"

"Coming!" she said, giving one last look at the disappearing ears as she squeezed Black Wind farewell. Then Mulan, the great warrior, turned and ran into the warm yellow light of the tulou, transforming back to a daughter and sister.

EPILOGUE

ON THE edge of the desert, where hills of golden sand rose and fell like ocean waves, the bird that had once been the Red Fox landed.

She could never be the Red Fox again, she knew. Seeing Daji die — seeing the White Fox turn to that black puddle oozing insects — made her realize that she never wanted to be like Daji again.

Why didn't that girl kill me, too? she wondered. Mulan. The girl, Mulan, must have seen how helpless she was trapped under the gourd. She would have been easy to destroy.

But instead Mulan had let her go. She remembered how their eyes had met that last time. All the things that had reminded Xianniang of Bouyue were still there in Mulan's face — the sincerity, the innocence, the determination — but they had been tempered with something else. It had been sorrowful, but it was not pity, like the Rabbit. It had been understanding.

Xianniang stared toward the desert, but she was not seeing the shimmering, serpentine sands. She was thinking of Mulan. All this time she had believed that Mulan reminded her of Bouyue, but truly, Mulan had never been like him at all. Mulan had been like Xianniang. Mulan reminded her of herself.

Mulan would be returning home now, with a cure to save her sister. Perhaps she was already there. *What would my home-coming have been like,* Xianniang thought, *if I had not become entangled with Daji?*

But she was free of Daji now. Free from Daji's demands, her anger, her maltreatment. But somehow not free. While Xianniang had not loved Daji, she did, oddly, miss her. Because now, she was alone.

Without realizing it, Xianniang had let her head droop,

and a grey lizard slithered at her feet. It flicked its tongue as if scolding her and then disappeared.

Xianniang felt a strange amusement wash over her as she straightened. This lizard did not care that its existence was solitary; why should she? She was more powerful than any mortal in the kingdom. She had learned all of Daji's magic and she no longer had to play the part of someone docile and meek.

Nor would she be like Daji, either. Xianniang may have obtained Daji's same skills, but as she thought of Daji's beguiling and luring, she felt disgust. No, Xianniang decided, she would neither pretend nor hide.

She summoned her power and felt it surge through her as she transformed. Her black hair flowed from her head and her fingers stretched as if unused to feeling only the weightless air. Her robes were not the delicate silk of a noblewoman's maid, but a plainer cloth of graduated greys, as if night had bled onto a white mourning dress. It was adorned with scalelike armor — much like the lizard she had just seen. She closed her eyes and felt a band of white form at the top of her face. *For Daji,* she thought. Because Xianniang felt a strange twinge of something like grief for her dead mistress. No matter what, Xianniang knew that the White Fox would always be a part of her.

In the distance, a storm of dust surged into the blue sky. A silhouette of a man on horseback came into view. More men and horses joined him, one carrying a banner waving wildly in the wind. Xianniang could not see the emblem, but she knew it would be the head of a wolf. These were Rouran warriors.

They called me a witch, Xianniang thought. *Let me show them what a witch can do.*

And then Xianniang stepped onto the burning sands to join the warriors.

Author's Note

When Disney's animated *Mulan* was first released, I was much too old to be its target audience. I had already graduated from college and was working toward getting my first book contract. But beneath my veneer of adulthood, I was absolutely thrilled with the delight of a child. A Disney movie with Asian characters? There was an Asian Disney princess *(gasp!)*? Had all my dreams of seeing someone who looked like me as heroine finally come true?

Well, yes and no. Seeing Disney's *Mulan* was wonderful. For the first time in my life, I saw an Asian character championed and beloved, but it also made me hungry for more. And it reinforced the question I had begun to ask myself: why were there so few Asian characters in the stories around me? Why did it seem like Mulan was the only one?

For, of course, there have always been thousands and thousands of Asian characters — heroes and heroines, gods and goddesses, villains and demons. I found this out as I began to delve into Asian myths and legends and write my own stories. Following the threads of my own culture, I found an endless treasure trove of magic and wonder — a true "embarrassment of riches" that has fed all of my books, including this one.

For example, the Rabbit is based on a popular figure in Beijing, "Lord Rabbit." If you are there during the Mid-Autumn Moon Festival, you may see in the shops little clay statues of a white rabbit dressed as a stately lord and riding a horse, a tiger, or even a dragon. He is the Moon Lady's companion, sent to the Earth to save the people from a deadly plague, and — just as I have written in this book — able to change into anyone from a young girl to an old monk to accomplish his task.

Lu Ting-Pin is a character from Chinese mythology as well. There are many legends and stories of the Eight Immortals — a group of eight extraordinary beings with divine powers who dispense justice, alleviate suffering, help others find enlightenment, and generally cause havoc. Lu Ting-Pin (also referred to as Lu Dongbin or Lu Tung-Pin, depending on the transliteration) is often considered the leader of the group and always carries a double-edged evil-killing sword. He is also very typical of the Eight Immortals — kind, powerful, fun-loving, and brash, with a history of adventures. The sea beast that Mulan kills with the sword-boat is a reference to the giant octopus that Lu Ting-Pin is persuaded not to attack at the end of the famous "Eight Immortals Cross the Sea" saga. And while Xianniang is a new invention, her lineage was inspired by the story of Pai Shih — an ill-fated forbidden son of Lu Ting-Pin.

Daji is, unfortunately, inspired by a real person. Chinese history is littered with stories of ignoble emperors and kings whose final downfalls were influenced by their selfish and spoiled consorts. The last ruler of the Shang Dynasty (1600–1100 BC), Emperor Zhou, became enamored of a woman named Daji, who was so cruel that people could not believe she was human (she really did go boating on a pond of wine!). They began to say that she must be an evil fox spirit in disguise, for no person could be so wicked, and the infamous legend of Daji was born. However, the true story of the emperor causing a war just to amuse his beloved was not about Zhou and Daji. That was a different ruler, Emperor Murong Xi of the Later Yan dynasty (AD 384–407).

Oddly enough, we don't really know if Mulan herself was a real person. Her first known mention comes from a folk song, "The Ballad of Mulan." This tale of a girl who took her father's place in war became a source of hope, encouraging soldiers to fight invaders in the fourth, fifth, and sixth centuries, and has never been forgotten — so much so that Mulan has continued to be a cherished character, showing up in plays and novels in the late Ming dynasty (1590s) to now. Hundreds of storytellers have added and embellished onto Mulan and her story, reinventing and rewriting variations of her story with romance, tragedy, and humor. Without a doubt, she has sparked endless images and stories from countless artists and writers.

Including me, of course. Disney's *Mulan* introduced me to the possibility of an Asian heroine that could be embraced by all. That, in many ways, has fueled almost all the books I have created. From my first picture book, *The Ugly Vegetables* (published only a year after *Mulan* was first released), to my novels like *Where the Mountain Meets the Moon* and *When the Sea Turned to Silver*, I have been attempting to add to the line of Asian characters in American stories — that line that Mulan began for me.

Which is why I am so thrilled to share this novel with readers! To write about the character that inspired me before my first book was even published is an incredible full circle that truly delights me. I hope it does the same for you!

Best,
Grace Lin

A partial list of books that inspired *Mulan: Before the Sword*:

The Eight Immortals of Taoism: Legends and Fables of Popular Taoism, translated and edited by Kwok Man Ho and Joanne O'Brien. New York: Meridian, an imprint of New American Library, a division of Penguin Books USA, 1991.

The Eight Immortals Cross the Sea, illustrated by Chan Kok Sing, translated by Koh Kok Kiang. Singapore: Asiapac Books, 1999.

Infamous Chinese Emperors: Tales of Tyranny and Misrule, compiled and illustrated by Tian Hengyu, translated by Dai Shiyan. Singapore: Asiapac Books, 2006.

Tales of the Taoist Immortals, by Eva Wong. Boston, MA: Shambhala Publications, 2001

Tales of the Dancing Dragon: Stories of the Tao, by Eva Wong. Boston, MA: Shambhala Publications, 2007.

The Ballad of Mulan, retold and illustrated by Song Nan Zhang. Union City, CA: Pan Asian Publications, 1998.

Tales from 5000 Years of Chinese History, Vol. 1, by Lin Handa and Cao Yuzhang. New York: Shanghai Press and Publishing Development Company, 2010.

ACKNOWLEDGMENTS

Special thanks to my editor, Brittany Rubiano, who thought of me for this book; my agent, Rebecca Sherman, who brought the project to me; my good friends Jarrett Krosoczka, Lisa Yee, and Mike Curato, who encouraged me to take it; and the Highlights Foundation Unworkshop that gave me a place and peace to finish it. Many thanks to my Middle-Grade Mojo Writer friends: Jackie Davies, Molly Burnham, Ali Benjamin, Leslie Connor, and Lita Judge, for their support while I struggled through, as well as dear friend Libby Koponen who was willing to be a sounding board for my early ideas. But the most thanks go to my partner, Alex, and my daughter, Hazel, who accepted my neglect as I created!

Thanks to Soyoung Kim and Scott Piehl for their design and art direction; managing editor Cathryn McHugh; copy editors Rachel Rivera and Warren Meislin; the studio franchise team, Sarah Huck and Dale Kennedy; the Chinese cultural consultants; and all the hardworking people at Disney for making my story into a book.

Lastly, thank you, the readers of this book. Stories must be shared to live, so it is only with you that my work comes to life. I am so glad that my words have found a way to you . . . so much so that you are even reading the acknowledgments!